D1107698

If I Can Give You That

For any trans kid who's ever felt alone.

Typography by Laura Mock
23 24 25 26 27 LBC 5 4 3 2 1

First Edition

MICHAEL GRAY BULLA

If I Can Give You That

Quill Tree Books
An Imprint of HarperCollinsPublishers

One

"YOU CAN BAIL ANY TIME you need to," Nicole reminds me for the fourth time today.

I nod. I don't tell her that I really can't—at least, not without feeling bad about it—but I know what she means. She means I can escape to the bathroom, that I can slide out of the space quietly and lock myself in a stall until the meeting is over, or I can leave and catch the bus to downtown and walk back to my apartment. I can even call my mom to pick me up if I really want to.

But even if I *can* do that, I won't. I have no idea how this group will respond to a new guy showing up out of nowhere and then leaving halfway through, and I'm not gonna chance it. But I know my best friend well enough to get that she means well. So I just say, "I know," and Nicole smiles as I hold the door open for her.

Glenwood's only youth center is small. The building is unimpressive from the outside, tall and gray and easily overlooked. Inside isn't much different, but the owners—the workers? The volunteers? Whoever's in charge of decorating?—they've clearly tried their best to make it as lively as possible. In the lobby, colorful afghans are slung over the backs of second-hand couches and delicate lights are strung over the chipped countertop. Art lines the walls—figures of people dancing, splatter-painted self-portraits, flowers and buildings and things, all with their artists' names and ages displayed under their art.

I look at it all while Nicole talks with the woman behind the front desk. The paintings are throughout the lobby, and I follow the artwork until I'm in a hallway. The pieces change to photography, black-and-white images of teens in various generic poses—arms crossed loosely, sitting on curbs, talking to one another, looking directly at the camera with somber expressions. I guess it makes sense that this is the kind of artwork they display here, especially when the whole point of having the youth center available and free for the public is to actively help at-risk teenagers in the city.

Am I an "at-risk teenager"?

I don't know. Maybe.

Across from the photographs are two doors. From the lobby, I hear Nicole wrapping up her conversation. She finds me, and we head through the doors together.

The room is large and mostly empty, save for some round tables and a rolling whiteboard at the front. A few kids are already here, sitting on the floor or standing around. I don't know any of them, but they obviously know Nicole. They're quick to greet her, launching into more pleasantries and conversations while I stand around awkwardly.

Everyone looks to be either my age or younger, placing Nicole, at twenty, as maybe the oldest person in the room. More kids trickle in from the lobby. Nicole finishes exchanging all her polite *how are you*s and *that's good to hear*s and slings an arm around my shoulder, pulling me close to her.

"Hey, asshole," she says, which is Nicole-speak for *Come join the conversation*.

"That's me," I say, which is Gael-speak for *Please don't make me do that*.

She snorts and opens her mouth to say something when a boy I recognize from school comes up to us, grabbing Nicole's attention.

"Aww, hey!" she says brightly. Nicole says most things brightly. "You made it!"

"Yeah! My mom ended up taking my brother instead, so," the boy says. We're in a class together, but we've never really talked. He's shorter than me, with a bright smile and deep dimples, his blue raglan shirt pushed up to show off warm brown forearms. His dark corkscrew curls are pulled into a short ponytail at the base of his neck.

Nicole is telling him something, still with her arm slung over my shoulder. She chokes me a little when she tries to use both hands to talk, but this is par for the course for her.

"Oh! And this is Gael," she says, finally letting me go, only to do something worse: motion broadly toward me, in that here's-what-I'm-presenting-for-you gesture, which I didn't realize I hated until this exact moment.

"Hey." He extends a hand for me to shake. "I'm Declan."

"Gael," I say, taking it, and then, a moment too late, "Nicole already said that."

He laughs a little, like he's not completely sure if he should or not. "You go to GHS, right? I'm pretty sure we're in the same AP Lit class?"

"Oh." I blink. "Yeah, I think we are."

"How are you feeling about senior year so far?"

I shrug. We only started back at school this Wednesday, but I don't say that. "It's all right. You?"

From the corner of my eye, I can see Nicole watching this interaction between glances at her phone, a smile forming on her lips. No doubt she's happy that I'm talking to someone new.

"Good so far. I'm hopeful about the year." Someone behind us laughs way louder than necessary, and Declan and I both glance at them. More people have arrived since we started talking. A few are sitting down already, some with backpacks next to them, clearly getting here straight from school. He turns back to me. "I guess we should get settled so the group can start. But it was nice talking to you!"

"You, too."

Declan heads to the opposite side of the room and sits next to a girl I recognize from my Environmental Science class. Nicole takes a seat on the floor, and I follow her example, keeping as close to her as I can.

"All right, everyone." Nicole claps her hands together. "Circle up, circle up."

Slowly, the chatter dies and the group calms. Nicole leans

4

back on her palms, the room's attention on her.

"Hello, and welcome to our first Plus meeting of the school year!" She aims her blinding smile around the circle. "Before we get started with group discussion, let's go around and do introductions: name, pronouns, and for today's icebreaker . . . something you like to do to relax. I'm Nicole, my pronouns are she/her, and when I want to relax, I go for a long drive with my music playing."

A few people in the room express their approval of her answer with polite snaps, and she turns to me expectantly. I'm hit with a wave of nervousness.

"Um." I run my finger over an eyebrow nervously. "I'm Gael, he/him. I guess to relax . . . I crochet?" I don't mean to end it uncertainly, but the eyes on me turn my statement into a question. From where I'm sitting, I can see Declan, pressing his shoulder to his friend's. He's looking at me—not weirdly, just in that way that you do when someone in a group has the floor, but it makes me blink and look away from him.

Nicole pulls me away from overthinking the moment with a hand on my arm. The next person is already speaking, and she squeezes my arm gently. She doesn't have to say it; I know she's happy I got through introductions okay.

It takes a while for everyone to go, but when we've finally gotten back around to Nicole, she announces this meeting's theme: "Arts and Expression," which she writes on the whiteboard in large, neat letters. "Can y'all think of any LGBTQIA+ artists, writers, musicians, or actors who inspire you? It can be anyone at all."

Hands are already up before she's finished asking. As Nicole calls on people, they offer different names, some I recognize, some I don't, and she writes every answer on the board. Janelle Monáe, Freddie Mercury, Audre Lorde. The list keeps going. Some examples come to mind, and Nicole makes hopeful eye contact with me, but when I don't raise my hand after a few seconds, she moves on to someone else.

Once she can't squeeze any more names onto the board, Nicole puts the cap on her marker and turns back to us. "Small group time! I want you to get into groups of four or five and discuss the role of the arts in the LGBTQIA+ community— what it means to you, why these people on the board inspire you, your own experiences with art, anything at all. And while y'all are talking, I want you to make something." She gestures to round tables with buckets of markers, crayons, colored pencils, and other various art supplies. "It can be a poem, a picture, a song—I don't care as long as you're creating. In thirty minutes, we'll get back together and share in the large group."

She gestures toward the tables in a final go-ahead, and people are already getting up and finding their places, naturally gravitating toward their friends. Nicole watches everyone for a moment, then glances at me, still sitting on the ground. She grins and offers her hand to pull me up. "Come on, loser." *You can stick with me.*

I don't say anything, but I know she understands what I mean. *Thanks.*

Nicole chooses a table in the back of the room, with a few containers of Play-Doh, some falling-apart boxes of crayons and markers, and white printer paper. Declan is already seated, rummaging around for the right crayon colors. His friend, who introduced herself as Jacqueline when we went around, is shorter than Declan, with box braids pulled into a bun on the top of her head and lots of ear piercings, and the neon pink Play-Doh she's already claimed matches her nails. Nicole plops into the chair across from Jacqueline. I sit next to Nicole.

Declan and Jacqueline talk, and Nicole starts on a drawing of her and her girlfriend, McKayla, while I go for the blue Play-Doh. I scrape out the last bits from the bottom of the container, then shape it into a cylinder. I pull it apart while half listening to Declan tell a story about his younger brothers.

Nicole is drawing two miniature lesbian flags for stick-figure Nicole and stick-figure McKayla to wave around when she says, "So, about the prompt . . . Gael, you have any thoughts on the whole arts thing?"

"Um." I press my thumb into the dough until it starts to fold in half from the pressure. "Not really."

"Nothing at all?"

If it were just Nicole and me, I wouldn't have any issues discussing this. We've talked about trans art and trans artists, all the musicians and actors we look up to. She knows that even though I don't consider myself artistic, I've still thought about this—how it helps, or doesn't help, or could help.

But Declan and Jacqueline are here, sitting across from us, looking at me—and I'm not looking up, my eyes still trained on the Play-Doh, but I can feel their stares, and the weight of it makes me press my thumb into the dough harder—and suddenly I can't think of a single thing.

So I just say, "Nothing," and hope she gets what I mean.

She doesn't push me after that. She talks about Laura Jane Grace while I just keep pressing into the dough, until it's so thin that it's almost falling apart. I don't say really anything at all until we're nearing the end of small group time and Nicole holds up her drawing to show off. "Ta-da!"

"It's cute," I say. "But, um, what's under McKayla's nose?"

"It's her septum ring." She gestures toward the image with a pink crayon.

"Oh, clearly."

"It sort of looks like a giant mole," Declan says.

Nicole turns the paper around to take another look. She frowns at the smudge.

"I think it's still cute," Jacqueline says, and Declan knocks her elbow with his.

When he looks up again, our eyes meet. I panic and look away, then worry that looking away so quickly was a weird thing to do. But he doesn't say anything, and a minute later, we're cleaning up our tables and heading back to the large circle, completed projects in hand.

He sits in the same spot as earlier, and for the rest of the meeting, I make sure our eyes don't meet again.

Two

WHEN I GET HOME, MOM is asleep on the couch.

She's curled up with her laptop still open on the coffee table, displaying a half-finished Word document with lesson plans for her music theory class. The TV is muted and left on the History channel. Despite the Tennessee August heat, it can get chilly at night, so I get a blanket and lay it over her.

After changing into pajamas, I sit on the floor in front of the couch and turn the TV volume up. The documentary plays quietly, the voice-over low and smooth while I run my hands over the carpet and listen to my mom's steady breathing.

I don't remember falling asleep or getting up in the night, but I guess I must have because when Mom wakes me up the next morning, I'm on the couch. The blanket is now draped over me, and early morning light shines in from the living room window. Mom stands in front of the coffee table with a mug in each hand.

"Good morning." She holds one out for me and smiles. From here, the light illuminates the countless freckles and moles splattered across her cheeks and forehead, making her look older than her thirty-seven years.

"Morning." I sit up and take the mug from her. She made me tea, thank God. I've never liked coffee.

"How was the thing with Nicole yesterday?" she asks, sitting down on the couch. "What was it again? A club?"

"Kind of. It's, like, a support group for LGBTQIA+ teens."

Mom brings her mug to her lips and blows gently on the coffee, nodding. "Was it fun?"

"I guess. I don't know that I'd use the word 'fun,' but I liked watching everyone interact." I've always liked people-watching. When I was looking at it from the outside instead of worrying about coming up with something to say, the group felt . . . I don't know. Comfortable. Like everyone knew each other, and there were no secrets when it came to sexuality and gender, personal information offered between jokes. People laughed a lot. And they got to celebrate their identities, even when the discussion got a little heavier. I don't think I've ever been able to do that.

"What is it Nicole does there?" Mom asks.

"She's one of the mentors. She led the group discussion. Usually there's another person there, too, I think. Or maybe they switch off? I don't know."

"Were there other trans people there, other than you and Nicole?"

"Yeah," I say. "But I didn't really talk to them."

Mom nods again. We sit together, sipping our drinks in silence. Between several pop-ups alerting me of critically low battery, my phone tells me it's just barely nine a.m.

Mom sets her mug down on the table. "Do you have plans for the day?"

"I have a shift at the restaurant at one. You?"

"One of my students has a recital tonight," she says. Glenwood is only twenty minutes out from Nashville, so even though we don't live there, she works as a piano teacher at an arts school there. "But other than that, I'm going grocery shopping in a little bit. Want to come?"

". . . Eh . . ."

She smiles. "I get it, I get it. You want to relax before work, it's fine."

She stands and makes her way to the bathroom, putting her half-empty mug in the sink on the way. She seems to be doing better this morning. Smiling. Talking. Nothing like she was just a few nights ago.

I found her sobbing on the kitchen floor, shakily picking up the ceramic shards of a broken mug she'd accidentally dropped, a cut on her hand leaving a trail of blood on the pieces. If not for the Band-Aid on her palm and the mug's remains in the trash can, I might've thought I dreamed the whole thing.

Half an hour later, she leaves for the store. Her pajamas are replaced with blue jeans and a blouse, her light brown hair brushed and braided, the bags under her eyes hidden with concealer. "I'll see you later, Gael." She grabs the car keys with steady hands and kisses my forehead on her way out.

I'm relieved.

I'd started worrying she was caving in on herself again.

When I was six years old, my parents opened a bakery.

I say "my parents," but I really mean my father. He bought a small space only a block away from our apartment. Back then, Mom was in college, but most days she still managed to pick me up from kindergarten right after school let out, and from there we'd walk to the bakery, my hand in hers. We'd push open the shop door and a bell would chime our arrival. I loved the sound of that bell, so dainty and content, like every person that came into the bakery was someone special, something good. That bell was my second favorite part of the bakery.

My first was when my dad would greet us, standing at the entrance to the kitchen, wiping his hands on a dishrag and smiling. Lucas Bailey had a way of smiling with his whole face: first at the corners of his lips, then stretching across his cheeks, dimples, the crinkle at the corners of his eyes, the scrunch in his nose. If he were faking it, I'd know—it wouldn't reach past his dimples—but he *never* faked it. He loved us.

I wouldn't waste time. I'd sprint as fast as my legs could take me and jump into his arms, shrieking with laughter, my backpack bouncing with me.

"Hey, kiddo!" He always caught me. He'd pick me up and throw me into the air. My father was strong. My father was a giant. "Did you miss me?" And he'd always tickle me right under my ribs.

My mom would watch this exchange, smiling softer than my

dad but just as warm. My parents were as warm as they came, but never in the same ways. Mom was quieter, almost timid, like she wasn't used to loving us yet. I wouldn't understand why until much, much later.

"Did you forget about me?" Mom would say to him once I'd stopped laughing, and he would grin.

"How could I ever forget about you?" And he'd lean over to kiss her with me still squirming in his arms.

All three of us would stand in the entrance to the kitchen for a few more minutes, talking about our day, then we'd shuffle over the threshold, me with my hand in my mom's or my dad's or both, and in the kitchen, he would show me the correct way to knead and roll and shape dough. I'd watch as he reached for more flour, his sleeves pushed up to his elbows, his careful fingers pressing and molding something previously shapeless into something he wanted.

My father could make miracles.

My father could make anything—except my mother happy.

When I get to work, Nicole is there to greet me, her hands on her hips.

"You're late," she says, raising a plucked eyebrow.

I've worked with Nicole at Joey's Pizzeria for about a year now, but she's been my best friend for much longer. Mom and I moved after my dad left, but Nicole was our neighbor at our old place. Our parents were sort of friends and there weren't many other kids in our apartment complex, so we saw each other around a lot. When I finally got my license and started looking

13

for a job, she helped me get hired at Joey's.

She's been pretty much my only friend since transitioning. There were other kids I hung out with in middle school, but we kind of fell out of touch after I moved, and besides, I was never close to them the way I am with Nicole. She's more like my big sister.

She looks the part, too. Along with the fact that we're both white with dark brown hair, we've got the same heart-shaped face, high cheekbones, and pale skin. We get mistaken for siblings a lot. The way she reprimands me doesn't really help, either.

I don't bother giving her an answer. I know I'm late. She knows I know I'm late. I head to the back room to clock in and get into my work shirt and apron, and she follows behind me. She turns around politely when I start to change, even though the binder I have on under my shirt keeps me from any indecency.

You'd think after three years of binding I would be used to it, but sometimes it's just as fresh as the first day I wore one, wriggling into the compressive fabric with the hope of feeling all right in my skin for once. It helped—like, *immensely*—but the tradeoff is that it's uncomfortable as shit. Back pain is expected, if not guaranteed; summers are hell because I'm *always* wearing a restrictive second layer, and Tennessean heat is nothing to mess around with. Sometimes, no matter how much I twist and pull and readjust, it just doesn't feel right. But the alternative, at least until I can get top surgery after I turn eighteen, is going out in public without a flat chest. Which means there's really no alternative at all.

Nicole stands facing the doorway. "Where were you?"

"At home." I pull off my hoodie and trade the shirt under it for a cotton T-shirt with the restaurant's logo on it. I should've changed before I got here, but I didn't remember until I was getting on the bus.

"You okay?"

"Mm-hmm." I don't usually forget things like this, but my brain's been . . . all over the place. Ever since my mom's breakdown the other day, I've been on edge. Mom doesn't always get the way she did the other night. She doesn't always break down at small mistakes, and she doesn't always go through these heavy depressive episodes. A lot of the time, she manages to go to work, teach her students, come home. Those days, she doesn't cry or stare vacantly at the TV or ask me to sit with her until everything feels a little less heavy.

But the other times—when she can't help crying, when the TV sits on until it becomes a permanent buzz, when my arm goes numb where she's been leaning against me for hours—when she gets like that, it's always scary. It always feels like it's going to be the thing to push her into some greater sadness, something I can't pull her back from.

So, yeah. I'm a little on edge right now.

"Oh." Nicole thinks about it. "Care to elaborate, or am I just gonna have to fill in the blanks there myself?"

"You can look now," I say. She turns back toward me. "I was with my mom." Mostly just sitting with her. She seemed more tired than usual after grocery shopping. I wanted to try to pull her out of it a little before leaving her all alone at the apartment.

There's a pause. Nicole knows what that means, everything I'm not saying out loud.

"Well, at least you're here now" is all she says about it. I'm glad.

I slide my apron on and fumble to tie the strings in the back.

"You need help there, kiddo?" There's a grin clear in her voice.

"Shut up."

"That's a yes. Turn around."

I roll my eyes but do as she asks. She ties it for me, a little too tightly, but I don't complain. "Thanks."

"You're welcome. Buuut, just so we're even . . ."

"No."

"You don't even know what I was gonna ask!"

"No, but I know *you*."

"Rude." She reaches out to flick my ear, but I manage to dodge out of the way. "Anyway, I was gonna invite you to join us for Plus again next week."

I pause. "I don't know. . . ." It's not that I hated the meeting. I think that if I had the option to be invisible and just sit there and watch the group, I might really like it. But going back with Nicole means I can't just be an observer. I know her, and I know what she's trying to do. The first meeting wasn't to get me to talk; it was to let me get used to it. Now she's going to expect some kind of effort to socialize.

And I don't know how I feel about that yet.

At my hesitation, she singsongs, "I'll buy you Chipotle afterwaaard. . . ."

Dammit. She knows me too well.

"I'll think about it" is what I settle on. "But no promises."

She beams. "Good enough for me."

After Nicole disappears to actually do her job, my manager, an older white woman named Lisa who I wouldn't mind so much if she didn't always insist on calling everyone "sugar," tells me we're training a new guy.

"I'm gonna have him shadow you while you're waiting tables, okay, sugar?" she says more than asks. I nod.

I don't know who I'm expecting, but it definitely isn't Declan, dressed in a dark blue button-down and nice jeans, his hands shoved in his pockets as he makes his way to the back of the restaurant. He smiles at Lisa as she greets him with a pat on the shoulder, and I don't realize I've been watching them until Lisa gestures for me to come over.

"This is Gael," she says. "You'll be shadowing him today."

Declan nods, rocking back on his heels, and gives me a smile and a small half wave. The smile is awkward, one that says: *I know we know each other from somewhere, and I know you know we know each other from somewhere, but I'm not sure if we should acknowledge it.*

The best I can offer is "Um, hi."

Lisa pats me on the back encouragingly. "I'll let you get to it."

Despite my worries, it's all right once we get going. I make sure to tell him what he needs to know, and I don't try to make small talk. For the most part, he doesn't, either. It's only after

17

I've given a group of college students their check that he says, "You make this look so easy."

A little twinge of pride needles through my anxiety. Apparently, my nerves aren't immune to compliments.

"Thanks." I shrug, leading us around a large group that's just gotten up to leave. "It's just practice. You'll get used to it."

"I hope so," he agrees.

I look at him. He's holding his phone in one hand and tapping the back of it with a finger. His nails are painted, neat and unmarred like he did them recently, the bright purple complementing his brown skin.

"Is this your first job?" I ask.

"If you don't count dog-sitting for my neighbors a few times."

I don't know what compels me to keep talking, but I ask, "Are you nervous? About this being your first job, I mean?"

"Oh, absolutely." He laughs a little. The bell chimes as the group finally exits, the sounds of their conversation disappearing as the door closes behind them.

I look away and start again to the kitchen. "You'll be fine," I say. "It's not so bad once you get used to it."

I don't know that it's reassuring, but when I glance at him, he's smiling something small and grateful.

At the end of our shift, Nicole takes me home. On days where our schedules align, she usually offers me a ride, which I appreciate. Riding the bus isn't exactly fun, Ubers add up quickly, and I let my mom have our shared car as much as I can, so she doesn't end up stranded at the apartment. If I really needed to, I could ask

Mom to pick me up, but I hate inconveniencing her. Even when she says she isn't bothered by it, it always makes me feel bad.

As we're heading out to the parking lot, Nicole stops. "Shit."

"What?"

She pats all her pockets before pulling her purse around and digging inside it. When she comes up empty-handed, she groans. "*Ugh*, I left my phone inside. Be right back."

I wait for her outside the entrance. Joey's is part of an outdoor shopping center, next to a Publix, a laundromat, and a small hair salon. I stand under the sidewalk's awning, scrolling through my Twitter feed absentmindedly. The laundromat and Publix are both still open, but I'm all alone out here.

There's the familiar ringing of the pizzeria's door being opened, but the "Hey!" isn't Nicole's—it's Declan's; he's letting the door close behind him with a small smile in place.

"Oh, um, hi."

"Thanks for helping me out today," he says.

I look down, my gaze landing at his shoes—worn-looking Doc Martens with rainbow shoelaces. "It's no big deal," I mumble. "It's part of the job."

"Still. You could've, I don't know, been a dick about it, and you weren't. So thanks."

I look up. "You thought I was gonna be a dick about it?"

His response is immediate. "No! Sorry—not what I meant." He winces, and I realize with sudden clarity that he *also* doesn't really know what to do with this conversation. "I just wanted to say thanks. For helping me out. I appreciate it."

I suppress a grin. "You already said that," I point out gently.

"Yeah." He sighs. "I did."

There's something comforting about knowing that he's just as nervous right now as I was all day. I relax a little.

He shifts his weight from foot to foot. "Would it be weird if I asked for your number? Just—I mean—about work. Lisa told me—"

"To get in touch with your coworkers?" I finish, and he nods. "Yeah, Lisa has this whole thing about everyone 'getting in touch.' When I started working here, she made me get to know everyone and get their numbers."

I get out my phone, pull up the Contacts app, and hand it to him. He enters his number quickly and returns it to me.

"I guess I'll see you tomorrow, then?"

I nod, and he smiles one last time before heading out. I try not to watch him walk to his car, afraid he'll notice and it'll come off as creepy, so I look at my phone. He put his contact in as *declan o'connor*.

As he's starting his car, Nicole returns, looking flustered. "You find it?"

"Finally," she grumbles. "You wanna know where I left it? The bathroom. *Why* did I leave it there?"

Declan backs out of the spot, and I can just see him in the window. He doesn't look at us before driving off. "Not sure," I say.

"Let's get home."

I follow Nicole to her car. I don't bring up the interaction with Declan.

But when I get home, I shoot him a quick text so he'll have my number, too.

Three

MY PARENTS WERE YOUNG WHEN they met.

They were young when they married, too, and when they had me. They were high school sweethearts, and I'm told that they were madly in love, always together, joined at the hip.

When my parents first got together, Mom was in a bad place. Her family wasn't abusive, but she never felt like anything but an outcast with them. It was the way she didn't look like her dad, she'd told me, the way she didn't carry herself how her three older sisters did. Things only got worse when my grandma admitted the secret that Mom's father was not her sisters' father. She was fourteen when she found out, and her family hasn't worked the same since. She never admitted it to me, but I know a rift was created, one that only widened with time. It's palpable even now. I don't know my maternal grandparents, and the only person we talk to on that side of the family is my aunt Isabella.

Maybe that secret, that rift, was what triggered her initial decline. But then again, maybe she was always going to start showing symptoms at that age. Regardless, she was fifteen when things really went downhill.

I don't know exactly what she felt back then, how the symptoms showed up, in what order, what she struggled through. She doesn't like to talk about it, and I've never asked. What would I even say? Hey, Mom, tell me about your suicidal ideation? Hey, Mom, did you go days without sleeping? Hey, Mom, did your grades drop? Did you isolate yourself? Did you become scared, withdrawn, anxious? Hey, Mom, how often did you think about killing yourself?

What I do know is that my father met her that same year. I know that he never knew her before she was sick. He only ever saw the shaking, the noise, the constant collapsing and rebirth—and I know that he still looked her in the eyes and promised her the world.

Instead, they got me.

Monday comes too fast.

Before AP Lit, I'm on my phone, avoiding anyone's eyes as kids trickle into the classroom, so I'm startled when a voice says, "Hey!"

It's Declan. He smiles at me as he makes his way to his desk, a few in front of me. The students who sit between us aren't here yet, so he turns around in his seat to face me. I hadn't even realized he sat there.

Too late, I remember I'm supposed to respond. "Hi." It sounds stiff, almost harsh coming out, and I wince internally.

But Declan doesn't seem bothered. "How was the rest of your weekend?"

"Um. Fine. You?"

"Pretty good."

Unsure what else to say, I just nod. Thankfully, the teacher enters, saving me from having to come up with something else. Declan gives me one last smile before turning to face the whiteboard again.

For the rest of the period, I can't help glancing at the back of his head every now and then. When class ends, Declan waves to me as he heads to the door. I wave back, and he smiles before disappearing down the hallway.

Mom almost always gets home from work after me, and this afternoon is no exception. She slips her shoes off at the door, the tension in her shoulders clear. Somehow, she still manages to smile.

"Hey, honey. How was your day?" She makes her way into the kitchen. It's more of a kitchenette than anything, with an open floor plan that connects it to the living room. I'm at our kitchen table, crocheting what will eventually be a blanket. Even though I've been crocheting since I was fifteen to help with nerves, I've only ever finished one blanket—currently thrown over the couch, because Mom loves it—but it's not exactly the best, so I've been trying my hand at another one for the past month. I'm a little less than halfway done now.

"Fine," I say. "How was yours?"

"It was . . . a day." That's her way of saying it sucked.

"Sorry."

"Oh, that's not your fault."

She reaches into her school bag and pulls out a mug, half

wrapped in tissue paper. I watch as she places it on the kitchen counter.

"Um," I say, staring.

"What's up?" She throws out the packaging and pours soap into the mug.

I can't find my voice. I just watch her wash it and set it on the counter to dry, nestled in the recently empty space between a blue *World's Best Teacher* cup and the plain white one I use for tea.

Mom finally seems to understand what I'm confused about. "Oh—you remember my student, Caroline? The sophomore?"

My mom tells me so much about her students that I can't keep them all straight in my head, but I nod anyway.

"She asked about the cut on my hand the other day, and since I said I'd broken a mug, she brought me this." She ends the story by gesturing to it.

I didn't realize how worried her behavior had me until my shoulders drop at the explanation. I don't know what I'd thought about her suddenly coming home with a replacement mug, or why I thought she would've wanted to buy a new one when— even if she and I won't acknowledge it out loud—the old one was a long-ignored gift from my dad, given to her years ago when they were still pretending to be in love. I just know that it felt like a bad sign, some kind of proof that she's getting worse.

It wasn't like Mom had *tried* to break the mug the other day. I think it just slipped out of her hands while she was doing the dishes. I don't know for sure, since I wasn't there when it happened; I was doing homework in my room with my headphones in, and the crash got my attention. I rushed into the kitchen and found her kneeling over the remaining pieces, her chest heaving with thick, sputtering sobs as she gathered them up and sliced her hand on a shard.

I knelt next to her and rubbed her back, trying to get her to calm down. *Mom, it's okay, it's gonna be okay.* I didn't even know why she was crying, but I think having me there and hearing my voice helped calm her down some. After a few minutes of kneeling on the kitchen floor and trying to take deep breaths, she finally composed herself enough to get up. Of course, that was when we realized she was bleeding everywhere.

The two of us haven't spoken about the episode. Most of the time, we don't really speak about *any* of her episodes.

"That was really nice of her," I say.

"It was," she agrees. "But tell me more about *your* day. Anything interesting happen?"

"Not really." I pause. "Well, except . . ."

I start to tell Mom about Declan talking to me in class, but then I think—what happened isn't a big deal, but maybe talking about it would make it one? It must mean something if I want to bring it up to her, right?

"Except . . . ?" she prompts, grabbing a pitcher of sweet tea from the fridge.

"Just . . ." I grasp for something else to say. "This kid in my class—I saw him at Plus the other day."

The ice dispenser whirrs in violent protest when she goes to fill her glass up. It's been broken for weeks now, but she either forgets every day or refuses to acknowledge that it doesn't work, and neither of us has bothered fixing it, leaving us to manually reach in to get ice, as she does now.

"Oh," she says. The ice clinks at the bottom of her glass. "That's good! Did you talk to him?"

"No," I lie.

"Oh, you should," she says. "There aren't that many LGBT kids at Glenwood, right?"

"Not that are open about it."

Mom nods like that proves her point and raises the glass to her lips. "It would be nice to have friends outside of Nicole, don't you think?"

"Yeah, I guess." I agree with that in theory. Friends at school, a group to sit with at lunch, people to spend my weekends with getting into shenanigans or whatever it is high school seniors are supposed to do—I think I would like that. Or, at the very least, I would like to *try* having that.

Unfortunately, agreeing that it would be nice to have friends outside of Nicole is different than actually *making* them.

"I'll think about it," I tell her. I'm glad that I had the foresight to leave out how he's working at Joey's now, and that I *technically* have his number.

I set my half-finished blanket down. "Did you take your meds this morning?" I get up and reach for the green pill organizer in the cabinet above the sink. Even though Mom has been on antidepressants for longer than I've been alive, she still sometimes forgets, so I like to check.

The box reading *MONDAY* is empty. I flick it closed again and put the organizer back.

"I remembered," she says. She holds the glass between both hands, and she's looking at a spot to my left, some place away from here.

She's going to retreat into herself, I can feel it. She's going to revert to her silence.

Distantly, a panic builds.

But she just sets her glass on the counter. The moment is over. "How do you feel about going out for dinner tonight?"

My panic subsides. "I'm fine with that."

"I'm going to lie down for a while before we go, then." She smiles one last time at me and heads off to her bedroom. I watch the half-empty glass of sweet tea on the counter. The condensation on the sides. The ice, already melting.

Sometimes I wonder if my mom realizes just how much I worry about her. Maybe she doesn't notice how much of my time I spend analyzing her behavior, looking for any sign of feeling better or worse or nothing at all, scrutinizing all her comments and looks and tones so I don't miss something crucial.

Maybe she's convinced herself I don't think about it. That it doesn't affect me.

I don't know. But I know that it's better if she doesn't worry about me, too.

That night, I get a text. I assume the buzz from my bedside table is Nicole or a Twitter notification, so I don't really know what to do when I see it's Declan.

declan: Hey! What math class are you in?

It's occurred to me that, if I were someone else, I could've just . . . texted him. Started a conversation. Talked like a normal person. Maybe it's what my mom said about befriending him that's got me thinking about reaching out, or the smile he sent me in AP Lit, or how nervous he was about starting at Joey's—whatever the reason, it's been on my mind. I hadn't figured out what I was going to say, if I even decided to go through with anything at all, but I've entertained the idea a little more than maybe I should.

But I hadn't expected *him* to text first.

I stare at the message, the glow of my screen the only light in my room. It's 1:09 a.m., and if I were smarter, I'd be asleep. Instead, I'm sitting up in bed and swiping my phone open. My thumb hovers over the keyboard for a good few seconds before I tap out a response.

> **gael:** im in algebra 2. why?
>
> **declan:** Oh. :/
>
> **declan:** I'm in Pre-Cal. I was just wondering if you could help me with something.
>
> **gael:** this early in the quarter?
>
> **declan:** Yeah, lol.
>
> **declan:** Mrs. Emerson is NOT going easy on us.
>
> **gael:** that sucks. sorry i cant help
>
> **declan:** Don't worry about it. :) Sorry for texting so late!
>
> **gael:** its cool, i was still awake
>
> **declan:** Can I ask why you're up?
>
> **gael:** can't sleep

I pause at my message. Tap out another.

gael: what about u?

declan: I got distracted by BuzzFeed personality quizzes and
    forgot the homework I have due tomorrow.

declan: Now I'm falling asleep trying to finish this page and
    text at the same time.

declan: But hey, at least I know what princess/Marvel
    character combo I am.

gael: whats the combo

declan: Cinderella and Captain America, lol.

declan: Neither of those feel accurate, but I don't know that I
    can expect much else from a quiz made, like, 4 years ago.

declan: (If you wanna take it:)

His message is followed by a link, and because I have nothing else to do, I click it. A few minutes later, I text back.

gael: i took it

declan: What'd you get?

gael: spiderman/merida

declan: Aw, nice! That's a good combo.

gael: ill have to take your word for it

gael: i havent seen most disney movies, and the only
    superhero movie ive seen is thor ragnorak bc nicole made
    me watch it with her.

gael: she loves that movie but i think its mostly cuz she has a
    crush on tessa thompson

declan: And she's so valid for that.

declan: I'm incredibly gay and even *I* have a crush on her.

We keep texting, Declan going on about the most recent movies Tessa Thompson has been in, and even though I haven't seen any of them, I manage to keep up. Once the conversation reaches a lull, I glance at my phone's clock to find that it's been almost twenty minutes since he originally messaged me.

gael: arent you supposed to be doing homework?

declan: I am! Kind of. I'm almost done.

gael: its almost 2am

declan: I'll have you know it's no more than a crisp 1:30.

gael: crisp?

declan: Walk outside right now and tell me you wouldn't describe this 1 am temperature as crisp.

gael: crisp enough for you to go to bed yet?

declan: Fiiine, fine, I'm going. You've twisted my arm.

declan: Good night! Sorry to bother you so late.

declan: Get some sleep, and also watch Into the Spider-Verse because it's the best Spiderman movie!

gael: night

I smile as I plug my phone in before bed, and I make a mental note to ask Nicole if we can watch *Into the Spider-Verse* sometime soon.

Four

"CAN I SIT HERE?"

I look up from my work. Declan is standing at my table, a hand hovering over the back of the chair across from me and a hesitant smile on his face.

"Sure," I say, once I remember that I'm supposed to respond.

Wednesday's AP Lit class has taken an unexpected class field trip to the library. Our teacher had to leave early, and because of GHS's chronic shortage of substitutes, we have to spend the next fifty minutes here, much to the librarian's dismay.

Everyone is still getting settled, some people standing around instead of sitting, others looking through the bookshelves, most with nothing to do. We weren't given any assignments, so I'm treating this like a study hall and attempting to plow through my algebra homework, which is no easy feat. I'm absolutely shit at math.

It only gets harder when Declan sits across from me. He

hasn't texted me since Monday night. I'm not sure if things are as awkward as I feel like they are, or if my anxiety is just morphing every interaction into its worst possible iteration—but either way, we sit in silence, working on our own things. The library's clock ticks down the time until our class is out. Five minutes pass. Ten.

Fifteen minutes pass, and I tap my pencil against the desk and blurt out, "I didn't know you wore glasses."

He looks up and blinks. "Hm?"

". . . Your glasses?" I gesture to my own face and then to Declan's. He showed up to class today wearing them. If he wears them often, I never noticed before now. Although, to be fair, it's not like I was paying any attention until recently.

"Oh." He touches the round, dark brown frames gently as if he'd forgotten they were there. "These, yeah. My eyesight's not that bad, so I don't wear them all the time. I really only need them if I'm trying to read something far away or driving."

"Oh. Cool."

I want to say something more, ask why he's wearing them now if he doesn't need them often, maybe. Just *something* to make conversation.

But as it always does, my mouth shuts on its own, locking tight, and I run my index finger over my eyebrow. I just need something physical. Something to ground me. That's sort of what crocheting is for, but when I don't have my needle and yarn with me, I have to make do with other tactile things.

Declan pushes his glasses up on the bridge of his nose, then leans forward. "Is it cool if I ask you something?"

My pulse quickens, but I nod.

He lowers his voice a little. "Are you gonna be at Plus on Friday?"

"Oh." I don't know what to say. "Um."

"It's cool if you aren't!" His voice rises there, enough that I worry other people can hear him. "Just thought I'd ask, since, you know, I've been going for a while, but I hadn't seen you there until last week's meeting. . . ."

"Yeah, no, I'm . . . new."

"What made you want to start going?"

"Nicole asked me to check it out." I don't tell him this was only after I'd expressed to her how lonely it is being at GHS, where there's always a feeling like one wrong move and something bad could happen.

It's not that Glenwood High School is the *worst* place to be as a trans kid. At the very least, I'm not getting harassed every day, even though I'm pretty sure it isn't a secret that I'm trans. I started transitioning the summer before freshman year, right before my dad left and my mom and I moved to a new apartment forty minutes from our old neighborhood. The kids I grew up with don't go to GHS, and after I moved, I lost contact with the few friends I'd had. So, starting here, I was a new person.

But still—freshman and sophomore year, I was getting misgendered constantly. Junior year was when things started getting better (probably because my voice dropped), but I doubt everyone's just forgotten. My guess is that people don't really know what to do with me, so other than substitutes occasionally misgendering me or some teachers strategically avoiding any pronouns when talking about me, I'm left alone. I've been lucky.

Lucky, and lonely. I could definitely have it worse, but it's not like I feel welcomed or accepted. Here, trans people are an arguing point. Bathroom stalls are a breeding ground for scribbled slurs and offensive graffiti, and class discussions on anything "political" are an invitation for blatant admittance of prejudice with a "that's just my opinion" thrown on like a Band-Aid. Last year, in AP Language and Composition, my teacher made us do a class-wide debate on one of the many recent transphobic bathroom bills proposed by the state, and she didn't seem to realize why I didn't want to sit through kids arguing about whether or not people like me deserve to use public restrooms— especially since I'm not even technically *allowed* to use the men's restroom at GHS. Freshman year, the administration told me that, instead of the men's, I'd have to use the nurse's. I ended up skipping class that day, but the work I had to make up at home was worth missing that conversation.

"Yeah, it makes sense that she introduced you. Nicole's pretty enthusiastic about getting people involved in the community and everything," Declan says.

"She is," I agree.

"Are you two close?"

"Yeah. It's complicated, but—I mean, she's my best friend."

Declan leans forward, setting his elbows on the table and lacing his fingers together. "How's it complicated?"

I shrug. "It's a little weird that my best friend's a sophomore in college, right? Most people's best friends are their age. And it's usually a mutual best-friendship."

"You don't think Nicole thinks of you as her best friend, too?"

"McKayla," I say.

He twists his mouth to the side in thought. "I guess that's true. But they're also, like, super in love, so it's different, right? And someone can have more than one best friend, you know? I mean, I have three."

I think about Jacqueline and him at Plus, elbowing each other and laughing to themselves. I want to ask if she's one of those three, but I don't know if that would be weird to mention—maybe it would make it seem like I've been paying way too much attention to him and his business.

Instead, I just say, "Maybe."

He unlaces his fingers, setting his chin on a fist. "How long have you known her?"

"About five years. She and I were neighbors when I was a kid, and we kept in contact even though I moved." I pause. "You?"

"I started going to Plus at the beginning of sophomore year, so two years now."

"What made you want to start going?"

"Jacqueline heard about the group online and didn't want to go alone, so she invited me to go with her. We've been to almost every meeting since."

"Wow. You must really like it there."

He nods. "It's a welcome reprieve from . . . well, you know." He gestures around us.

I glance across the table at the notebook he's resting his elbow on. I can't read whatever he's gotten written down, but it reminds me that we're supposed to be doing work right now.

He notices my glance, and I think he catches on that the conversation's extended way past what I expected. He smiles, a little sheepish. "But all that to say, I was wondering if you're going to the meeting Friday?"

I look at him, at the striped sweater he's wearing even though the Tennessee summer is going strong and it's still in the eighties, at the way he's rolled his sleeves up to his elbows, the bright purple polish on his nails, one hand tapping against the table gently as he waits.

I don't know what I'm gonna say until I've opened my mouth. "Yeah. I'll be there."

He grins. "Cool."

This Friday's Plus activity is called "Identity Linking." Basically, everyone spreads out around the room and closes their eyes for a few minutes while we think about our identity. Once the time's up, we're supposed to go up to someone we think shares something in common with us and link hands, and once everyone's paired up, we talk about our similarities and differences.

This, unsurprisingly, sounds like my worst nightmare.

After Nicole's finished explaining it, I give her a pleading look. But unlike last week, she can't save me from having to branch out; she has to get the timer going, and because of how many people there are today, if she plays, she'll make it an odd number. Meaning, I can't default to her.

Shit.

Since Wednesday, my feelings about Plus had solidified

36

somewhere between tentative excitement and dread. Excitement, because the more I thought about last week, the more I came to terms with the fact that it was kind of interesting being here. My conversation with Declan made me feel a little better about it, too. But the dread stayed because I knew I couldn't get away with not participating this time around.

And, evidently, that feeling was warranted. I spend the entire silence wishing I hadn't agreed to come tonight.

I haven't decided what I'm going to do when Nicole says, "Time's up!"

People start moving to one another, some of them clearly friends, others friendly enough that they don't seem uncomfortable linking arms or holding hands or whatever else. It's more obvious than ever that I'm new here.

Double shit.

Before I know it, half the room is happily done with the activity and I'm still just standing there, my fingertips tingling with anxiety.

From behind me, Declan says, "Being a GHS kid has gotta count for something, right?"

When I turn around, he's smiling and holding his hand out expectantly. I glance around for Jacqueline—I assumed the two of them would've paired up—but Jacqueline's hooked arms with someone else.

I take Declan's outstretched hand, but he seems to catch on pretty quick that I'm not comfortable with the physical "linking" part of this activity; he drops our hands and hooks our arms together loosely like some other kids are doing. I breathe a small sigh of relief.

We watch the last few people find their partners. From her spot near the whiteboard, Nicole is watching everyone too, and when she catches my eye, she gives me a thumbs-up. I stick my tongue out at her in response.

"You think she wants us to talk about it?" Declan asks.

"What?"

"Like, about the activity," he says. "Do you think Nicole wants us to try to talk about our 'shared identity' and stuff?" He uses both hands to do the air quotes, which means it jostles me a little, too, where our arms are hooked.

"Probably," I admit.

"Do you have any thoughts on being at GHS?"

"It's school."

"It's school," he repeats, like I've said something profound.

"What about you?" I ask. "Do *you* have any thoughts on it?"

He thinks about it for a moment, twisting his mouth up to one side. "I don't know. I mean, it feels kind of weird saying that part of my 'identity' is being a Glenwood student. I don't usually like to think of Glenwood as a part of me, since it's not exactly the most welcoming place to be a gay Black kid. Honestly, if it weren't for band and my friends, I don't think I would've stayed all four years."

GHS is known for its marching band. From what I've overheard people saying, our football team sucks, but almost everyone goes to the games just so they can see the band play. I've never been, mostly because I've never had anyone to go with, and I don't think a crowded place with lots of screaming and loud noises is really my thing anyway.

But I don't say that part. Instead, I ask, "What instrument do you play?"

"Mellophone. It's kind of like the marching version of a French horn."

"How did you know I wouldn't recognize it?"

He grins. "I've yet to meet a non-band person who recognizes the mellophone by name."

I laugh a little. I want to ask more, but Nicole calls, "All right, that's time! Let's head back to the group!"

We all go back into the large circle to discuss what that was like. Other groups say the activity was hard, or that they liked it, or that it made them think about their identities, and one group talks about what it was like to discover what they had in common. One person talks about being nonbinary, and how different they are from the other nonbinary person they paired up with, and it makes me think about how I'm more or less trying to go stealth—here and at school—and the times when I see someone in public that I recognize myself in, how I want to convey to them that we're alike, that they aren't alone, and I think about how I never really can. I think about GHS and the way I've moved through the hallways like a ghost for years now. Suddenly, my hand itches to raise.

I want to say something about the bathroom situation—about the AP Lang teacher who looked lost when I tried to tell her I wasn't comfortable with having my humanity debated; about the substitutes who have accused me of trying to trick them when I ask if I can change my name on the roster; about the email my mom received a week into freshman year, explaining why I couldn't use a restroom where other people could see me, why I needed to be pushed out, hidden.

And I know I won't talk about it here, with everyone else. I know that at most I'll discuss it with Nicole on the drive to Chipotle.

But I realize that it's new, the desire to talk about it. New, and not exactly bad.

The meetings always last an hour and a half, so by the time Nicole drops me off at my apartment, it's just starting to get dark. I slide my shoes off at the door and make my way to the couch, ready to watch *The Great British Bake Off* while I recharge from the day, when I hear Mom's voice from the hallway.

"I think that's something you should discuss with him when you get a chance to talk," Mom says, and then she comes into view, fresh from the shower and already in her pajamas with her hair in a wet braid. Her phone is balanced between her ear and her shoulder as she carries her laptop bag and other schoolwork into the living room.

She halts when she sees me on the couch. "Oh, sweetie. I didn't realize you were home."

"Nicole drove me," I say.

Whoever she's talking to says something. "Well. Um." She sets her bag down on the coffee table and takes her phone away from her ear, cupping the speaker with her hand.

"Everything okay?" I ask.

She pauses, just looking at me. Then she says, "Gael. Your dad's on the phone."

I stare at her. My fingers tingle with the familiar mix of anger and anxiety that makes me stand up and start toward my bedroom before she can even offer me the phone.

"Good for him," I say as I brush past her.

"Gael, he just wants to talk—"

"I don't have anything to say to him."

That's not entirely true. I have a lot of things I want to say. Just nothing I think would do any good.

"You can't even give him a minute? Just to explain himself?"

Mom has followed me down the hallway, and now I stop at my door. "Explain what? Why he dropped off the face of the earth for four months? Why he hasn't called or attempted to talk to me? Or you? I don't think there's anything *to* explain."

The words come out quick and harsh and frantic, which just makes me even angrier. I hate that my dad has this control over me. That I haven't even heard his voice and I'm already this upset. I hate that he can do anything or nothing and it'll affect me.

"He's been busy," Mom says quietly.

"Whatever," I mumble. "Just . . . whatever."

I go into my room and close the door, and Mom doesn't try to stop me this time. I sit on my bed with my head in my hands, pressing my palms into my eyes until the black behind my eyelids is bursting with stars. Some of it is because it feels good, the pressure, the physical sensation. The other part is because I don't want to cry, even if they're angry tears, even if I'm alone.

Outside my door, I hear my mom's footsteps receding.

Five

THE FIRST TIME I HEARD my parents fighting, I was nine.

They were in the kitchen. I watched from the cracked doorway, my father's back to me. Our apartment's walls were thin. From my bedroom, I'd heard something like a door slamming and had gone to see what was wrong.

Mom was crying. I couldn't see Lucas's face, but I could see the tenseness in his shoulders, the way he leaned toward her. She pulled her robe tight around herself, like she was trying to make it a second skin, some kind of armor. Most of what they said was gibberish to me, things I didn't understand until much, much later.

"I'm doing the best I can," Lucas said. It might have been an attempt at calming her, maybe at defending himself. "You don't know what it's like—"

"*I* don't know what it's like?!" Mom was still crying, but she took a step toward Lucas, jabbing a finger at his chest. "Have you *met* me, Lucas? Do you know me at all?"

I didn't know what they were talking about. What was making them like this. Even now I wonder—was it something small? The dishes, who did the laundry last, who forgot to pack my lunch? Or was it bigger—a woman at the bakery that slid Lucas her number, Mom spending too much time at work, an unpaid bill or deadlines fast approaching?

There's no clear answer. The truth is that it could have been anything, or a combination of things, just a rising of tension to the surface. Another blowing of the top.

And besides, I don't think Mom could tell me even if I asked. Every distinct problem at the time seemed to melt into one another until there were no concrete images, no tangible instances, only an overarching feeling of—I don't know. Anger, maybe. Resentment. Loneliness.

I was certainly lonely, watching them through the doorway.

Lucas went quiet. Mom forcefully wiped the tears from her cheeks. "Don't answer that. We both know—" Our eyes met, and she shut her mouth abruptly.

For a moment, I stayed there, afraid of coming out and admitting I'd eavesdropped. Mom smiled at me encouragingly, but it was watery and too thin to be anything but forced. Lucas turned to face me, his anger replaced with shock.

"Come here, sweetie," Mom said, holding her arms out. I shuffled along the floor slowly, sheepishly, ashamed. I buried my head in her robe, clinging to her.

"I'm sorry," I mumbled. "I didn't mean to . . ."

Lucas cleared his throat. "It's okay. It was . . . our fault for speaking so loud. We're sorry."

I didn't look at my dad. I couldn't stop hearing his voice in my head, the tone, the defending. I didn't look anywhere but at the floor when I asked, "Were you guys fighting?"

"Of course not," Mom assured. "We were just . . . having an important conversation, that's all." She squeezed my shoulder gently. "It's past your bedtime. You need to go to sleep or you'll be tired tomorrow."

I nodded, and she led me to my room, where she tucked me into bed and kissed me goodnight and told me she loved me.

For a long time after that, I couldn't go to sleep. I couldn't get rid of the image of Mom's anger, the echo of her bitten words, the tears, and I couldn't stop thinking about Lucas, and his tense shoulders, and the shock he wore when he realized I had overheard them.

Sometimes, even now, I still think about that.

The next day, Mom and I don't talk about the phone call.

When I wander into the kitchen for breakfast, she's working on a puzzle in the living room. It was a birthday gift from Aunt Isabella, and even though Mom got it in June, she only recently started it. "Good morning," she calls. "How'd you sleep?"

"Fine."

"Any plans for the weekend?"

I shrug. "Just work tonight."

She nods and goes back to her puzzle. That's it. No bringing up Lucas.

I'm not surprised. It's like this when something with my dad happens. The next morning, or an hour later, or when she gets back from work, she'll pretend nothing was ever wrong. This is one thing we'll never agree on, and I don't think pushing it will do much good. Sometimes, like today, I don't mind it so much.

But I've never understood why she isn't as angry at him as I am. His most recent offense is forgetting about us for four months straight—no contact since my birthday back in April. It's just one asshole move in a string of many, and every single one of them proves over and over again that he doesn't care about us.

But somehow, she always answers his calls. Always talks to him like things are fine. Always acts like he didn't do anything to her. I hate it—for her, as much as for me.

But we don't talk about it.

As I'm making myself breakfast, my phone buzzes.

> **declan:** Have you done the homework for Monday yet? I'm trying to get through the essay we have to read, and I am not enjoying it in the LEAST.
>
> **gael:** yeah i read it. it was alright
>
> **declan:** Ah, yes. "it was alright." Classic code for "I hated it."
>
> **gael:** i didnt hate it
>
> **gael:** it was just SUPER boring
>
> **declan:** Which means you hated it. :P

"Have you had breakfast yet?" I ask Mom.

She pauses—which means she hasn't but doesn't want to tell me that.

"I'm making oatmeal right now, so I can make you a bowl," I say, already pulling out another packet.

There's a quiet "Thank you."

declan: What kind of stuff do you find not super boring?

I add water and oatmeal to both bowls and put them in the microwave. Then, looking back at my phone, I type out my response.

gael: i watch a lot of cooking shows and documentaries
gael: and i listen to a lot of music
declan: What genres?
gael: mostly alt rock i guess. ive been into big thief lately
declan: I've not heard of Big Thief! I'll have to check them out. :)
gael: what about you? what kinds of stuff do you like?
declan: I usually end up reading and watching more classic sci-fi and fantasy, but that might be because my parents were REALLY into them when I was growing up. That, plus superheroes.
declan: And for music, I like a lot of different genres, but I end up listening to a lot of rock and folk.
gael: that explains the marvel/disney thing
declan: A little, lol.
declan: I still think you should watch them when you can! You can't be a Merida/Spiderman combo and NOT see the movies!

46

declan: I mean, granted, Brave isn't . . . my FAVORITE
movie, but it's still worth a watch.

gael: good job selling me on that

declan: I only speak the truth!

declan: I don't want to give you false impressions about it
going in.

gael: how noble

declan: Very!

I smile, and the microwave beeps. I take a bowl to Mom. She looks up from her puzzle. "Thank you." She starts to say something else, but my phone buzzes again. "Who's that?"

I look between her and my phone screen. "Just . . . Nicole."

The lie is obvious, but she doesn't call me out, the same way I don't bring up Lucas. She just nods and returns to her puzzle.

I leave her bowl on the table in front of her and take mine to my room so I can continue texting Declan.

That night, I'm wiping down a table at Joey's when I hear Nicole's footsteps behind me. I don't startle when she pokes me in the side and yells, "Boo!"

"Hi to you, too."

"Oh, you're no fun anymore." She steps into view. "Declan and I are going to grab some food once we get off. You're coming."

"Is that your way of inviting me?"

"Not inviting so much as telling. Since I'm your ride and all."

"Then I guess I don't have a choice."

She grins. I won't admit it, but I kind of like the idea of going out with them. Declan and I were texting before work. Just small stuff, mostly about school or his friends or the shows we're watching. I think we're friends now. Maybe? We didn't sit together in AP Lit yesterday or anything like that, but he waited for me after class so we could walk out together, and when we're texting, it's . . . nice. Kind of comfortable.

Once we get off work, we meet outside near Nicole's car. "How does everyone feel about getting Cook Out?" she asks.

Declan looks between us. "Cook Out?"

"I *know* you're not being serious right now." When he just smiles sheepishly, she shakes her head. "This is just sad. Even *Gael*'s been."

"I think I'm supposed to be offended by that," I say.

Nicole ignores me and explains, "It's a fast-food place where all the cool kids hang out after partying or whatever, since it's open 'til three a.m. And the milkshakes?" She kisses her fingers like a chef finishing a dish. "Phenomenal."

"Guess I can't argue with that," Declan says.

Cook Out is, predictably, very busy. It's so loud that when each person's order is ready, the employees have to use a megaphone to call out the number. Even then, it's hard to hear them.

Declan's number is called just as I'm sitting down with my order, and the second he's gone, Nicole nudges my foot under the table. "Okay, spill."

"What are you talking about?" I say, struggling to open the Styrofoam box containing my three chicken quesadillas and more fries than should be legal.

"You've been in a weirdly good mood the past few days." She leans forward conspiratorially. "What happened? You're legally obligated to tell me, as your best friend, mentor, group leader, *and* coworker."

I finally get the box open. I take the lid off my milkshake, shove a fry into it, and offer it to her.

"I think Declan and I are friends now," I say as she takes my fry.

Almost instantly, her face lights up. "Aww, Gael! That's so sweet!"

"Just let everyone in the whole restaurant know, that's fine."

"As if anyone could hear us over the megaphone." But she's still smiling like a proud mom. "I knew you two would get along. Didn't I tell you you'd get along?"

"I really don't think you did."

"Still. That's so great." She pauses. "Why do you say you 'think'?"

"I don't know," I mumble. "It's very . . . new. But I think he considers us friends. I mean—we texted earlier today, and he's talked to me at school. That's a good thing, right?"

"I'd say so. But you're not feeling like it's a good thing?"

"No, it's just . . ." I stop, dip another fry in my milkshake, and pop it into my mouth. I try to arrange my thoughts in a way that makes sense. "You're basically my only friend. Suddenly having someone else here is *good*, but weird. I don't remember how to do all this . . ." I wave my hands around my head, hoping she gets what I'm trying to say. "I don't know. New-friend stuff.

I mean, you know how the few friends I had in middle school just sort of *decided* we were friends, so I never really had to make an effort. But it's different now. I'm making an effort."

"I think that's normal," she says. "I also think it's really cool you're making connections with other people now, even if you're a little lost sometimes. You know what you would've done if I'd introduced you to Plus last year?"

"Not gone," I say.

"Absolutely refused to go," she agrees. Then she smiles. "You're opening up a little! I'm proud of you."

Before I can say anything else, Declan slides into the booth next to me, our shoulders bumping. He's holding his container and a milkshake.

"Ooh, what'd ya get?" Nicole asks.

He opens his container, revealing a burger that can only taste good late at night. Most of the food here is like that. "Ta-da."

"Hold on, don't take a bite yet." Nicole rustles through her purse for her phone. "I want to capture this moment."

"The moment I eat a burger?" Declan laughs.

"The *first* moment you eat at Cook Out. It's, like, a rite of passage. Right, Gael?" She looks to me pointedly, her phone now out and poised to take a photo.

I dip a fry in my milkshake and tell Declan, "Yeah, I'm pretty sure she did this when I came here the first time, too."

"Well, if it's tradition . . ." He gives me this look like he's holding back laughter, and I offer the fry to him. He takes it, and Nicole snaps a photo of us.

Nicole gets her meal, and we eat and talk for a total of fifteen minutes before Nicole's phone buzzes. She frowns at it. "Aw, shit."

"Something wrong?" I ask.

"Kind of." Nicole taps something on her phone quickly. She has her nails done, so they're long and probably difficult to type with, but somehow, she doesn't seem hindered by them. "One of my roommates forgot her keys, so I gotta run back to let her in," she explains, already standing up and gathering her trash. She stops when she realizes that Declan and I haven't finished eating. "Oh. Hm."

"I can drive you home," Declan says to me. When I blink at him, he continues, "Nicole was your ride, right?"

"You're sure that's okay?" I ask.

"Yeah, no biggie." He leans over and grabs a fry from my pile.

"That would be perfect," Nicole says. She gives me and Declan quick half hugs. "Sorry to leave so suddenly. See you guys later!"

And then she's gone, and Declan and I are left alone in the bustling, almost uncomfortably loud restaurant. Over another order being called out on the megaphone, Declan says, "I do *not* envy her."

"Nicole?"

He nods. "The whole sharing-a-place-with-someone-else thing doesn't really sound appealing to me."

I think about the story he told at Plus that first Friday I went. "You have siblings, right?"

"Three of 'em."

"Jesus." I swirl one of my last fries in my half-finished milkshake.

"It's a lot," he agrees. "Although, I've never had to share a

51

room with them. The twins get to deal with that."

"Roommates in college will be a first," I conclude.

"And I'm not at all looking forward to it." He cracks his knuckles, *pop pop pop*, then laces his fingers together and sets them on the table. "What about you?"

"No siblings," I say.

"And college?"

"What about it?"

"Looking forward to roommates? Not looking forward? Indifferent?"

I run a finger over my eyebrow. "I . . . don't know what I'm doing with college. I'm not even sure I'm going, really."

"How come?"

I shrug. "I don't know if there's anything I'm passionate about enough to do long-term. I don't want to work at Joey's forever, but it's not like I can be a doctor or lawyer or something. I don't have that kind of drive. And I don't have any talents I can make into a career."

He unlaces his hands, starts to reach for me or maybe the fries, then stops himself. In response, I offer him my milkshake. "Want some? I'm not gonna finish it."

"Thanks." He takes it. "I think that's probably normal."

"Not finishing my milkshake?"

He grins a little. "About college. It's normal that you aren't totally sure what you want to do for the rest of your life right now, you know? I mean, people *go* to college without knowing what they want to do, and they change their minds when they're there, too. So, it's not so bad that you don't know yet. I think part of college is figuring out who you are and what you want to be. And if you don't want to go, that's fine, too. It's not for everyone."

I'm silent for a moment. An order number is called three times over the megaphone before the customer finally claims their meal.

"You sound like you have these kinds of conversations a lot," I say.

"A couple times, yeah. My one friend, Annie, has been talking about college stuff since, like, basically freshman year, so I've gotten used to thinking about life after high school."

"Well, what about you? How are *you* feeling about all of it?"

"Pretty okay," he says, popping off the lid of my—now his—milkshake to scoop it out with a spoon instead. "I mean, as okay as I can be. I'm excited for college, I think? At the very least, I'm excited to leave GHS. Not my friends or band, obviously, and there are a few teachers I'll miss, but overall, I'll be happy to get out of here."

"I'm assuming you're not gonna miss pre-cal," I say.

He snorts. "Oh, *God*, no."

We spend the rest of our meal talking about our classes and Declan's siblings and working at Joey's. I realize, as we're getting up to throw our trash away and finally head home, that I didn't shut down that whole conversation like I normally would. I didn't shut him out. And, despite all my anxiety . . . I'm glad.

Six

DECLAN DROPS ME OFF HALF an hour later, and Mom's in the kitchen when I get home. There's a pot of boiling water on the stove, but she doesn't seem to be cooking anything. She's bent over the counter, her hair curling around her face. Her grip on the side of the counter is tight.

"Mom?" I step into the apartment and shut the door quietly. She pulls her head up, but she's looking at the pot of water. "Mom," I say again, not a question this time. I'm behind her, and she's still not looking at me.

Gingerly, I set a hand on her shoulder. The touch pulls her from wherever she'd been, whatever world she'd trapped herself in this time, the way my voice couldn't—but it doesn't do anything to alleviate my building panic.

"Mom, what's wrong? What's going on?"

"Gael" is all she says, and then nothing else.

I turn off the stove and carefully dump the pot of hot water

54

into the sink. When I turn back, she's blinking rapidly, tears welling up quicker than she can ward them off. "Your father called again," she says.

"Awesome," I say dryly. I turn the faucet on and reach for a dirty plate, one of the many that have piled up this week. I need to do dishes more often. "What's he want this time?"

"He's moving back."

I turn around.

"What?" I whisper.

I stare at her, her eyes bloodshot, her expression so painfully open, and I feel the blood in my face drain, then feel it burn. I turn away again so she doesn't see how my face contorts into something angry. My mouth is dry. I pour a generous amount of soap onto a plate and scrub with more force than necessary.

"He wants to be . . . closer to us again," she says.

"So, what, you're just gonna let him move back in with us like nothing happened?"

"Of course not. He has an apartment set up, out in Bellevue."

"Oh, great, so now it'll only take him a thirty-minute drive to ruin our lives again."

"Gael . . ."

"What?" I snap. I finish washing the plate and start on the next one. I need something to do with my hands that doesn't involve breaking anything.

Mom is silent. Then, "He misses you."

I slam a plate into the rack of dry dishes. "Why are you defending him?!"

Mom flinches, and I feel it even from here, the weight of her recoil. Guilt bubbles in my stomach immediately. I'm going to be sick; I'm going to pass out. I need to get out of here.

I twist the faucet off. "I'm going for a drive."

She doesn't say anything as I grab the car keys from the kitchen table, or as I slam the door behind me. She just watches me leave.

Nicole doesn't answer her phone.

"Dammit." I end the call and stare at my contact list. I only have four numbers I actually use saved: *declan o'connor, joey's, mom,* and *nicole fletcher.* My options glare at me, the bright light of my phone like a torch in the dark, empty park I've found myself in.

I'd unintentionally lied to Mom earlier—I didn't go for a drive. I pulled into a public playground a few blocks from our apartment, threw the car into Park, and trudged my way to the swings. Being away from the apartment helps calm me down a little, but being alone doesn't.

I stare at my screen with my thumb hovering over the list. I make a decision.

Declan shows up in his pajamas ten minutes later, his glasses on. It's a weird sight, especially when I compare it to the image of him only an hour ago. I've never seen him look anything but put together, so seeing him in flannel pajama pants and a ratty *Star Wars* T-shirt makes him more real, somehow. I'm thankful for that.

"Are you okay?" he asks once he's within earshot of me, his keys jingling in his fist.

I shrug, unsure what to say. It's so dark out, and the only light is from the streetlights on the road, my phone, and the flashlight I got from the trunk of my car. I wave the flashlight around now, shining it on Declan, who doesn't so much as flinch.

"You sounded really upset on the phone," he says. He tosses his keys to the ground and sits on the swing next to me, the chains groaning under his weight.

"Sorry," I mumble. "You probably didn't want to see me again so soon."

"On the contrary." I can't even fake a smile, and that seems to worry him. He glances at me. "What happened?"

I'm quiet.

Some part of me regretted asking this of him the moment we hung up, but I'd just . . . I'd figured we're friends enough for something like this, right? Only an hour ago, we'd been sitting next to each other in those shitty vinyl seats, talking about GHS and *Bake Off* and Declan's siblings. I know I haven't exactly had the most experience with friendship, but it can't be that much of a stretch to say we're close enough for something like this. To lean on each other, or something. To ask for help.

But if we're friends enough for this to be okay, then we're friends enough for Declan to deserve a real explanation.

Shit.

"I freaked out on my mom," I say. "Just . . . totally freaked out, and I took the car and drove out here to calm down and . . ."

"Called me," he finishes.

"I didn't know what else to do," I mumble.

57

I feel it when he turns to look at the sky. A minefield of stars peeks out to wink at us. I look at the moon and try to remember the difference between waxing and waning.

"Did it help?" he asks. "Driving out here to calm down."

I think about it. "Yeah. It helped."

I can't keep track of how long we sit in silence after that, swaying on the swings, the moon watching us. Minutes feel like seconds feel like hours. I replay the conversation with my mom in my head, and time is pointless. All that matters is that she was crying, she winced at my voice. All that matters is that *I* did that. All that matters is that *Lucas* has done that.

"You don't have to say anything if you don't want to," Declan starts. "I can just sit here if that's all you need from me right now. But if you're cool with sharing . . . why'd you freak out?"

I open my mouth, but the words don't come. Where do I even start? With Lucas, with Mom—with myself? And for that matter, where does this story start at all? With my mom's depression, my parents' marriage, their divorce?

"My dad called today," I say, because starting anywhere else feels like bleeding.

"Oh."

"They're divorced."

"I figured." Declan pushes back and forth with the tip of his toe, swinging gently. "Can I, uh, ask what he called about?"

I look at the flashlight I'm still holding.

"He's moving back."

"Oh," Declan says again. Then, "Shit."

"Yeah." I flip the flashlight off and on a couple of times.

"Did he say why?"

"Not really." On. Off. On. "My mom just said he misses us, but I don't understand why he'd decide to come back *now*. What's even the point?"

Declan seems to think about that. "How long has he been away?"

"He moved to Buffalo after my parents split up, right before my freshman year."

"That's . . . Shit. That sucks, Gael."

I don't think I've ever heard him say my name before. For some reason, I get stuck on that. I like that he said my name. It makes all this more real. And, weirdly enough, I also kind of like that he doesn't know what to say. Somehow, it's validating, like his loss for words proves that I'm not upset over nothing.

We swing for a while. I keep playing with the flashlight, pressing the pad of my thumb into the switch's black plastic, sliding it up, hearing it click as the light is born then dies again a second later. It's what I need right now. A tactile distraction. A beginning and an end. Something to control.

After a while, I ask, "What about you? I've just been talking about my family drama for a long time. What's your family like?"

"We're all pretty close. Although, when it comes to my parents, I'm a little closer with my mom. My dad and I have kind of a weird relationship. I mean, like, it's good now, but it wasn't always, and I don't tell him what's going on in my life the way I do with my mom. But we still get along and everything."

I nod. "I get that. And you have three siblings, right?"

"Two brothers and a sister, yep. And I'm the oldest."

"Jesus. I can't imagine having that many people in one house."

He laughs a little. "It can get a bit crazy sometimes, that's for sure." His phone buzzes. "Speaking of siblings, my brother's calling for some reason. Sorry, one sec."

While he answers his phone, I point the flashlight upward. The beam stares toward the sky and disappears somewhere in the clouds.

"Yeah, I'm, uh . . ." Declan glances at me. "With a friend." A pause. "He goes to my school. No, you haven't met him. And I already told Mom where I am, stop freaking out." He rolls his eyes toward me. I turn the flashlight off again in reply.

"I'll be home soon. Yeah, love you, bye." He ends the call. I see his lock screen is a picture of a German shepherd, its tongue lolling out of its mouth happily. *10:46 p.m.* is plastered over the photo.

"Is that your dog?" I ask.

He nods, shoving his phone in his pocket. "What about you? Any pets?"

"No, my dad's allergic to fur, so we could never get one growing up."

"You aren't allergic, though?"

"Nah, no allergies."

"In that case, you should come over sometime to meet Ant-Man." Declan stands from the swing, the seat still swaying as he gets off.

"I'm sorry, what?"

He pushes his glasses up, looking unsure of himself for the

first time. "Only if you want to, obviously—"

"No, no, not that." I stop him. "I'm just—*Ant-Man*?"

"Oh, yeah. That's my dog's name."

"Declan."

"Yeah?"

"What," I turn the flashlight on, "the fuck?"

He laughs, loud and sudden and genuine, like I'd surprised him. The sound is infectious. And despite everything that's happened tonight, I can't help joining him.

Growing up, I hardly ever came home to an empty apartment. If Lucas wasn't home from the bakery, Mom was home from work. I spent time at after-school care if they couldn't get me, but once I started middle school, they decided I could handle staying home alone some days. Mom fretted over my safety, her anxiety making the prospect worse—*remember to lock the door, don't answer it for anyone, call us if you need anything, my number is on the fridge, you remember what to do in case of a fire?*—and Lucas, with his infinite culinary knowledge, began teaching me snacks to make if I got hungry before dinner, and then dinners to make if Mom had a recital or if he was in charge of closing, or on another bowling excursion with his friends, or simply just "out." He was "out" a lot those days. I wouldn't become suspicious of that for another year.

An empty house meant fighting. When my parents were still feeling the aftereffects of a particularly bad "discussion," Lucas would stay at the bakery after closing, cleaning up or stress-baking, and Mom might stay after school to get a lesson plan done, or else come home and lock herself in her bedroom. Thinking back on it now, I can't help wondering if she was trying to save me from having to handle her anger, her sorrow—or if she was just too depressed to get up.

She took a lot of showers those days. I understood that. The need to scrub anger from your skin. To wash out the bad, or at least numb it a little.

This is how I know the two of us have had a fight: when I get home from the park, I can hear the shower running. The apartment is quiet, too reminiscent of middle school. The pot is still sitting in the sink, and I try my best to ignore it on my way past the kitchen, but I think about it while changing into pajamas, while sitting down at my desk, while trying to finish some homework. I'm still thinking about it when I hear the water shut off.

I can't concentrate on studying. I'd been riding a weird sort of high after seeing Declan; it was like being with him and talking like that covered up the bad stuff for a second, painted over it with the same thing I felt when he texted me and when we sat next to each other at Cook Out. I don't know what to call the feeling, exactly, because it's not just that I'm happy. It feels like the answer to some of my loneliness. Despite the anxiety, despite the weirdness sometimes—it feels *good*.

We said goodbye at the park a few minutes after his phone call, and I started coming down the moment I got back in my car, left alone with my thoughts. Even with the radio playing as loud as I could get it, I couldn't keep the good stuff from leaking out, all that emotion sliding off me until I was left with the guilt and fear and anger underneath everything. I think maybe it's always underneath. Or at least most of the time.

It's 11:20 before I finally get the courage to knock on Mom's door.

She answers in her pajamas, her hair still wet from the shower. She looks tired. But not sad, thankfully.

Before she can say anything, I say, "I'm sorry for yelling at you."

She looks at me, wringing the ends of her hair out with a towel. After a second, she nods. "Okay."

"And I'm sorry for leaving without telling you where I was going. I shouldn't have done any of that, and I shouldn't have gotten so upset. None of it was your fault. I was just taking it out on you because . . ." Because Lucas isn't here to take it out on. But she knows that already.

She takes the towel away from her hair, folding it over her arm, and hugs me tightly. "It's okay, sweetheart. I understand."

I hug her back, holding on just as desperately. Things are always like this when Lucas is involved—heightened. Everything more desperate. Everything more intense.

"Let's both get some rest, okay?" she tells me once she's pulled away. The towel left water stains on my T-shirt, but I don't care.

She brushes hair away from my forehead gently, the way she did when I was little, and gives me a watery smile. I nod, but when I go to my room, I'm still thinking about Lucas, and my mom's smile, and the boiling water.

Seven

WHEN I WAS A KID, there was always a feeling in my gut, a trace of wrongness. I knew I was feeling *something*, that there was a disconnect between the body I was growing into and who I was, that there was something off about the way people saw me and the way I saw myself. But it was a small thing. A twinge in my stomach. A kind of hurt that was felt, but softly, quietly, and only on occasion. I ignored it, or wrote it off as something everyone else felt.

I was twelve when I first realized what was going on.

My parents were fighting, and I was in my room, staring at myself in my floor-length mirror, fresh out of a shower with the towel still wrapped around me. I looked at my body. The pale skin. The hips, already widening. My legs were free of hair since I'd shaved ten minutes ago, but I already wished I hadn't; something about the nakedness felt wrong. Mom didn't really want me shaving yet because she said I didn't need to worry about stuff like that as a seventh grader, but I did it anyway, trying to imitate the girls I passed in the hallways and the women on TV.

I'd never been a particularly feminine kid growing up, but then, I'd never been overtly masculine, either. Maybe I just needed to get better at being a girl, I thought. Maybe if I did what the girls at my school did—shaved my legs, bought push-up bras, wore something other than a T-shirt and jeans—maybe something would click. The only friends I had in school, Brianna and Neema, were all right—nice, and funny, and they'd invited me to sit with them at lunch at the beginning of seventh grade, but we weren't that close. At school, we talked about homework and the music we liked and the shows we watched, and every now and then Neema would tell me about a boy she had a crush on, but we never got into anything more personal than that. I couldn't tell them about these feelings I had, about how I was doing girlhood wrong, I was doing gender wrong, I was wrong, wrong, *wrong*.

So, instead, I buried the feelings, imitated the girls around me, and prayed it would get better.

But I'd been trying that for months, and nothing had changed. The wrongness was still there, and the older I got, the harder it was to ignore, until every moment I was aware of just how uncomfortable *everything* was.

Something changed when I stared at myself in the mirror that day, though.

Nicole had lived in our apartment complex with her parents and sister for as long as my family had, but she and I didn't become friends until a few months after she started her transition. I'd already known of trans girls, although mostly from stereotypes and transphobic jokes in sitcoms my dad watched. But I hadn't realized that there were trans *boys*, too.

At least, not until halfway into seventh grade, when I saw a documentary about this swimmer at Harvard. He was a transgender man, the TV told me, showing his before-and-after photos. He was smiling so much wider in the second photo, and the scars across his chest were unlike anything I'd ever seen. I couldn't get over how much happier he seemed in the "after" photos. Mom made a small comment, something like "Oh, good for him," as the narrator continued to discuss the man's performance on the men's swim team, but I didn't say anything, still watching the television.

It was the first time I'd ever seen those scars. I was drawn to the pink, healing lines and the swimmer's jawline, the way he stood next to his teammates without looking at all uncomfortable. The documentary said a lot about him—*surgery* and *hormones* and *transition* and a million other things I'd never realized were part of the whole "transgender" thing. I watched, mesmerized, without knowing what I was so drawn to.

I don't know why it took me so long to come to the realization that if that man could be transgender, then I could, too. But it wasn't until I was in front of the mirror, staring at myself, at the body budding into something I knew wasn't right, that I made the connection.

I want to be a boy.

It was a juvenile thought. The kind you have before you're

old enough to realize that, most of the time, *wanting* to be a certain gender is a sign of *being* that gender. But even admitting that much lifted a weight off my shoulders, lightening this heavy discomfort I'd carried with me.

I thought about Nicole, who I'd only started getting to know for a month or two at that point. She talked to me a little bit about being trans—just a quick comment here or there, but enough that I understood that this girl in my life was similar to that man on the documentary.

It would be a while before I brought up my feelings to Nicole, but here, standing in front of the mirror, I thought about those "after" photos of that man. I thought about how happy he looked. How alive.

Wednesday night, Mom stands in my open doorway. "Everything okay?"

I pull my head up from where I was looking at my phone. "Yeah, why?"

Her eyes flit between me and my phone. "You've just seemed . . . preoccupied lately."

There's an undertone in her voice that I pinpoint as being related to Lucas. The two of us haven't talked about him since Monday. A small part of me wants to know when he's moving back, so I can at least *feel* like I've prepared myself for it. The other, larger part wants to pretend it isn't happening at all.

"No," I say. "Just, you know. Busy with school. Senior year and everything."

She seems to think about that, then sits at the foot of my bed.

I quickly send the text I'd been composing and sit up, crossing my legs.

"You've been going to that group with Nicole, right?" she asks.

"Yeah."

"You've seemed . . ." She pauses. "I don't know, a little different since you started going. More distracted." She glances at my phone. "I mean, I wouldn't blame you, what with college applications and your dad—"

"It's not that," I interrupt. "I haven't started my applications. And Lucas . . ." My phone buzzes. Without thinking, I look down, scanning Declan's text before I realize Mom can see it, too. I don't try to explain anything, even though I can tell from her expression that she has a million questions. "Nothing's happened," I say. "I've just . . . I don't know."

She bites her lip and looks away, folding her hands in her lap. "I don't mean to push you. I just wanted to check in."

I smile. "I'm fine, really. Plus is good. You don't need to worry about me."

That seems to relieve her. Her shoulders drop with the breath she releases, and she stands as if to leave. Her eyes are a little wet, I realize, and I stand to comfort her immediately.

"I'm glad you're liking it there," she says, waving off my concern before I can even ask. "I just . . . I'm really glad."

I want to hug her, to stop whatever emotion overwhelmed her suddenly, but she swipes the budding tears away with her thumbs before they can even fall.

The thing is—I worry Mom more than I'd like to admit

when it comes to my social life. It's pretty obvious that I keep to myself, that I'm quiet at school. I know she's always wanted me to have more friends, people to lean on. That's maybe part of why she adores Nicole as much as she does. Nicole's presence in my life calmed Mom's fears for a while, but there's only so much Nicole can do for me when we only see each other outside of school.

I pull out my phone, go to my photos, and scroll up until I find the ones Nicole took at Cook Out. In most of them, Declan is mid-bite or laughing, but there are also a few with all of us, Declan grinning widely while I throw up a lazy peace sign in the background, Nicole's eyes and forehead just making it into the corner of the photo.

"You remember how I said a kid from my school also goes to Plus?" I ask her. She nods, and I hand her my phone.

She stares at the photo, and I run my finger over my eyebrow as I watch her reaction.

"Is that him?" she asks, sounding a little in awe.

"Yeah. His name's Declan." And I don't exactly mean to, but I tell her everything.

By the time I've caught her up, she looks like she's gonna cry again. I gently take my phone back from her. "I just . . . I don't want you to worry."

She hugs me tightly. "I won't," she says into my hair.

"Good." I hug her back.

"I'm glad you like it there," she says when we pull away. "And that you're making friends."

She leaves my room a minute later, and I sit back down on

my bed. When I open my phone, it's still on the selfie. I survey the photo, how we're locked in that moment: Nicole's eyebrows raised and her eyeliner smudged just a little; Declan's arms crossed as they rest on the table, the corners of his brown eyes crinkled from the force of his wide grin, his dimples deep; my faint, almost-smile and the way I'm not looking at the camera, exactly, but somewhere a little to the left of it.

I look at the photo for a long time, content.

At Plus on Friday, Declan, Jacqueline, and I play Jenga while we wait for the group to start.

As Jacqueline sets up the final Jenga piece, she says, "Who wants to go first?"

"Not me," I say.

Declan shrugs and easily gets a piece out, then nudges my knee with his. "What are you doing this Sunday?"

"Nothing, currently," I say, while Jacqueline slides out a middle piece. Declan and I text all the time now, and we've walked out of AP Lit together every day this week, but despite our shared Environmental class, I still haven't hung out much with Jacqueline, so my anxiety has kicked up a little. She seems really cool, and I don't want to come off as weird or annoying. But I'm trying my best to keep it from getting to me too much.

She motions for me to take my turn. I manage to get one piece out without knocking anything over, and she claps at my success.

"Give it time, I'm horrible at this game," I say, turning to Declan. "But, yeah, not much. Why?"

"We're gonna get lunch Sunday," he says. Unlike me, Declan can talk while taking his turn.

"And by 'we' you mean . . . ?"

"Our friend group," Jacqueline says. "Me, you two, and our friends Annie and Jeremiah."

"As long as we're not eating at Joey's," I say.

Declan laughs. It wasn't that funny, but he still laughs. He always laughs at my almost-but-not-quite jokes. "Great! I'll text you more about it tomorrow. We were thinking around noon."

This time, when I feel his knee bump into mine, I can't tell if it was intentional or not. I smile. "Cool."

We keep playing until Plus starts. During the group discussion, I sit next to Declan, with Jacqueline on his other side and Nicole on my right. And, to my surprise, it doesn't feel new or unusual. It just feels . . . nice.

Eight

SATURDAY MORNING, I WAKE UP to Mom playing piano.

The melody pulls me from sleep. It's a song I've heard a million times, but I don't know the name of it. I lie in bed for a few minutes just listening, looking at the ceiling. I get up as the song trails off into a new one.

In the hallway, I watch as she plays. This one is less somber than the other, the tempo picking up. She's sitting on the bench, her back straight, her hair braided down her back. Despite the upbeat song, she doesn't look happy. She's only in her late thirties, but she looks so much older sometimes.

She was more, before Lucas left. Before their marriage fell apart. I remember it: her eyes so dark they swallowed the pupils, lips full and smiling, face covered in beauty marks and freckles. She wasn't healthy back then, but she was healthi*er*.

I look more like Lucas; I have his nose, his eyes, his

cheekbones. When I was little, Mom would poke the mole sitting above the left side of my mouth, the only marking I have, and tell me it was a part of her I'd taken with me. I'd pout, because she has planes and planes of freckles and moles, and I wanted more of her to myself.

"You have enough of me," she'd say, "but I'm glad you want that now. When you're older, I bet you'll want to get rid of me."

I'm older now, but I still don't have enough of her.

The song ends. She sits at the piano bench with her hands hovering over the keys. I watch her, trying to find meaning in her stillness.

I remember what it was like when I was younger—when she was really, really bad. She was so quiet. She didn't sing for me. She didn't do much of anything but hole herself up in her room and argue with my dad. When she cried, she always did it silently. Once, when I was in fifth grade, I walked into the living room to see her at the piano, tears slipping down her cheeks, so quiet I almost didn't notice.

She isn't crying now, though. Just sitting there. Still.

I don't know what to say. Lucas brought this on, I can tell. And now that he's moving back, there's nothing I can do to stop it.

As silently as I can, I go back to my room.

When I was eleven, Mom ended up in the hospital.

At the time, I didn't understand why she was there. All she would say was that she'd taken the wrong medicine, mistaken Prozac for Advil. *I didn't mean to take that*, she'd promised Lucas, her hands still shaking, her voice cracking. *It was an accident; I wasn't in my right mind.* He was calling the ambulance even as she gave him excuses. I wondered why, even if she *had* thought it was Advil, she had taken so many.

I was just a kid then, but while I waited for the ambulance to arrive, I kept staring at the newly opened bottle, at the number on the side. Seventy pills, the wrapper said. The bottle held seventy pills. I counted the ones left on the counter. Seven. I did the math.

"She took sixty-three of them," I said, to nobody but myself.

While I'm on break at work that afternoon, I check my phone. I have three notifications: two texts from Declan letting me know where we're meeting tomorrow, and one missed call from an unknown number. I ignore the call.

I manage to put the call mostly out of my mind until I'm at home that night. Mom did laundry while I was at work, so when I get home, I help her fold it. I'm sitting on the floor in front of the coffee table, Mom on the couch, when my phone rings.

"Who's that?" She folds a washcloth.

"Don't know." It keeps ringing—once, then twice. "I'm gonna take this real quick."

In my room, I press Answer. "Who is this?" I say, instead of hello.

"Gael?"

My breath hitches. It's been a while since I've heard my father's voice, but it sounds the same as I remember it. Warm.

Low. I want to think it sounds like nails on a chalkboard or something equally as grating, but if I'm being honest, my father's voice is just as familiar as it has ever been. The only problem is that it doesn't calm me anymore. It just makes me angry.

"Gael?" Lucas tries again. "Are you there? I didn't know if you had this number saved or not but—"

"I don't," I interrupt.

"Uh, right . . ." It's clear that Lucas isn't sure how to respond to that.

"Why'd you call," I say, not a question.

"I can't call my son every once in a while?"

"You haven't in four months."

Lucas is silent. Then he says, "I'm calling because I miss you."

I could hang up right now. I almost do. I pull the phone away from my ear and stare at the screen, the red End button taunting me. All I'd have to do is tap the screen and this would be over. I wouldn't have to listen to an apology I don't want, a forcing of normalcy I've been actively avoiding, a lie that reeks despite the miles between us.

Lucas's voice comes muffled from the phone. "How's school been?"

I put the phone back to my ear. "Horrible. I dropped out."

"Gael . . ."

"How's your girlfriend?"

"We're, uh, taking a break right now. She needed space."

"Sounds familiar."

"Gael . . ." Lucas sounds tired. I take some pride in knowing that I'm getting on his nerves. "I called because I'm genuinely interested in how you've been. I know you're angry with me, and I get it, I really, really do—but can you please, just for this conversation, pretend it's okay?"

Jesus fucking Christ.

Pretend it's okay? I've been pretending it's okay every day since I was fourteen. I've been pretending it's okay because Lucas wouldn't, because Mom couldn't, because *I had to*. I don't need him to tell me to *pretend*.

But I don't say that.

I almost do—I open my mouth, blood rushing to my ears. But then I think about Mom in the living room, sitting with piles of laundry, and I remember what she told me when they decided to separate—that we were still gonna stay a family, that she wanted me to try my best to get along with Lucas. She didn't want to burn bridges; she just wanted to cross them. She'd dealt with a family that left her once, and she never wanted to go through that again.

Please just try, she'd said. *If not for your dad, please, at least for me.*

I take a breath.

"Sorry about your girlfriend," I mumble. I just barely refrain from jabbing the "ex" in there.

"It's okay," he says, almost like he's trying to convince himself, too. "Um. I guess your mom told you about my plans, right?"

What an odd way to talk about it—his *plans*. "She told me." I pause. "Why now?"

He's silent. I don't know if he's just thinking, or if he doesn't plan to respond at all.

I continue: "I mean, what made you decide *now*'s the best time to move back when you've been MIA for so long?"

"I haven't been MIA," he defends immediately, which is funny to me because what else do you call it when your dad moves seventeen hours away only to go four months without checking on you and your suicidal mother? What do you call it when he leaves you to take care of her, when he shrugs off all responsibility like a coat he's outgrown?

"Call it what you want," I say. "It doesn't change my question."

Lucas is quiet for so long I start to think he's hung up on me. "Well . . . things in Buffalo weren't great, and—you remember my friend, Abdul? The place he works at had an opening for a food service manager, so . . . here I am. And, I guess . . . I don't know. Like I said, I miss you guys."

Bullshit, I think. *Bullshit bullshit bullshit.*

Lucas's voice crackles through the silence. "Did Ana tell you where I'm moving?"

"Yes."

"So—" He pauses. "So, you understand . . . Well. I'm getting into town next week, and . . . your mother and I have been thinking about us all getting together. Maybe next Saturday?" He pauses, waiting for my response. When I give none, he says, "Gael?"

"I can't. I already have plans," I lie. "With my friends."

I can hear the cogs in his brain working, trying to piece

together when it was, exactly, I started having *friends*, plural. The lie feels so obvious to me, but it must be solid enough because after a moment, he says, "Oh. In that case, I, uh . . . I guess we'll have to reschedule."

He doesn't even sound disappointed—just intrigued. Before he left, he was always kind of weird about my lack of a social life. He wanted me to experience all those traditional rites of passage, so the fact that I barely ever hung out with Brianna or Neema outside of school always bothered him. As far as he knows, I'm finally doing what he's always wanted for me.

I guess that's why he doesn't argue with me or push to reschedule. If nothing else, I'm thankful for that.

Lucas sighs. "Well . . . I should probably let you go. I'll talk to you later."

I don't say anything. He hangs up.

Mom is still on the couch when I come back into the living room. She looks up from the laundry, a neatly folded stack placed on the cushion next to her. "Who was that?"

As casually as I can, I say, "Just Declan. Figuring out stuff for tomorrow."

"Oh, that's good." She sets a folded towel on the stack. "I feel like I don't know anything about him. What's he like?"

I fold a washcloth, set it in the pile, and reach for another. "Annoying," I say, except it comes out much fonder than I mean it to.

"Of course," she says. "You think everyone's annoying."

"Not you. Or Nicole."

She folds a towel in half, then thirds, fitting it into a perfectly neat parcel and setting it aside. Her voice is softer when she says, "I'm happy you're talking to him. It's good that you've made a friend, even if you think he's annoying sometimes."

She smiles, so sincere that I feel bad for not giving her a serious answer.

"Yeah, I guess so," I agree.

We continue in silence. From the corner of my eye, I see when her smile falls back into a neutral expression a moment later, leaving blankness as we go through the motions, picking up towels and folding them into thirds, setting them aside then reaching for another.

I can't stop thinking about her piano playing this morning. It's only the beginning of fall, and I'm already worried about her. Summers are hard—school being out lets her slip into bad behavior easily—but fall is bad in different ways. Her moods are so capricious. I feel like I spend all my time at home watching her, fearing and waiting for the twitch in her jaw or the crack in her voice that will confirm what I already know.

She's declining again.

Nine

I HAVE A DREAM THAT I'm on a roller coaster.

It's bright green with cartoonish faces painted on it. I sit at the very end and next to me, Nicole is putting her hair in a high ponytail. In front of us is Lucas's ex-girlfriend, but because I've never seen her before, she's faceless. She's talking on the phone the whole time to someone that sounds like Lucas.

My dream shifts, and the end result is that someone tries to stick a gun to the roof of their mouth and ends up shooting through their cheek instead. The bullet doesn't reach their brain, but the person—my dream doesn't specify who—dies as quickly as if it had. There's no blood. No screaming. No theatrics of death. There's only a gunshot and a soft *thump* as a body hits the invisible ground. The gun is lost somewhere in the commotion. In my dream, I wonder if the person swallowed it.

When I wake up, I'm covered in sweat. I stare at the ceiling for a long time. Birds chirp outside my window, and I can hear my neighbor's music, some rock band and heavy bass line muffled through the walls. Eventually, I pull myself up from bed, the blankets sticking to my sweaty limbs. My phone says it's 10:03 a.m.

It occurs to me that the person in my dream could've been Mom. I mean, maybe not. The person was faceless, genderless, voiceless. But I can't ignore the feeling it was meant to be her.

Mom isn't in the kitchen. She's not in her room either, and for a brief moment, I panic that my dream came true somehow. I can't get the image of the gun out of my head, and I keep imagining walking into the bathroom and seeing Mom on the floor. But when I check, the bathroom's empty. There's a note on the kitchen counter, saying that she's running errands and she'll be back soon. At the bottom of the page is her neat, curling signature followed by a scribbled heart. It doesn't make sense, but for some reason, seeing it makes my chest constrict like I'm going to cry.

My phone rings and lights up with a picture of Declan under his contact name.

"Hello?" I sit down on the couch, still trying to relax from my panic. It's too early for me to be this tense. I should crochet. Or at least do *something*.

"Hey!" I can hear the smile in his voice. "I'm surprised you picked up, it's so early."

"It's ten."

"Like I said, early."

"What are you doing up, then?"

"I promised my little sister I'd take her to get bubble tea if she did well on a test, and the place will be closed by the time we're done getting lunch, so early morning boba it is."

"Right. So, what's up?"

"I just wanted to make sure you're still good for today. You didn't text yesterday, so . . ."

"Oh, shit." I told myself I was going to text him back when I got home from work, but then everything with Lucas happened . . . "Sorry, I meant to reply, but—"

"No, you're fine! Just figured I'd check."

I lean my elbow on the armrest and run my finger over my eyebrow. "Yeah, I'm still good for today."

"Awesome! Do you need me to pick you up?"

"Um." I think about Mom. She might not be home by then, but if she isn't, I can just take the bus. "Nah, it's fine. I can meet you guys somewhere. Text me the address."

"All right, cool. See you soon!"

For a while after he hangs up, I sit on the couch, my phone still pressed to my ear.

I meet Declan and his friends in downtown Glenwood. The city was founded in the 1800s, so most of Main Street is one restored Victorian building or antique shop after another. We end up at Puckett's, a restaurant that doubles as a small grocery store, and it's already packed by the time we get there. There's a small stage at the front of the restaurant, the wall behind it covered in signed acoustic guitars, and a young man with a beard is setting up, his own guitar in his lap.

Inside, Declan introduces me to Jeremiah and Annie. Jeremiah is a tall, lanky white guy with red hair and too many freckles to count, and he nods his head to me in greeting. Annie is Latina and even taller than Jeremiah, with long, bright-blue hair, her roots a dark brown.

The host seats us at one of those extra-long booths, so Declan sits next to me while the other three sit across from us.

"So, Annie," Declan says, lacing his fingers together and setting them on the table. "How was your *date*?" He wiggles his eyebrows, grinning widely.

Annie's ears redden. She picks up her menu, placing it like one of those desk dividers kids are given in elementary school. "Can't I order something first?"

Jacqueline plucks her menu away from her. "Nope."

Annie opens her mouth, but a waiter comes by before she can answer. After we've ordered our drinks, she snatches the menu back. "It was fine. Sydney's nice."

"Where did y'all go?" Declan asks.

"Bowling."

Jeremiah laughs. "On the first date? Ann, you *suck* at bowling."

"I knooow," she groans. "I didn't want to, but she's apparently really into bowling, so I just . . . dealt with it."

"So, how'd that go?"

She wrinkles her nose. "I lost."

It's Jacqueline's turn to snort a laugh, and Annie rolls her eyes, but she's smiling. I watch them without saying anything. It's nice, just listening to them talk, even if I don't have a lot of context. The man onstage starts playing a quiet country song, just loud enough that I can hear it over the restaurant's chatter.

While they're discussing Annie's date's Instagram profile,

Declan breaks away from their conversation to tap my menu. "You wanna split something?"

"Oh. Um, sure." I glance at the options for the first time. "What were you thinking?"

He leans toward me, and his arm brushes against mine as he points to a burger under the lunch section. Maybe I'm just imagining it, but it definitely feels like he's closer than usual, which is saying a lot. Declan isn't afraid of casual contact, and it extends all the way into how he engages in conversation; he's always looking at people with such intensity, putting all his focus onto one person and what they're saying. During Plus, he's so focused when someone speaks, and when he looks at you while you talk, he makes you feel like you've got something *actually* important to say.

I think a part of me might like all that attention, because when Declan nudges my shoulder again, I realize that it's . . . kind of nice. It's nice, having him so close.

"You can have most of the fries. I'm not big on them," he says.

"Ooh, can I jump in on those?" Jacqueline asks. "If I order my own, it's way too many but I still want, like, a couple."

"Help yourself," I say. Declan shifts away from me a little, and I try to ignore the pang of disappointment at the space between us.

Once we've gotten our drinks and placed our orders, Annie asks me, "You go to Plus with Declan and Jac, right?"

"Yeah. I started going, like, a month ago." I unwrap my straw slowly before putting it in my drink. The ice clinks together.

"Nicole's my best friend, so she wanted me to try it out."

"Do you like it there?" Annie continues.

"Yeah, it's nice."

"What have the meetings been like so far?"

"Um." I stir my drink, trying to find a good answer. "They've been fun. We've just been doing activities and having group discussions about certain topics each week, so . . . pretty standard, I guess?"

"Sorry, I don't mean to interrogate you." She offers an apologetic smile. "I just ask 'cause I've been thinking about going."

"You should come!" Declan tells her. "It'll be fun with you there. And if Jeremiah would join us, we could have the whole squad!"

"You already know what I'm gonna say to that," Jeremiah says, giving him a look.

Declan pouts. "Yeah, but you never had a problem going to the GSA after school."

"That was different. Barely anyone ever went to those meetings, so we ended up being half the group, and we didn't do anything but sit around and talk. Y'all actually have, like, activities and shit at Plus."

"I didn't know there was a GSA at Glenwood," I say.

"It's a work in progress," Jacqueline says. "Not a lot of people go, and I've heard there've been issues with leadership and stuff."

"They're trying their best, but I definitely prefer Plus," Declan says.

"You've met a lot of cool people through Plus." Jacqueline

looks between Declan and me.

My face heats, and I sip my drink, trying to seem busy.

But Declan just grins. "Yeah, I have."

An hour later, I check the temperature on my phone as we're walking outside: eighty degrees, and only climbing until the sun goes down. Annie glances over my shoulder and sees my screen. Declan, Jacqueline, and Jeremiah are walking a few feet ahead of us, discussing the new Marvel show that just started airing.

"Did you take the bus?" Annie asks.

"Um." I lock my phone and put it back in my pocket. "Yeah."

"Do you want a ride home? I don't have anywhere to be after this, so it wouldn't be a problem." She must see the surprise in my expression because she gestures to my clothes. For a second, I think she's going to criticize my outfit—one of the loose T-shirts I always wear to avoid attention to my body, and my favorite pair of jeans (because shorts make my dysphoria about my hips worse)—but she just says, "It's too hot for you to walk all the way to the bus stop in that."

"It's just a few blocks. I'll be fine."

Jacqueline comes over, putting a hand on Annie's shoulder. Annie's got more than a few inches on her, so she has to tilt her head down to look at Jacqueline.

"What's going on?" Jacqueline asks.

"I'm offering him a ride since it's hot as hell today."

She grins. "Aww, you're such a mom."

Annie blushes, and she looks back to me, moving past the

86

comment. "Anyway, Gael, it's no trouble—"

"It's okay," I interrupt. "Really. I don't mind walking."

I'm lying through my teeth—today is the worst kind of weather you get from September in Tennessee: oppressive humidity, heat that sears through your clothes, the air stagnant and breezeless and wet all at once—but I'll take the heat over sitting in a car with someone I only sort of know. Annie's nice, and I had a good time with everyone, but I can already feel the anxiety building at the thought of the awkward small talk.

And, yeah, maybe if I said yes, it wouldn't turn out so bad, and I'd get to know her better, and we'd get along the way I get along with Declan. But there's no guarantee, and I don't exactly feel like risking it right now.

They both look a little uncertain, but Annie nods. "If you're sure."

Jeremiah leaves with Jacqueline a minute later, and Annie heads off after them, but not before pulling me into a hug. I hug back awkwardly. I don't love hugs, mostly because they draw too much attention to my chest, but I try to act normal about it. She seems to mean well.

After she's left, Declan slides up next to me. "You need to get home?"

"In a bit. You?"

"Not yet."

We stand next to each other, not saying much for a moment. He shifts his weight from one foot to the other. "I know Annie already threw it out there, but if you need a ride . . ."

I brush my bangs back and look up. The sky is completely

cloudless, an upside-down ocean. We're in the shade under the restaurant's awning, but it's barely keeping the heat at bay. I wiggle my shoulders, trying to surreptitiously readjust my binder, but it sticks to my skin, sweat pooling under the fabric and making me all the more aware of the pressure on my chest.

I can sense Declan looking at me. I think about his arm brushing mine at lunch, and the night at the park when he sat with me until I calmed down, and the dream I had last night, the empty apartment I woke to this morning. I realize, suddenly, that despite the heat, and the anxiety, and the newness of everything, I don't want to go home. I don't want to be alone yet. I want to stay with Declan. Just for a little bit longer.

I'm still looking at the sky when I say, "If you're sure it's not a big deal . . ."

From the corner of my eye, I see him smile. "Definitely."

Ten

gael: are you up?

Outside my room, I hear Mom padding down the hallway, and then the sound of the TV playing. It's Sunday night—well, technically Monday morning now—and I grab my phone and leave my room.

Mom is on the couch, her breathing heavy, her eyes closed. She opens them when she hears me coming, but she seems to look through me. "Gael," she says, her voice hoarse. "Did I wake you?"

"No. I was already up."

"You should be asleep by now. . . ."

"I was doing homework," I say, making my way to the kitchen for some water. "How are you feeling?"

The only light comes from the one over the kitchen sink and the TV. The screen's glow casts an eerie blue on her skin. She looks like a ghost. "I'm all right."

I pass her the water, and she takes it from me with both hands. Mom has always been beautiful, and I think her hands were something Lucas used to love about her, before—but like everything else, they're washed-out now.

"You're sure?"

She drinks. When the cup is half-empty, she sets it on the coffee table. I follow her gaze; it seems like she's staring vacantly at a scratch on the glass table.

"Just . . . stress from school," she mumbles finally.

Because it's the only thing I can think to do, I say, "I'm going to get a thermometer."

There's one in the kitchen drawers between an unused mousetrap and some paper clips. We don't keep a lot of medicine in our apartment, other than the occasional painkiller and our prescriptions—Mom's antidepressants and my testosterone. She's been on antidepressants since she was first diagnosed as a teenager, but the prescription's changed a few times. I think the last time it was changed was when I was eleven and she was admitted to the psychiatric hospital. She doesn't go to therapy anymore—she used to, back before Lucas left, but I think she fell off the wagon and just never got back on. But she still sees a psychiatrist every few months to make sure her prescription gets refilled.

I don't have a therapist, but I have a physician I see every six months. It's mostly for blood work to make sure I'm not running into complications, and refilling my prescription for testosterone, which is taken as a shot in my arm every two weeks. Mom administers it because when I first started T, I was freshly sixteen and severely freaked out by needles. After a year and a half of this, I'm way less bothered by it, but we still haven't changed our method.

Her temperature is normal, but that doesn't make me feel any better. She doesn't say anything else, only lying back down on the couch, her face toward the TV. Even from across the room, I can tell she's shivering. I get her a blanket and drape it over her.

I stay in the living room for another half hour before she falls asleep. My phone buzzes in my pocket.

> **declan:** Yeah, what's up?
> **gael:** nothing. couldn't sleep

I stay where I am and watch a few more minutes of TV while I wait for a response. The ellipses bubble pops up, letting me know Declan is typing. It's 1:43 a.m. We have class later today, but I try not to think about that.

He's still typing. I get up, switch the TV off, and head back to my room, where I crawl under my covers and throw them over my head until I'm completely submerged in blankets.

> **declan:** Any reason you can't sleep?
> **gael:** i had a weird dream last night
> **declan:** Do you want to talk about it?

I sit up and look at the text message. The time goes from 1:48 a.m. to 1:49 a.m. and I'm still not sure how to respond.

Surprisingly, no bubble pops up. I kind of want to know where Declan is right now. If he's in the dark of his room, too.

I start typing.

> **gael:** someone shot themself
> **declan:** In your dream?
> **gael:** yeah. through the cheek
> **gael:** i dont know why it was through the cheek though
> **gael:** it didnt make a lot of sense
> **declan:** Is that the part of the dream that's been bothering you?
> **gael:** yeah

Even as I send the message, it feels wrong. Like a lie. It's *part* of what bothered me, but it's not *all* of it. It wasn't just *someone*.

> **declan:** I'm sorry. That must've really sucked.
> **declan:** Have you ever heard about that thing that says that, like, anyone in your dreams is someone you know?
> **declan:** I don't know if it's a fact or a theory or what, but I read somewhere that your subconscious can't make up faces. So in dreams, it just reuses people you've seen before, even if it's just random people on the street or teachers you had a billion years ago or something.
> **declan:** Was it someone you've seen on the street?

The last question stares back at me, and before I realize what I'm doing, I call Declan. The phone only rings once before he answers.

"Hey." He sounds tired, but his voice comes over clear. There's no background noise. Just him. "Is something wrong?"

"Nothing's wrong." I run my finger over my eyebrow, again and again. "Sorry. It's late. I shouldn't have called."

"No, it's okay, I don't mind. Besides, something must be up for you to call me."

I don't respond. I'm not sure whether Declan's assumption is right, but it feels close enough to the truth that my chest constricts.

"Are you okay?" Declan asks. When I don't respond to that, he continues, "It's okay if you aren't. And it's okay if you don't want to tell me, either. We don't have to talk if you don't want to. I'll stay on the line until you hang up, though."

If you don't want to, he keeps saying. *If you don't want to.* I'm not sure what I do and don't *want.* They always seem to get so mixed up in my head.

"I don't know," I admit. "I don't know if . . ."

There are a million ways to finish that sentence. *I don't know if I want to tell you. I don't know if I should tell you. I don't know if it'll help. If it will make me feel any less shitty. Any less scared for my mom.*

Declan stays quiet, waiting patiently for me to get my thoughts together.

"Can you just . . . talk to me?" I finally say. It doesn't make my chest any lighter, but it sounds closer to what I want.

"We are talking," he points out.

"I mean, like, tell me something." Thumping in my ears. It might be my heartbeat. "Never mind. That was weird."

"It wasn't weird," he rushes to assure me. "What did you

mean, like, you want me to just talk?"

I lick my lips. Bring my hand up to my eyebrow. Tangible. "Yeah. Like a story. About your family or your friends or . . . something. Whatever you want to tell me."

He doesn't even pause at the request. "Okay. Did I ever tell you how we got our dog?"

"No."

He launches into the story.

I don't know how long I sit there with my phone against my ear, but Declan tells me about Ant-Man, about his little sister, Ellie, and his brothers Joshua and Jordan, about Jacqueline's girlfriend, Maggie, and their complicated relationship, about prom last year, about his family's trip to Ireland over the summer to see his paternal grandparents, about his fears for college and the Spotify playlist he started making today. He tells me a million and one things about himself and the world around him and I catch as many as I can.

I fall asleep, and Declan is still telling me.

When I was in seventh grade, Lucas came home drunk one night.

I'd gone to sleep early and woke up around two a.m. to the sound of the front door opening. He'd left after dinner that night, saying he was going out with some friends. Footsteps sounded down the hallway, and I pulled myself out of bed. When I poked my head out the door, I could barely see him in the dark, but he was leaning against the wall with his head down.

I hadn't come out to anyone yet, so Lucas called me by my dead name when he saw me, the sound coming out slurred.

"What're you up for?" he asked, blinking like he couldn't believe I was there.

"I couldn't sleep," I lied. I came out of my room, closing the door behind myself quietly. I pressed my back against it, a hand still on the knob. "Did you, um . . . have fun?"

"Oh, yeah. Loads. We went bowling."

"Um, that's good," I said. I could smell the perfume on him even from here—strong and pungent and floral and startling. Mom hadn't worn any since she started getting worse again a few months prior. She could hardly get up most days, let alone get dressed up enough to put on perfume. "With who?"

"You know, Abdul, Nathan . . ." He waved his hand dismissively, named a few more "college buddies" I'd never met, and started toward his room again. "You should head to sleep, kiddo. G'night."

"Good night."

I went back to bed, but not before watching my father's retreating form. The dark of our apartment swallowed him, and he disappeared for the second time that night.

The next morning, Mom left for work early, so it was just Lucas and me at breakfast. I couldn't help but eye his neck. Purple and red bruises bloomed on his skin, peeking out from the collar of his button-down.

And he still smelled like that perfume.

At school, Declan texts me as the bell rings for lunch.

declan: Hey!

declan: Where do you sit for lunch?

95

Before I can admit to him that I've spent the past three years eating lunch by myself, tucked away in a corner next to a broken vending machine, he sends four more texts.

> **declan:** My friends and I are at one of the round tables near the gym.
> **declan:** You should join us. :)
> **declan:** But only if you want to!!
> **declan:** No presh.

Instead of responding, I head to the cafeteria. Declan is sitting by himself with his backpack on the seat next to him, like he's saving it for me.

Walking up to him, I say, "'No presh'?"

He beams. "A low-pressure way of saying 'no pressure.' The best literature does what it's writing about."

"I'm not sure if I'd consider text abbreviations 'literature.'"

He laughs and moves his backpack, and I slide into the seat next to him.

Jacqueline and Annie show up a few minutes later, and Jeremiah's the last to join us, holding two Taco Bell bags. Declan looks at the bags, surprised. "How did you already get off-campus lunch?"

Jeremiah shrugs. "We weren't doing much in class, so I snuck out early."

"Please tell me you're sharing," Jacqueline says.

"Hell no." He starts unpacking the bags while she pouts. "You were gonna eat all my nachos anyway, so I just went ahead and bought everyone food. Easier on me in the long run."

Annie bumps his shoulder with hers, grinning. "Aww, Jer, that was so nice of you!"

"Yeah, yeah, just don't ask for any of my chips." He starts passing everything out—a burrito for Declan, nachos for Jacqueline, a quesadilla for Annie, and cinnamon twists for everyone to share. He slides an extra bag of cinnamon twists my way. "Sorry, Gael, I didn't know what you'd want, so . . ."

"Oh." I look at the bag. "No, that's okay, these are good. Thank you."

He nods. "Don't mention it."

When I glance at Declan, he's smiling at Jeremiah, soft and fond and a little proud. I don't know why, but I suddenly feel a little like an outsider, like I've walked into a private moment between Declan and Jeremiah, and my stomach does something weird. I look at the table.

As much as I like Taco Bell, cinnamon twists aren't a full meal, so halfway through lunch I go to one of the vending machines to get chips, a granola bar, and a water. I don't usually remember to pack my lunch, and the school's food is abysmal at best, so I'm no stranger to a vending machine meal. There's a line for the machine closest to our table, and while I'm waiting, Annie and Jacqueline join me.

"Hey," Jacqueline says, sliding up next to me. My five-foot-seven height suddenly makes me feels giant next to her—she can't be over five feet. It doesn't help that she seems to always be next to Annie, who has a few inches on me. "What's up?"

I glance at her. "Not much. Why?"

97

"You've been pretty quiet," Annie says. "Something on your mind?"

The person in front of us finishes getting their food, and I punch in the number for the chips I want. "Um, not really."

We're quiet while I get my food. Only when it's Annie's turn does she say, "Is something going on with Declan?"

I'm not sure how to answer, so I don't say anything.

She shakes her head, her blue ponytail shaking with it. "What'd he do this time?"

"He didn't do anything," I say. It's the truth; nothing's happening. I mean, nothing that should make me act this way. It's been good, eating lunch with everyone, meeting them yesterday. And this morning, Mom seemed to be doing a little better than last night. I haven't heard anything about Lucas since his call.

Everything's fine.

I should be *fine*.

But Annie gives me a look.

"We've been friends since we were kids," she says, "so I've dealt with a lot of shit vis-à-vis Declan. If you're up for talking about it, I promise I'll understand, whatever it is."

Jacqueline hums her agreement. "I've known him since middle school, which is arguably the darkest time of everyone's life. We get it."

I can't imagine what kind of "shit" they could've dealt with from Declan; he's always so understanding and considerate. But it's not like I've never been wrong before. Maybe there's a part of him that I wouldn't like if I met it.

How much do I really know about Declan?

How much do I *want* to know?

No one says anything. I run a finger over my eyebrow and finally say, "I don't know what's wrong. Nothing happened."

"But something *is* wrong?" Jacqueline asks. I pause before nodding.

I think about Plus and the phone call last night and the boiling water my mother stood in front of. I think about the fond look Declan was giving Jeremiah earlier. About lunch with everyone yesterday and Declan talking to me until I fell asleep and getting Cook Out together and his laugh, bright and clear.

The girls are quiet while I think. I shift my weight from one foot to the other and ask, keeping my voice down, "Are Jeremiah and Declan, um . . . dating?"

Jacqueline snorts. "*God*, no. Was that what was bothering you?"

"It wasn't *bothering* me. I just . . . wasn't sure. I mean, I thought Declan would've told me by now if they were, but it's not like I've actually asked, and with the way the two of them act sometimes . . ."

"Yeah, they've been close forever," Jacqueline says. "Like, they pretty much grew up together. But there's nothing romantic there. Trust me."

"Jeremiah's our token straight friend," Annie adds.

"Oh, okay." My shoulders fall.

Jacqueline pokes my shoulder good-naturedly. Her nails are painted a warm pink, matching her lipstick. "If I can ask, are you?"

"Am I what?"

"Straight?"

"Oh." The question catches me off guard. Save Nicole, I don't think anyone's ever asked me that. I fumble over my words, but what I land on is, "Um, I guess."

Maybe that's not the greatest response to a question about your sexuality, but I don't think I want to tell them I'm trans just yet, and *I guess* is a much easier answer than *I highly doubt I'll ever be in a relationship, mostly because I'm trans and who would want to date me, but also because I don't think I've ever felt that way about anyone and it's not something I really think about anyway, and I don't know if that makes me straight, exactly, but it's definitely the easiest thing, so maybe if I'm lucky, once we've graduated, I'll, I don't know, find a girl who likes me for God knows what reason, and maybe I'll like her back, and that'll be it, or else I'll just be alone, which doesn't matter too much because I can't imagine ever letting someone touch me anyway.*

Because the truth is, I don't think of myself as someone with sexuality. I'm just Gael. And so much of *me* is wrapped up in being trans because it's *had* to be, and so many of people's ideas about trans people revolve around the assumption that we're all straight—and I *know* that's absolute bullshit and not at all true, I *know* that being trans has nothing to do with sexuality, that there are gay trans people and bi trans people and asexual trans people and every-other-sexuality trans people—but . . .

I still don't know. Sometimes it feels like I'm not allowed to have those feelings. Like, until I've had all the surgeries I can possibly get and grow up and become this hypermasculine poster boy for trans men, then I'm not *allowed* to want sex or a relationship. I'm not allowed to feel anything for anyone.

Certainly not anything that would be considered not straight.

Hence the *I guess*.

To Jacqueline's credit, she doesn't seem confused by the clear lack of conviction in my answer, and she doesn't try to push me. She just nods.

I ask, "You're not straight, right? I mean—Declan mentioned that you have a girlfriend, but I didn't wanna assume . . ."

"I'm bi," she answers easily. "And thank you for asking."

I don't know if "you're welcome" is the appropriate response, so I don't say that, but I can't think of anything else. Her question has got me all in my head now.

We finish getting our food and head back to the table. When I sit back down, Declan nudges my shoulder, and I manage a smile.

But I don't relax. I just keep thinking about all the gaps in that *I guess*.

Eleven

WHEN I GET TO THE youth center on Friday, Nicole is already there, cleaning off the whiteboard. She grins when she sees me, and when she pulls me into a hug, her perfume is strong and very floral. "I was starting to think I'd go this week without you," she says.

"You can't escape me that easily," I reply, looking around the room. People are hanging out in the lobby, and a handful of kids I recognize as Plus regulars have trickled into the room. "Do you know where—"

"Where Declan is?" she guesses, then laughs at my surprise. "Not sure. I kind of figured he'd get here with you."

"Why?"

"'Cause you're together all the time?" she says, like it's obvious.

"We work together, and we go to the same school."

"So? I work with him too, and *we're* not together all the time." She grins.

I'm not sure what to say to that.

Nicole returns to wiping down the board. "It's not a bad thing that you two are close," she says.

"I know," I mumble, but I can't help the way her reminder makes my anxiety kick up, like I've been caught doing something I shouldn't.

When she's done, she sits at one of the tables, tucked away in the back. I sit across from her, the metal chair digging into my back. Someone in the lobby laughs loudly.

"There was something I wanted to talk to you about, actually," I say. She looks at me, curious, and I run a finger over my eyebrow. "It's about . . . um. Well. Jacqueline asked me if I'm straight?"

"Oh." She pauses. "And . . . is that what you wanted to talk about?"

"No. It's just . . . what I said."

"Well, what'd you say?"

"'Um, I guess.'"

"Pardon?"

"That's literally what I said. 'Um, I guess.'"

Her eyebrows go up. "That's . . . certainly more noncommittal than I was expecting," she says. "*Are* you straight?"

"I mean, yeah. It's just—it's weird, liking people and all that when I'm . . ." I gesture toward myself.

Her expression softens. "I know what you mean."

I want to ask her more—find out what it was like with her, maybe—but Declan's voice filters in from the lobby, and a second later he enters with Jacqueline and Annie in tow, the three of them talking. Nicole and I turn to see them, and his face lights up when our eyes meet.

"Hey!" He joins us at the table. "Sorry we're a bit later than usual. I had to give these two a ride after I got out of band."

"No worries! We're not gonna start for another few minutes, anyway." Nicole smiles at them. She catches my eye, and I give her a look to mean *Please don't bring this up with them.*

She nods subtly. *We'll talk more later.*

Declan jumps into introductions between Nicole and Annie, and my shoulders relax.

Saturday night, while Declan and I are cleaning up at Joey's, we get to talking about *Star Wars*—by which I mean *Declan* is talking about *Star Wars*; I'm just listening to him explain why the original trilogy is still the best and trying to pretend that I'm following anything he's saying.

"Sorry," he says at the end of his explanation, giving me an embarrassed smile. We're putting up the chairs on one side of the restaurant, the other side already done. "I'm probably boring you."

"Not at all." I set a chair upside down on its accompanying table. "I've just never seen any of it."

"Oh, shit, that's right! I still need to get you to watch them."

"I'd probably follow along a little better," I agree.

"Probably." He smiles, but it's not embarrassed this time. "Hey. What're your plans for the rest of the night?"

"Other than clock out? Go home and do nothing."

"Wanna come over and watch *Star Wars*?"

I place the chair on the table. I haven't been to Declan's

house before. I've thought about it a little, though. What his house would look like. What his family would be like.

I think about Mom at home by herself. When I left the house today, she was still in bed, and she barely responded when I told her I was headed to work. Things have felt worse lately. Some days, she's fine, better than fine—but she comes down from that just as quickly, then it's back to blankness or sudden crying or sleeping in past noon.

The other day, I checked to see if she was still taking her meds, just in case. She hasn't skipped any days, but that's just made me even more worried. If she's still this depressed on her medication, that must mean something else is causing her to decline. Something I don't know how to fix.

"Sure, but I need to stop by my house real quick first, if that's fine," I say.

He puts his hands in his pockets. "Whatever works for you is cool with me."

We drive to my apartment separately, but once we're both parked, I get out to let him know he doesn't need to go inside with me. "I'm just gonna be a sec."

"No worries." He smiles.

I can't help smiling back. I'm thinking about how excited he is to show me the movies as I'm unlocking the front door, and how much I kind of love that he wants to share the things he likes with me. But all that disappears when I open the door.

Lucas is standing in the kitchen.

Mom sees me before he does, his back to me. I only have half a second to register her slack-jawed expression and surprised "Gael!" before Lucas is turning around, facing me.

He looks different than I remember. Older. His hair has grown out, and there are lines on his cheeks that weren't there before. It's been almost a year since I last saw my dad in person—he wasn't in the habit of visiting us before he moved, only coming by once a year for Christmas—but I guess the possibility that he could've changed since I saw him never occurred to me. He's always been untouchable, in my mind. Unshakable. But he looks shaken now.

Then the moment ends, and his face is shaping back into his regular, pristine expression. Cool and collected and intact.

Warmth spreads up my fingertips. Anger catches up to me. "What the *fuck*?"

"Gael," Mom says.

Lucas is just standing in front of me, his mouth pulled into a straight line and his hands half clenched on the counter, skillfully neutral, my body like a funhouse mirror of his—all my features warped into anger that's already threatening to overwhelm me. I can feel the anxiety attack coming on, building. It always starts with that warmth in my hands, moving up until I can't control it, and I clench my fists in an attempt to find something physical to ground me, but it doesn't work.

"Honey." Mom's hand is on my shoulder now. I know she can feel how I'm threatening to fall apart. "He was just here to talk. I thought it might be nice to welcome him back to town so—"

"Stop. Just stop. Just stop." I wrench myself away from her and run down the stairs to the parking lot. I trip over my feet on the way, but I don't care, and I run past Declan's car and don't look him in the eyes and get in my car and start the engine and I'm trying to get myself to go somewhere but I'm shaking too bad, the worst I have in a long time, and I just slam my hands on the wheel—I need something—to *touch* something—and lean my head back against the headrest and cry.

I don't know how long it's been, but my brain is still swirling when there's a tap on the driver's side window.

I jump. It's dark out, and I hadn't seen Declan coming. He's bent over so I can see him all the way, hooking his thumb in the direction of his car, and I take it to mean I should follow him. He mouths something, but I don't catch it. I just nod. He leaves.

For a moment, I just stare out the windshield. It can't be more than five minutes after I stormed out, but it feels like I've been sitting in the dark for days. I take a second to compose myself before I turn the car off and head to Declan's.

I slide into the passenger seat silently. He's got his music going, something alternative, quiet and almost uncomfortably melancholic.

"Hey" is all he says.

"Hey," I mumble back.

"What happened?"

After a moment, I say quietly, "My dad came over. He was there when I went in to . . ." The thought doesn't need finishing.

"Oh. Shit."

Silence again. The music is loud in the gap.

I sigh. "Can we . . . can we just go to your house?"

"You're sure? We don't have to if . . ."

"I want to."

Declan nods. He turns the music up a little and backs out of the lot. We're quiet the rest of the drive, the songs folding into each other. I stare out the window as Glenwood passes us, streetlights and houses blurring. Now that I've come down from my panic, the world feels sharp and painful, like everything is poking at me.

"How are you feeling?" Declan asks suddenly.

The abruptness paired with the simplicity of the question pull a laugh from me. "Not great," I admit.

"Yeah, I guess I could tell that without asking. Sorry."

"Don't be." I pause. "I'm sorry for . . ."

For losing my cool in front of you. For dragging you into my shitty family drama. For being a little bit of a dick even as you try to help after being put through all that.

"All of it" is what I end up saying.

"Don't be," he parrots.

When we get to his house, his mom and dad are in the living room watching TV, and a German shepherd lies on the floor in front of the couch.

"Hey, honey, I didn't realize you were having someone over," his mother says when she sees us. Mrs. O'Connor is a short Black woman with a heart-shaped face and dreadlocks pulled into a loose bun, and when she turns a smile to me, I can see where Declan gets his. Mr. O'Connor—a white guy with pale blond hair and laugh lines around his eyes—turns the TV volume down a little.

The dog runs over to greet Declan, his tail wagging almost violently in happiness.

"Hey, buddy!" Declan gets down to pet Ant-Man. To his parents, he says, "Sorry, I forgot to text you. This is Gael."

"It's nice to meet you," I say.

"You're Declan's coworker, right?" Mr. O'Connor asks. I nod. "How is it at the restaurant?"

"It's nice. Declan's really good with the customers."

"Oh, stop," Declan says, a laugh in his voice. Ant-Man jumps to lick his cheek, just barely getting him. "You too, bud, I don't want your slobber all over me."

"Well, Gael, it's nice to finally have you over," Mrs. O'Connor says. "We were wondering when we'd get to meet this new friend Declan hasn't stopped talking about."

Declan gives her a pleading look. "Mom . . ."

Mrs. O'Connor laughs. Ant-Man finally decides he's gotten enough attention from Declan, and heads over to me as Declan stands. I hold out my hand for him to sniff and try not to cringe too much when he licks my palm. I'm not used to being around animals.

"We should actually get going 'cause we were going to watch a movie and it's already a little late, sooo . . ." Declan starts toward the stairs. I wipe my palm on my jeans.

"All right, you two have fun," his mom says. As we're turning to head up the stairs, Ant-Man trailing after us, she calls, "Remember to leave the door open!"

Declan grimaces, but he just answers, "Yes, ma'am!"

Once we're in his room, he says, rubbing the back of his neck, "Sorry about that."

"Does she make you do that with all your friends?"

"Only the guys. Well, other than Jeremiah. But I think that's 'cause she's known him so long, and she knows there's no, like, romantic intention or whatever." He laughs, but it's obvious that he's a little embarrassed.

Ant-Man hops up on the bed that's pressed against the far wall, and I survey the room. There's a messy desk to my right, and the walls are decorated with posters, mostly of Marvel movies and a few miscellaneous films. He has a framed poster for *The Adventure Zone*, a podcast he's told me he listens to, and another for The National, his favorite band. A big black instrument case—I'm assuming his mellophone—sits against one wall, next to a bass guitar propped up on a stand.

"You play bass?" I ask, coming over to get a better look at it. It's solid black, and I don't really know anything about instruments, but it certainly *looks* fancy.

"Oh, yeah. I taught myself when I was in middle school, so I'm not exactly good, but I can bang out a few tunes here and there."

"That's really cool."

"Thank you." He smiles, and it hits me just how much he looks like his parents—I can see his mom's smile and honey-brown eyes, his dad's chin and dimples.

I look away. "Um, are your siblings home?"

"Yeah, but they're usually asleep by now. Well, maybe not Joshua and Jordan. They both stay up pretty late, probably playing *Minecraft* or something. Classic twelve-year-old activities."

"Was that what you were up to at twelve?"

"Nah, I never got into *Minecraft*. I was more into beating Jeremiah at *Mario Kart*."

I nod. "So, you've been friends a long time, then?"

"Oh, yeah, we basically grew up together 'cause our parents are friends. Then he recruited Annie to our group when we were ten, and she introduced us to Jacqueline when we were twelve. It's been us four ever since."

"Jesus. I can't imagine staying with a whole group of friends that long."

"What about you and Nicole?"

"She's the exception," I say. "I've had other friends, but they all sort of . . . disappeared after a while."

He frowns. "How come?"

"I moved right before high school started, and I'm not big on social media or texting, so we just lost contact."

What I don't say is that we stopped talking because, even after I came out to my family and Nicole, I didn't tell Neema or Brianna I was trans. I just couldn't find the words. And then my parents separated, and suddenly my mom was talking about moving, and it's not like I was ever super close with my school friends anyway, so I just . . . left it alone.

If I'm honest, I was scared. Scared of what they'd say. Scared that if I got a bad response, it would sap all of the courage I'd managed to drum up. My decision to transition felt so new then, so fragile, like one wrong move and it would all be reversed. I know now that, no matter what anyone says or thinks, transitioning was the best thing I ever did for myself. But back then, when my parents were falling apart and I was just starting my transition, I think I worried that if I let these two friends in on who I really was, and they rejected me for it, it would tear down everything I'd worked so hard to build.

So, I shut them out. I stopped responding to their texts, and after a while, they stopped sending them. It just seemed easier that way, like the safer option.

"That sucks," Declan says.

I shrug. "It's not a huge deal. I don't think about it that much."

He nods, and, thankfully, doesn't push the topic. He picks up the laptop on his desk. "Do you mind if we just watch the movie on my computer?"

"Go for it."

We get settled on the floor, our backs pressed to his bed as he pulls up *A New Hope* on the screen. According to Declan, it's best if we watch the movies in order of when they were released.

While he's waiting for the page to load, he turns to me. "About what happened earlier . . . you know I'm here if you want to talk about it."

When he looks at me, it's so open, so obviously concerned, that part of me wants to give in and tell him what I've been dealing with. Mom's mental health, Lucas's moving back. All of it.

But the movie's loaded on his computer, and the option is open: I can ignore it all. I can turn my brain off for two hours and enjoy my time with Declan.

So I tell him, "I'm okay now, but thank you. Really." And I promise myself that if I need to, I'll explain it all sometime soon.

He turns the movie on after that, and we watch in comfortable silence.

Declan drops me off at my apartment three hours after I stormed out.

Lucas isn't there anymore, and Mom isn't in the living room. The place feels eerily empty, everything just a little bit off. I don't go looking for Mom, instead heading straight to my room where I lie in my bed and stare at the ceiling for a long time. Declan texts me goodnight, thanks me for coming over, says we should watch the rest of the trilogy later. I tell him we can do that. I don't fall asleep for a while.

In the morning, Mom doesn't bring up what happened.

I don't know why I'm surprised. It's not like we don't do this with most family issues anyway. Bury it all. Keep it quiet.

I guess I just hoped that it would be worth talking about this time. That *something* could change.

But Mom makes her coffee like normal. Gets dressed. Sits down at the table to finish her schoolwork. And when I look at her for a long moment, taking in the bags under her eyes and the strands of hair escaping her loose braid, she tilts her head at me.

"Something up?" she asks, the mug her student bought her—the replacement—cupped in her thin hands. Like there was never any broken glass. Like nothing happened.

A knot forms in my stomach. I turn to head back to my room.

"No," I lie. "Everything's fine."

Twelve

declan: On a scale from 1 to 10, how cool would you be with me adding you to a group chat with Jeremiah, Jac, Annie, and me?

gael: 1

declan: :(

gael: im kidding, that sounds like fun

gael: also, u didnt say which end of the spectrum is negative

gael: for all u know that was a positive response

declan: I can't believe I cordially invited you to the BEST group chat available, and you used it as a chance to tell jokes . . . . Rude.

gael: how long did u have to hold the period key to type that

declan: A while. And was it worth it? Yes.

declan: Anyway!!! I'm adding you now. Be prepared for a LOT of messages, lol.

gael: sounds like fun

declan: It will be now that you're there! :)

The following week, Jacqueline sits next to me in Environmental Science class.

"Good morning!" She seems surprisingly awake, considering it's barely eight a.m. "You mind if I join you from now on? Don't tell anyone, but my lab partner has been getting on my last nerve."

"No, of course." I move my backpack off the table so there's more space for her.

"You're a lifesaver." She sets her elbows on the desk and leans her chin in her palm. Her nails are painted gold, and her box braids are gone, replaced by two Afro puffs.

"So, how was your weekend?"

"Fine, you?"

"Good! I slept in until three on Saturday, so overall a success." Her phone buzzes with a text. "Oops, hold on."

She taps out a reply, but she must receive another message immediately after that because I watch her eyes quickly scan over the screen, her eyebrows furrowing in confusion.

"Is everything okay?" I ask, but she's already typing again. This goes on for another minute before she finally looks up from her phone, blinking like she'd forgotten where she was.

"Uh, sorry about that. My girlfriend just dropped something on me out of nowhere and I'm just trying to . . ." She waves her hands around her head vaguely. "Process it?"

"Do you want to talk about it?" I look around the room. Kids are trickling in, and we still have another five minutes before the bell rings. "We've got some time."

Jacqueline glances back at her phone again before sighing deeply. "Okay. So. *Basically.* When we started thinking seriously about college, my girlfriend and I made an agreement to not let our relationship impact where we apply. I mean, I don't think it's too controversial to say it's not a good idea to base our college decisions off of our relationship?"

"That sounds reasonable to me."

"Well." She taps the back of her phone case. "I just now found out that, *apparently*, Maggie has decided to stop looking anywhere but at places she knows I'm for sure applying to."

"Oh." I pause. "That's . . . not ideal."

"Right! That's what I'm saying! But then she said that it isn't that big of a deal because we want to try to stay together after graduation anyway, and I'm like, yes, but that shouldn't affect what we decide to do with our whole *lives*, you know?" She takes a deep breath. "I'm not overreacting, am I? Like, am I in the wrong here for thinking this is a weird thing to spring on me out of nowhere?"

"No, I'd be upset, too." I don't know that for sure—it's hard for me to imagine myself in her shoes, dating someone, worrying about relationships after high school—but it feels like the right thing to say. "Especially since y'all already decided you weren't gonna let it affect you. Why did she change her mind all of a sudden?"

"I don't know, and that's the weirdest part. Like, why right now? Or has she been feeling like this the entire time and just

116

hiding it from me?" She runs a hand over her face. "I just think we shouldn't make the assumption we'll be together forever. . . . Messing our expectations up is the last thing we should do right now, especially since we don't even know *where* we'll get accepted."

"Where are you applying?"

"It's kind of a long list, but right now I'm really hoping for Duke, Brown, or Vanderbilt."

"Holy shit. Those are all insanely hard to get into, right? And she's only looking at them because you are?"

"Not *totally*—she was already looking at Vanderbilt, but I don't think she'd be looking into the rest of them if they weren't on my radar. But who even knows if I'll get into any of those places, let alone if she will, too? And then what if *she* gets accepted into a school that I really wanted, but I don't?" She looks down at her phone again.

"I'm sorry you're dealing with this. Especially this early in the morning."

She manages a smile. "Yeah, me too. But it'll be all right." She sighs. "Probably."

The teacher enters after that, and as class begins, I'm still thinking about Jacqueline applying to Vanderbilt and Duke and Brown. I wonder if she knows what job she'll eventually get. How far in the future is she looking? How far has she planned? And am I wrong if I'm not looking that far ahead, too?

The other night, I finally started compiling application dates for a few in-state colleges. If I apply early action, I have a month and a half before most of the deadlines. If I wait, I have until after Christmas.

I wonder if Declan is applying early action. If he's planning on staying in state, too.

That afternoon at Plus, Nicole is joined by someone else in leading the group, a nonbinary person named Dakota who's older than Nicole and just as extroverted. Before the meeting starts, Nicole tells me Dakota has been absent because they were recovering from top surgery, and a pang of envy hits me the way it often does when I hear about other trans people getting care I can't access yet. Not that I resent them—I'm happy for them. But it makes me think about my own body. I can't help looking at Dakota, trying to imagine myself in their position. I wonder what it'll be like to breathe with that new chest.

My mom and I have been trying to see if I can get top surgery after graduation, but because it's so far in advance, and because of how Tennessee is when it comes to trans healthcare, my first appointment won't be until after I turn eighteen next April. So, hopefully, if everything goes right, I *will* be in Dakota's position pretty soon. But I've been trying not to get too excited for it. There's still a lot of time before my first appointment.

I sit between Nicole and Declan, Jacqueline on Declan's other side, and watch Dakota write on the whiteboard in curling letters, "Gender: Roles, Expression, and Identity." They cap the marker and turn back to the group, hands on their hips. I run my finger over my eyebrow.

I know what this discussion topic means for me. I'm gonna sit here while other people talk about their experiences, and I'll listen, and appreciate hearing it, and feel a little bit better, a little less alone—but never less alone enough to feel like I can say something. And then, once the meeting is over, I'm gonna wish I'd said something, and then I'll relay all my thoughts to Nicole in an attempt to make up for the fact that I can never get myself to speak, even when I want to. Even when I need to.

I hate that I'm like this. Hate that my mouth clamps itself shut with anxiety. I run my finger over my eyebrow again and again.

Maybe it's the fact that even my weird eyebrow thing isn't helping my anxiety, or maybe it's because Nicole starts talking about how she came out, or maybe it's because I'm so irritated at myself for never speaking, never doing what I want—whatever it is, something makes me raise my hand when the girl across from me starts talking about the way her school's administration handles restrooms with their trans students. Dakota calls on me.

"GHS is like that too," I say, quick enough that I can get the words out before my anxiety catches up to me. "My freshman year, administration told me to only use the bathroom in the nurse's office instead of the men's restroom. I never end up doing that, though. It's too out of the way."

"Exactly!" The girl nods emphatically. "It's like—using the nurse's office is not convenient, or even possible when I have class on the other side of the building, but they won't just let me use the women's. It's so gross."

She keeps going, and then someone else adds their own two cents, and the conversation moves forward. I've faded out of the discussion again, but my heart is still thudding like I've run a marathon. This is the first time I've mentioned being trans in front of Declan or Jacqueline. I'm too nervous to look at them, but I'm able to look at Nicole when she puts a comforting hand on my knee. It's a subtle attempt to calm me down, and it doesn't make my heart rate return to normal just yet, but it does make me smile at her a little. She looks proud that I've finally spoken up.

The weirdest part is that I kind of am, too. Despite all the anxiety, I'm glad.

Since Declan gave me a ride from school to Plus, he takes me home afterward. Declan's been making playlists for everyone in the friend group, so I turn on the one he sent me, titled "to: g." We listen to the music for a few minutes in silence, and I wonder if he's thinking about what I said during group discussion.

I don't think he's going to be weird about it—after all, he's friends with Nicole, and it's not like he's ever given me a reason to think he'd be transphobic. But, still, it's the first time I've told someone I'm trans since I changed schools, and I can't help the way my anxiety increases as our silence grows. I wish he would just *ask* already.

The song reaches its bridge, and he's tapping his finger against the steering wheel to the music when he says, "I didn't realize that about GHS."

My tongue flicks over my teeth. "Yeah. They're pretty shitty."

It gets a small laugh from him, but it's more restrained than usual. I pull my legs up, prop my heels on the seat, and wrap my arms around my knees.

He finally asks, "So . . . you're trans?"

I nod. "I thought maybe Nicole might've told you at one point, but I wasn't sure, and I sort of didn't know when to bring it up, so . . ."

"She didn't tell me," he says. "I mean, when you first showed up, I asked her why you were at Plus, you know, just out of curiosity, but all she said was that she asked you to go for her, so I thought maybe you were just an ally or something."

"Nope. Just . . . you know. Part of the acronym."

"Can I ask if you're out at school?"

"I mean, kind of? I started transitioning right before high school, and there aren't really any people I grew up with around here, so most people don't know, like . . . what I looked like before, or my dead name, or anything like that. But I wasn't on testosterone until last year, so I was getting misgendered all the time freshman and sophomore year. I doubt people have just forgotten. But I'm *trying* to go stealth, kind of. I don't really talk about it." I pause. "You're the first person at GHS I've told, actually."

I don't know what I expected him to do after hearing that, but it's not for him to reach over and set a hand on my forearm, just long enough to be a comforting weight. He takes it away before it can become overwhelming or awkward, and I'm left sitting there with my skin tingling where he touched me.

"Thank you for telling me," he says, and it sounds like he means it.

I let go of my knees and stretch my legs out as much as I can in his small car, rolling my ankles to crack them. "Are you out at school?"

He nods. "Yeah. I don't usually tell people right away, but I don't really hide it either, and there was this whole thing about it in middle school, so somehow it just kind of seeped into GHS, too."

"What happened in middle school?" I think back to what Annie and Jacqueline had said to me at the vending machine the other day.

"It's . . . a long story," he says.

"We have time. If you want to talk about it, I mean."

For a moment, he doesn't say anything, and I worry that I've pushed him too far, asked for something he's not ready to give—but we come to a stop at a red light, and he takes a deep breath before speaking.

"I had a *huge* crush on one of my friends all throughout middle school," he says. "Like, I thought I was in love with him, it was that intense. So, in eighth grade, I finally said fuck it and told him how I felt. I wasn't even trying to ask him out or anything—I knew he was straight; I knew he didn't like me like that—it was just that I couldn't stand keeping this secret all the time anymore. And he was . . . okay about it, all things considered. His response was way lower on the homophobic reaction scale than it could've been. But he started avoiding me, and then I guess he told his other friends, and then *they* told *their* friends. . . ." He sighs. "So, word spread fast. I was already an outsider, what with the whole being-one-of-four-Black-kids-in-the-entire-school thing. After that, I was also our class's first 'out' gay kid, even though I never got the choice to tell anyone."

"Shit, Declan, I'm sorry. That's horrible."

"Yeah, it was pretty bad at the time. Other than, you know, the bullying, one of the worst parts was that I didn't get to decide for myself when and who I told. That entire year, and even a lot of freshman year, it seemed like all anyone knew about me was that I was gay. Now I don't give a shit who knows, but back then, I was still new to understanding myself, so it felt . . . violating."

The light turns green, and the road in front of us stretches out. An Arlo Parks song floats through the speaker, a quiet undertone.

"At the very least," he says, "I still got to tell my close friends and family on my own terms. I told Jeremiah basically the day I knew, and I came out to my parents a few weeks before all the stuff at school went down."

"How was that?"

"They . . . weren't too happy. My dad, at least. My mom was a lot better about it. She still didn't totally *get* it, but she always supported me. She never . . ." He takes a deep breath. "Don't get me wrong. I love my dad, and he's cool about it now. He's definitely *trying* at the very least, and, like, that's way better than a lot of people ever get. I'm lucky."

"But?"

"But . . . it kind of messed me up. Finally getting the courage to come out to my family, only to have my parents argue over it. Dad thought I should hide it, try not to make myself an 'easy target' for the other guys at school, all that bullshit. Mom thought I just needed time to figure things out for myself. And . . . I don't know. My family's always been super close, so all of a sudden having this weird tension every night at dinner, and knowing it was *me* that caused it . . ."

"I'm sorry."

"It's okay. I know they love me, and things are a lot better now."

"That doesn't mean it didn't hurt you."

He glances at me and offers a small smile. "Yeah. You're right."

We drive for a few moments in silence. The song changes, and when I look at my phone, I see it's by The National. I think about the poster in his bedroom, and then I think about meeting his parents, and his mom's warm smile. I picture Declan in middle school, outed against his will and dealing with his dad's disapproval. With how he talks about his family now, I wouldn't have guessed that they'd gone through something like that.

"What about you?" he asks eventually. "How are your parents about it?"

"They're supportive," I say. "My mom was a little confused at first, but she got over it quickly, and she was really chill when I asked to start testosterone. I'm trying to get top surgery after graduation, and she's been supportive of that, too. She's gonna help pay for it, and I've been saving up money from Joey's, so hopefully it'll come together . . . but that's a while away."

"Still, though! That's really exciting."

"It is," I agree.

"What about your dad? Is he on board with all of it?"

I run my finger over my eyebrow. "He never calls me the

wrong name, and he's good about my pronouns and calling me his son and stuff. But if I'm honest, I've never really talked to him about it. I started transitioning right around the time my parents separated, so . . ."

"You two don't have the best relationship, right?"

I laugh a little. "Yeah, you could put it that way. He's an asshole."

"In what way?"

"It's . . . complicated."

"We have time," he echoes.

I wasn't expecting to talk about this tonight. I mean, it's surprising he made it this long without asking at all, since he must've been curious about it ever since that night at my apartment. But . . . he's here. He's made it clear he wants to know.

And, more than that, I think I *want* to tell him.

"They divorced about three years ago," I start. "My dad used to own a bakery, but it went under around the same time they split, so he moved away. He was living in New York until about a week ago. Now he lives here again. Out in Bellevue."

These are all textbook answers, clinical sentences. But I know this isn't what Declan wants. He wants something heartfelt. Something that feels like bleeding.

I'm not sure if I can give him that, but I try anyway.

"My dad cheated on her," I say. "On my mom. For . . . I don't know how long. I figured it out when I was thirteen. It was just little stuff adding up. Things like how he always said he was out with his friends, but he'd get home late, and he'd smell like this perfume, and he'd be so dodgy about it . . .

Anyway, I didn't tell my mom for almost a year because . . . I didn't know how. And maybe a little because I didn't want it to be real—like, if I just ignored it, and if my dad never said anything about it, then maybe it wasn't actually happening. But it didn't matter in the end 'cause she found out on her own. I don't know how. Maybe she saw them together, or she'd picked up on the stuff I'd noticed, too. But they separated after that, and he moved out. It's been my mom and me ever since."

The car stops. When I look up, we're at a park, the same one I ran away to that night I first called him. Declan turns off the engine and gets out, the door shutting quietly behind him. I follow hesitantly.

"What are you doing?"

Declan is halfway to the swings by the time I voice the question. He's silhouetted by the streetlights.

"I'm giving us a better place to have a heart-to-heart," he says, and he might be smiling. "Don't you think this is more appropriate than a car?"

"Barely." But I'm already making my way to him.

Declan chooses a swing and I take the one next to him, the equipment creaking under our weight. It's cool tonight.

We sit next to each other in silence until Declan prompts, "Go on. I brought us out here for you to talk. I'm here to listen."

"There's not really much else to say. He cheated on her, they divorced, my dad sucks. End of story."

"*Not* end of story. There's never an end to the story."

"You sound like an English teacher."

Declan grins. "Considering I'm gonna be one, I'll take that as a compliment."

"You want to be an English teacher?"

"Yeah, you didn't know that?"

"No," I say, and I'm at a loss, somehow. This isn't exactly the most important thing to happen tonight, but it's what I'm stuck on. That I didn't know such a simple thing about him. That I didn't think to ask.

"I want to teach college, so *professor*, technically, but yeah. That's the plan. I'm gonna major in English with a focus on literature."

"Professor O'Connor," I say. "That suits you."

He smiles, a quiet thing. I look at my feet.

"Anyway," he continues, "what I said is still true. There's more to it. You don't have to tell me if you don't want to, but . . ."

I don't know what the end to that thought might be, but I'd like to think it finishes with *but I'm here to listen,* or *but you look like you do,* or *but I still care.* Or all three.

"My mom has pretty severe depression," I say. "She's had it since she was a teenager. It was okay for a while when I was a kid, but she's always . . . struggled. I think my dad started cheating on her around the time it got worse. He hated that she couldn't control it or just ignore it for our sake. . . . I think they fought over it a lot. He didn't understand that it's not something she can turn off or just, like . . . will away. He's never said it, but I think when he married her, he thought she would just stop being sad because she had someone who loved her, so when she stayed sick, it really affected him."

127

There's a breeze. I rock back and forth on the swing gently, my hands wrapped around the cold chains. My throat tightens, my tongue slips, my mouth stays shut. My whole body tries to keep me from saying the next words, but I force them out anyway. I need to get them out. I *need* to.

"She tried to kill herself when I was eleven," I hear myself say. "I don't remember a lot about that day, except that the bottle—she'd taken so many pills. I counted them. I don't know why I counted them, but it was so important to know at the time. And it's just—she's been worse lately, just getting worse and *worse* and now my dad is back in town and trying to talk to us again and showing up at the house the other day and I'm scared it's gonna make it even worse and that she's gonna—"

Declan's hands are on my shoulders suddenly, and they're warm, combating the chill that swept across my body. I don't remember seeing him get up from the swing.

"Hey, hey," he's saying, not quite a whisper. "It's okay, you don't have to keep talking about it. It's totally fine. Breathe. You're okay."

His voice is soothing. Warm and low. My hands unclench around the chains, and I realize only now how they've dug into my palms, the metal biting into my skin and leaving little imprints. Declan's hands are gone from my shoulders, disappeared like he's afraid of holding contact for too long, but I wish he hadn't.

He returns to his swing. "I shouldn't have asked. I'm sorry."

"It's okay," I mumble. *I wanted to tell you. I wanted to tell somebody.*

I *needed* to tell somebody.

I've gone so many years holding back that information from everybody but Nicole, avoiding any questioning involving my family, shoving the memories out. Even when Lucas was around, I never told Brianna or Neema about Mom. It was the same as with my dad cheating: if I never brought it up, if I never thought about it, if I never told anyone—then it wasn't a big deal. It wasn't happening.

But it *did* happen. It was still happening with Mom. All the time. And my silence these past years hasn't done shit to help.

It felt good, saying that to Declan. Even with the shaking. It felt good.

"It's getting late," he says, checking the time on his phone. "We probably need to get home."

He stands and offers a hand to me. I take it, letting myself be hauled up to my feet. His hands are just as warm now as they were when they were on my shoulders, but the contact is lost quickly, the moment over before it's barely begun.

The walk back to the car is quiet. As we pull out of the parking lot, I say, "How'd you know how to handle that so well?"

"Handle what?"

I gesture toward myself. "When I freaked out. You were really quick to help."

"Ah." He taps his fingers on the steering wheel. "My brother Jordan . . . he gets pretty bad panic attacks. He's had them for a few years, but they've gotten worse lately. Mom thinks it's 'cause he's twelve and everything sucks at that age, so all the problems he already had are just made worse. . . . Anyway, she's really good at calming him down, but I've gotten used to trying to comfort him, too."

"You're always helping people," I say.

"Yeah. Probably a little too much. When I *can't* do anything to help, I get to feeling all mopey."

"Why?"

He thinks about it. "When I love someone, I want them to be happy, and I want to help them as much as I can. It's nice, you know? It's fulfilling. But if someone's going through something and I can't do anything to fix it . . . it starts to feel like I haven't earned the love they give me back. Plus, I *hate* not having control over situations, so it's, like, *the* worst combination for me." He laughs, light and casual like he didn't just make himself vulnerable.

"You know you don't have to earn people's love," I say quietly. "It should just . . . I don't know. Happen. Be."

"Yeah." He tries to give me a reassuring smile, but I can tell how it weighs on him. "I know."

I have more I want to say—more I want to tell him. I want to let him know he's loved regardless of what he does for other people, and I want to know more about his brother, and about his childhood, his relationship with his parents, his dreams of becoming a professor, where he wants to go to college next year. I want to know more, *say* more.

But I'm so tired now, all the energy zapped out of me, and Declan seems content to just drive. I lean back and let the music fill our silence.

As I'm getting out in my apartment's parking lot, Declan

tells me to wait. I watch him unbuckle and get out of the car. Standing up close, I'm reminded that I'm taller than him. I'm reminded even further by the hug he pulls me into.

"I'll text you when I get home, okay?"

"Okay."

"Good night, Gael."

"Night."

As he drives off, I touch my shoulder, where his hand rested.

Thirteen

I DIDN'T REALLY COME OUT to my dad.

Even before Mom caught him cheating, I'd grown away from him. Started to resent him. Started avoiding him, afraid to see more proof of what he was doing. And even before the affair was brought to light, I had a track record of taking Mom's side during arguments. This clear bias put a strain on our relationship, already so fragile by then.

So, I never really came out to him, at least not in the way that I came out to Mom. With Mom, it was something planned, a moment that I thought about for weeks before I finally sat down with her on the couch one afternoon and told her the truth between nervous, fluttering hands and tears that I couldn't quite conceal. *I think I'm a boy,* I said. Then, *I'm a boy. I'm trans.*

And there was more to it, of course—more explaining, more questions. Things like *How do you know for sure?* and *How long have you been feeling like this?*, but in the end, Mom just held me close and kissed the top of my head and told me that she loved me no matter what, that she was there for me, that we could try out a new name and new pronouns and a new wardrobe if it would help me feel more like myself. She had a leg up on a lot of other parents in that she knew what it was like to feel wrong in your body, to be miserable in it. Even if her understanding stemmed from depression instead of gender dysphoria, she got enough to know that what I needed was to be listened to and trusted that I knew what was best for myself.

So, she listened, and she trusted, and I told her my new name. *Gael.*

I don't know when she told Lucas, but she must have at some point, because within a week of Mom's sudden switch to my new name, he wasn't questioning it or giving me curious looks or staring too long when I left the house in clothes from the men's section, my chest bound with the new binder Mom gave me money to buy. And, although he avoided using my name or pronouns for the first few weeks, I eventually heard him call me Gael.

But he never asked me why I didn't come out to him myself. Sometimes I wonder if he knew, even back then, just how much I couldn't forgive him.

At school the next week, we go off campus for lunch.

"I'm, like, eighty percent sure this isn't Dr Pepper," Jacqueline says, holding up her Taco Bell cup.

"How can you only be *eighty percent* sure?" Jeremiah comes

to a very sudden stop at a red light. From my spot in the back seat, I hold on to the back of Jacqueline's headrest.

Annie says, "Can you *not* slam on the brakes, please?"

"I'm not."

"You are," Declan, Annie, and I say in unison.

It's the end of September, and I've fallen into a routine with Declan and his friends. I sit with them at lunch every day; Jacqueline walks with me to and from Environmental Science; Declan and I get lightly reprimanded for talking in AP Lit. I'm part of the group now, but I still can't totally believe it, sometimes. I keep waiting for the punchline to hit, for them to tell me it was fun while it lasted but now it's over, bye, leave us alone. But so far, there are no signs of disaster.

Jacqueline turns around in her seat and holds her drink out to Declan, who's squished between Annie and me. "Here, taste this for me. Is this Dr Pepper?"

He tries it just as the light turns green and Jeremiah accelerates again. Luckily, Declan doesn't lose his grip and spill soda all over me. He hands the cup back to Jacqueline. "Nope. That's Pepsi."

"See!"

"Okay, but"—Jeremiah makes a hard turn—"*eighty percent*?"

"I know we only have, like, two minutes to get back to school, but Jeremiah, I would actually like to show up *alive* to class," Declan pleads.

"Sorry, dude, but you're the one that wanted off-campus lunch in the first place."

"I didn't mean for *you* to drive," he mumbles.

We get to school with a minute to spare. AP Lit is right after lunch, and Declan and I have to all but run to class, still carrying our Taco Bell bags. We make it just in time, and I settle into my seat with a grin still lingering.

We're halfway through the class when I notice Declan keeps glancing at his phone, then trying to surreptitiously text. It's uncharacteristic of him—this is his favorite class. I can't see his whole face from where I'm sitting, but I can catch glimpses of worry starting to grow, his eyebrows furrowing, mouth down-turned. Just as the teacher finishes a PowerPoint about Mary Shelley's life, Declan slides the phone into his pocket and asks to be excused to the restroom. She nods, and he scurries out the door, head bowed.

Fifteen minutes pass, and he's still gone. The teacher starts discussing excerpts from the first chapter of *Frankenstein*. I send Declan a text.

gael: hey, u ok?

declan: Uhhhh, sort of. It's all good, though, I'm fine.

gael: u do know ur being extremely cryptic right

declan: Yeah . . .

gael: a "yeah" trailing off does not help your case

declan: It's just something with my family.

declan: Don't worry.

gael: do u wanna talk about it?

No response. When he still hasn't returned five minutes later, I ask to be excused, too.

The hallways are empty and silent, save the occasional sounds of teachers lecturing as I pass cracked classroom doors, and I find Declan in the nearest men's restroom, his rainbow-shoelaced Doc Martens visible under a stall. There's no one else, but I still stand close to the exit. I'm not technically allowed in the men's restrooms, and I don't use public restrooms often to begin with, so being in here is a little more uncomfortable than I would like to admit.

"Hey," I say.

There's a pause, then Declan steps out of the stall. His eyes are red and puffy, and he wipes his cheeks with the back of his hand hurriedly. "Hey."

"Everything all right?"

He offers an unconvincing smile. "Just . . . It's nothing. False alarm."

Through the mirror, I watch his expression as he washes his hands, his glasses sliding down his nose. He's wearing a pale yellow T-shirt and a jean jacket decorated with enamel pins—a shield from *The Legend of Zelda*, a stack of books, a star.

I focus on the shield pin as I say, "If you really want me to, I'll leave it alone, but . . . I'm here if you want to talk."

I feel his eyes on me through the mirror, and I look up and meet his gaze. Something about looking at each other through a mirror is more nerve-racking than normal eye contact, some-how. More intimate. But I don't look away. I need him to know that I'm serious about this. That when I say I'm here for him, it's not just talk.

He looks away first, his eyes flitting back to the sink. "You know how I said my brother Jordan gets these really bad panic attacks?"

I nod.

"Well, he had one during class today, so my dad picked him up early from school. Instead of telling me any of this, though, Joshua starts texting me, all freaked out, saying Jordan's not doing good and that he couldn't be at school, so *I* start freaking out, thinking something bad happened. . . . Anyway, it wasn't anything too serious. I mean, it sucked, but he's at home, and he's fine now. But I guess I just got . . ." He can't seem to find an adequate word, so he just ends the sentence there, his shoulders drooping.

"I know what you mean," I say. I lean against the counter next to him. "Sometimes, with my mom, I'll jump to conclusions and freak myself out."

"What do you do when you get like that?"

The honest answer is "usually, nothing"—I'm not very good at stopping the panic. Most of the time, I don't find a way to pull myself out of the fear until I know for sure that Mom is fine. But I don't think that would be very helpful for him, so instead, I imagine what I would want to hear if I were in Declan's shoes, and I try to draw experience from the times I *have* calmed my anxiety.

"I try to catch myself doing it. Sometimes, if I can notice that I'm catastrophizing, that helps me get back to being more rational. Or I'll focus on something else, usually a different, like, physical sense. I'm a pretty tactile person, so I crochet when I'm getting in my head about something, or I'll find other ways to ground myself physically."

"Is that why you do that eyebrow thing?"

"Oh." I touch my eyebrow. I hadn't realized Declan noticed me doing that. "Yeah, that is."

He nods and leans against the counter with me. We're facing the wall away from the sink, looking at the paper towel dispensers and the white-and-blue tiles.

"I just wish I could help him," Declan says. "I wish I could make it all stop for him. I hate not having control. Not being able to *do* anything."

"I know. It really, really sucks. But at least he's okay right now?"

"Yeah." He sighs. "That's true."

We're both quiet for a moment. Then he nudges my arm with his. "Sorry for making you come after me."

"You didn't make me. I wanted to."

He offers a small smile. "We should probably get back to class."

"Probably."

As we're leaving the restroom, another boy enters. I tense as he passes, keeping my head down and my eyes trained to the ground. *Please don't say anything, please don't say anything....* And luckily, he doesn't; he just mumbles a "thanks" when Declan holds the door open for him as we exit, and I let out a quiet, relieved sigh once we're in the hallway.

This is part of why, school policies aside, I don't use the men's restroom in public much. Even when nothing bad happens, even when I'm in the clear—I'm still holding my breath.

Declan notices my uneasiness. He doesn't say anything about it, but as we head back to AP Lit, he puts a hand on my shoulder and squeezes once, gently.

Lucas calls.

I'm at home that night, sitting at the kitchen table doing AP Lit homework, drowning in reading questions as I flip through Mom's old copy of *Frankenstein*. She's never had much time for reading, but there are a few books she particularly enjoyed that she keeps around the apartment, all with their spines broken in, their pages worn, and the margins filled with scribbles. I'm half reading Mom's annotations and half trying to find the answers to the questions when my phone rings.

I stare at it, but I know even before I turn the phone over that it's Lucas. On the fifth ring, I brace myself enough to hit Answer.

"Hello?"

"Gael," Lucas says. "Hey. How are you?"

"Fine."

There's a long pause, like he's lost his place in a script. I doubt he was expecting me to pick up.

He finds his footing again. "How's your senior year been treating you so far?"

"We're not even halfway through the semester." I watch my pencil roll down the table. My book stops it mid-journey, so I pick it up again and set it at the top. On its third roll down I say, "But it's been fine. Why did you call?"

"I wanted to talk to you. Do you know what schools you're

applying to for next year?"

"Not really." It's a little misleading, since I've been *looking* at places, but I haven't decided on anything yet, and I don't exactly feel like telling him the details of my research.

"Well . . . what about majors then? Have you picked one yet?"

"Nope."

"What? What do you mean?"

"Exactly what I said. I don't know what to major in, and I don't know where I'm going."

There's a pause. "Gael . . ."

His tone is what gets me. Disappointed, and yet not quite compassionate. Just condescending. It's what makes me snap, "Why do you even care?"

"You're my son, can't I care about what you're doing with your future?"

"You haven't before."

"You know that's not true."

"Do I?"

He's silent.

"It's not really your business what I'm doing with college right now," I say. "My life isn't exactly your business. You forfeited that when you left us."

"I didn't—"

"And just because you're back in the state again," I say, and even I'm surprised by the bitterness in my voice, "it *doesn't* mean you're suddenly allowed in my life."

Lucas sucks in a breath. The rebuttal must have landed

somewhere vulnerable because there's a long pause before he says, "I just want to know how you're doing."

"I'm doing fine. Isn't that what you want to hear?"

I stare at *Frankenstein*'s green cover in the silence.

"Your mom's not doing well."

Anger hits me sharp and quick. "Jesus, you don't think I know that? I live with her, in case you forgot—of course I know she's not *doing well*. She's *never* doing well."

I don't know why I say it. It's not necessarily true—she has her good days. She has her good *weeks*. Sometimes even a month will pass without her spiraling, leaving behind uninterrupted and fragile normalcy.

But . . . the bad days stick out so much more. In my memory, even the good moments are tinged with worry. With fear.

When I realize what I've said, shame eats at the anger. I don't want to think of Mom like that. I don't want to view her as just her illness. I don't want to blame her for something I know she can't control.

"Please," he continues. "Just—let me come by one afternoon. I can cook dinner for you and Ana. I miss you. Both of you. We can catch up."

"I have to do homework," I say. "Bye, Lucas."

I hang up before he can respond.

The phone doesn't ring again, but as I turn back to my homework, I keep glancing at it like it will.

At Plus this week, we're split into pairs for an activity— something where we roll dice to assign ourselves characteristics, ranging from economic status to clothing preference, and we're supposed to talk about how these things would or wouldn't change our experiences. I pair with Nicole.

"All righty," Nicole says as we find a spot near the back of the room. "You want me to go first?"

The activity is a little underwhelming, but that's pretty normal for Plus. They're really just meant to inspire group discussions, and those are what I like the most anyway. Nicole rolls, and she compares the number she got with the sheet we were given. "I'm cis now." She laughs. "Ew."

I love that Nicole loves being trans. I think a lot of cis people have this idea that trans people are supposed to hate being trans, that we have to wish we were cisgender, that our transness brings us nothing but pain—but Nicole refutes that in every way she can. Even when things are rough, she still takes pride in who she is. I wish I could, too. Not that I *hate* being trans, but I haven't gotten there yet in terms of acceptance or self-love or whatever you would call it. I know it wasn't easy for her to get to this place, but seeing her find so much joy in who she is, it makes me hope I can find that, too.

The dice assigns me the label of bisexual, and it reminds me of Jacqueline's question the other week. While Nicole is rolling again, I cross my legs and run my finger over my eyebrow. "There was actually something I wanted to ask you."

She looks up from her activity paper. "Oh?"

"How did you know you liked girls?"

She gives me this look, and I know that she's thinking about my *Um, I guess.* I look away, my face burning with the knowledge that I can't slide this past her.

But she doesn't bring it up. Instead, she nudges the dice toward me, and says, "Okay, well, do you wanna know how I knew I was a lesbian, or how I knew I liked girls?"

I pick up the dice, but I don't roll them. "Either. Both."

"Let's see . . . Well, you know about my whole thing growing up. Everyone assumed I was a gay boy for a long time, and when I came out as a girl, my attraction to other girls was seen, by some people, as somehow in a different category than a cis girl's attraction to other girls."

"Right," I say. She's talked to me about this before.

"So, for a long time," she continues, "I thought I was bi. Even though I'd never liked boys, people were telling me there wasn't a way for me to be gay *or* straight because they viewed my gender as something 'in between,' even though I fit in the binary. People would've labeled any other girl who liked only other girls as a lesbian, but people looked at me and saw the 'gray' area; I wasn't allowed into their narrow definition of 'lesbian' because of my transness. And because of that, I convinced myself that, in order to be a girl, I had to like men, and for a long time, I just told myself I liked both. It took me until I was almost out of high school before I realized that there *are* bi trans girls, but that's not me. I'm a big ole lesbian."

I pause for a moment, taking it in. I remember, two years ago, when she told me that she'd realized she was attracted exclusively to women, casually dropping the new information into something we'd been laughing about, but I'd never really asked *how* she knew. At the time, I didn't want to pry.

"Tell me what's up with you," she says. "What's this all about?"

She *knows* what this is all about, but I don't say that. This is her giving me an out, a way to backtrack or come up with an excuse or just plain lie.

"I don't think I've ever felt that way about anyone," I say finally. I'm still holding the dice, shaking them in my fist without ever rolling. "Or, I don't know. Maybe I *can't* feel that way. Or maybe it's just because . . . because liking someone, with my body is . . . It feels—impossible."

"Impossible," she repeats quietly. I'm afraid for a second that I've disappointed or upset her somehow, that I've let her down by admitting this. I rush to explain myself.

"It's like everyone else but me is able to feel like that. Everyone but me is allowed to. So I end up telling people I'm straight because I *guess* I can see myself down the line falling in love with a girl and getting married and having kids or something, but it's so weird, too, because the me down the line isn't *me*, it's just this—" I wave my free hand around in front of me, searching for the words. "It's someone else. It's an idea of what I 'should' be. I can't imagine a world where I'm thirty-five and married with a wife and two kids to come home to after I get off from whatever stable job I've got, but then again, I can't even imagine a world where I'm in college, and I'm supposed to go in less than a year now, so . . . I don't know how much validity any of this has. Any of the feelings."

"First of all," Nicole says, "*all* of your feelings have validity."

"Of course that's what you'd focus on."

She smiles. "I'm trying to be serious, asshole. You know what you're feeling isn't uncommon, right? Like, you know you aren't alone in thinking there's not gonna be a future?"

"It's not that I don't think there's gonna be a future—"

"Just that you won't be in it."

I don't say anything to that.

"Not in a suicidal way," she continues. "And it isn't about not *wanting* a future. It's just that you're so busy in the day-to-day that if you try to think too hard about what comes next, then you'll get overwhelmed, so it's easier to focus on the now and nothing else. The future doesn't exist as long as you don't think about it." She looks at me, wearing an expression somewhere between knowing and worried. "Did I get that right?"

"Yeah," I admit. "How?"

"You're not the first trans kid to feel like that. No, fuck that—you're not the first person, *period*, to feel like that. Gael, what you're feeling doesn't make you crazy or wrong or broken. I *need* you to know that. You're not broken."

Her voice cracks at the end. Oh God. The last thing I want to do is make her cry. "Nicole . . ." I put a hand on her forearm, trying for comfort.

"Sorry." She wipes the budding tears away delicately with her pinkies. "I'm about to fuck up my eyeliner."

I laugh, and she smiles back, but her eyes are still wet, and the pull of her lips is a little less genuine than usual. I take my hand back and glance at the group around us. Across the room, Declan and Jacqueline are laughing about something.

Nicole asks, "You know about asexuality, right?"

I nod. We talk about asexuality sometimes in group discussion, and a few of the people here are asexual.

"Have you thought maybe you could be ace?"

"I don't think so," I say. "It's more like . . . I feel like I'm not *allowed* to have a relationship or sex or whatever."

"Because you're trans?"

I pause, then nod. For a second, it looks like she's gonna tear up again, but then she looks down at her paper, and I see her compose herself. I can tell this is hitting close to home.

"Having a body is hard," I say.

She laughs. "You can say that again."

"Can I ask you something else?"

"Anything."

"How can you tell if you like someone?"

She blinks at me. "Like, how do I know when I'm attracted to a girl?"

I nod. Nicole gives me the rundown I should've known she would, all the symptoms of a crush I've read about and watched on TV and heard other people talk about, the racing heart and nervousness and desire for touch, but I frown. "But how do you know, like . . ."

She waits patiently for me to get my thoughts together. I manage finally, "How do you know that it's not just . . . a friend thing?"

"You don't usually want to kiss your friends." She pauses, tilting her head and giving me a curious look. She asks gingerly, "Is there someone you want to kiss?"

I sigh. "No. No, I'm . . . I'm just asking . . . how can you tell the difference?"

Nicole looks at me for a long moment, not saying anything. I think about Declan coming out to his parents when he was in eighth grade, and Jacqueline asking me if I'm straight, and my *Um, I guess.*

I didn't used to think about sexuality this much. About *my* sexuality. I never needed to, back when it was just me and Mom and Nicole. My parents' divorce, Mom's depression, and my transition kept me so busy that relationships and sexuality were just this background noise, a distant hum I didn't acknowledge. I didn't think about it.

And now . . .

Well. Now I am.

"Five more minutes!" Dakota says.

Nicole turns back to me. "You'll know the difference. When you like someone, *really* like someone I mean, you'll know."

"Before you all head home," Dakota says, after we've discussed the activity in the large group, "we're at that time of the year again where we need to start thinking about fundraising. Along with the gala in November, we're also going to be putting on smaller events."

I look to Declan next to me. "Gala?" I whisper.

"It's this big thing they do every year," he whispers back. "We all get dressed up and there are performances and an auction and food. It's, like, a way to get donors and sponsors and stuff. It's pretty cool."

I nod and turn back to Dakota, who's explaining the events they have planned.

"That means," Nicole says, "that we're really going to need

y'all's help. If you're interested in volunteering, we're going to talk about it more in-depth next week, or you can let us know outside of group."

They let us go after that. It's the beginning of October now, and finally a little bit cooler outside. Jacqueline had to leave the meeting a few minutes early, so it's just me and Declan heading to the parking lot.

"Do you think you'll sign up for the event stuff?" I ask.

He flips his car keys around his finger. "I'm not sure yet. Why, do you?"

I just shrug, but I already know I'm going to. I like Plus, and if it's as important as Nicole said it was, then my help could actually make a difference. The real concern might be time management, what with school and work and friends, but if Declan does it too, then it probably won't be all that bad.

I stop walking. "You should sign up with me," I say suddenly.

Declan stops, blinking at me.

"Just—if you want to," I backtrack, my face warm. I'm surprised by how badly I want him to volunteer with me, and by how much I want to help out in the first place. Maybe it was the conversation with Nicole, but I want to get more involved with Plus. To feel like I'm doing something to help. I admit, "It's just . . . It would be better with you there."

At that, he smiles. "Yeah, why not. It could be fun, right?"

I smile back.

Fourteen

THE NEXT MONDAY NIGHT, NICOLE and I are wiping down tables at Joey's when I ask, "So . . . if I wanted to volunteer to help with Plus, how would that work?"

She stops and turns to me. "Wait, are you serious?"

I shrink a little at her surprise. "Um, yeah."

"Gael!" she shrieks, pulling me into a hug. The rag she'd been using is still in her hand, and it leaves a soapy patch on my apron. "You don't know how much that means to me. Oh my God, and I'm *so* happy you want to get involved more! If I can be honest, things are not doing too hot this year and I've been stressing about it all summer and—"

"Wait." I pull away. "What do you mean?"

"We lost one of our sponsors, and we were already just barely doing good with that, so . . ." Nicole looks down at the table, taking a deep breath. "Things are pretty tight. If we don't raise enough money, we might have to shut down."

My stomach drops. "Oh," I say. "So. It's, like, really important, then."

"Yeah." She laughs a little. "We're trying not to let on how urgent it is because we don't want to freak the kids out and make them think we're just gonna stop being there for them if we don't even know for certain that's happening. A lot of kids that go to Plus really rely on it, you know? It's the only place they feel safe, where they can be themselves." She frowns. "They can't lose that."

"But don't you think letting them know how important it is will make them more likely to help out?"

"It could," she agrees. "But it could also cause unnecessary stress. For now, we're just going to organize our events and do everything we can to stay up and running until the gala. That's usually where we make the big bucks, but things are a little different this time around, obviously. But about what you were asking me—we need people to take shifts for some smaller events. You know the coffee sales we did last spring? Where Plus sold coffee and pastries outside of high schools?"

I nod. There was a table outside of GHS every morning for a week last April. I always bought a cup of coffee and a muffin even when I didn't want it, mainly because I knew how important it was to Nicole.

"We need people to take over some of those," she says. "There are openings for the seventeenth and nineteenth at GHS. Do you think you'd be open to covering those? Maybe you and Declan could do it together?"

"Yeah, no problem. I can ask if that's cool with him."

She pulls me into another hug. "Thank you, thank you, *thank you*. And thank you for listening. I don't mean to dump this on you all of a sudden, it's just been so hard not being able to talk about it. . . ."

"I get what you mean," I say.

"Would it be too gimmicky to talk about my sexuality in my college essay?" Annie asks while looking at her laptop, frowning as she types. It's Tuesday morning, and Annie, Jeremiah, and I are in the library. When Annie realized we all had study hall during the same period, she suggested we meet up at the library to get work done together. That leaves us here, at a table in the back, as far away from the librarian and any means of getting fussed at as possible. The place is quiet but well populated.

I glance up at her over my own computer. "Which question are you using?"

"The one that's like 'talk about an important part of your identity,'" she says.

"Then do it."

"You're sure?" She stops typing, looking up at me. "Because . . . I mean, what if a homophobe reads these essays and I get turned down based on that? Or what if they don't consider it, like, serious enough to be part of my identity so they say it doesn't fit the prompt or something?"

"No one's gonna do that," Jeremiah says. "And if that *were* to happen, then fuck them, they don't deserve you. You're too good for all these universities anyway."

"If it answers the prompt and you want to talk about it, go for it," I tell her.

"I guess. . . ." Annie runs a hand through her hair. She re-dyed her roots recently, so all of her hair is the same shade of cotton-candy blue. It's the same color as the pen she picks up, scribbling something down in her agenda.

Next to me, Jeremiah glances at my computer screen. "What prompt are you doing?"

"Don't know yet," I admit.

"Ah, putting it off. I gotcha."

Annie slides her water bottle over to Jeremiah, and he takes it wordlessly.

"What about you?" Annie asks Jeremiah, taking her bottle back. "Have you actually started on any?"

"Nah," he says. "But I signed up to retake the ACT in two weeks and found a few more schools I like, so I think I'm doing pretty good."

She nods. "What's your list looking like?"

"Of colleges? Pretty okay. Mostly places in the Midwest."

He lists a few different universities and recites their application requirements as Annie asks for them. I'm only half listening. It's kind of overwhelming to hear how well they have their lives together. All I know is that I'm staying in-state, but that's mostly because I'm not sure I could be far away from Mom for that long without worrying. Plus, it's way more affordable.

"I'm looking there, too," Annie says to one of Jeremiah's bullet points. "You think they'd let us room together?"

"Maybe. If we both get accepted, it'd be worth it to ask."

"Nice." They high-five across the table.

"What about you, Gael?" Jeremiah asks.

I look at my screen, showing a Google doc with the names of the colleges I've looked at so far. I turn my computer toward Jeremiah, and I watch his eyes skim from Middle Tennessee State University to University of Tennessee Chattanooga to Austin Peay State University.

After a pause, Jeremiah looks up. "All in-state?"

I shrug and pull my laptop back to myself.

"Man, I can't imagine staying here," he says, leaning back precariously in his chair so the front legs raise off the ground. "I've been looking forward to getting out of here since the moment I realized I could."

I don't say anything. I can't help being embarrassed now, for my list, for how little effort and thought I've put into this whole life-after-high-school thing. I was so busy trying to survive the present that I forgot to worry about the future.

"Hey." Annie taps my computer gently with her pen, pulling me out of my head. "What are you doing Thursday night?"

"Homework," I say.

"Want to go to the football game with us? Declan's been dropping hints that he wants us to come see the band perform soon."

"They're doing a witchy-ritual-possession kind of thing," Jeremiah adds. "It's really cool, from what I've heard."

"Oh." I blink. "What time?"

"The game goes from five to seven, but we'll probably get food afterward," Annie says.

"Yeah, that sounds good."

"Awesome! I'll let Declan know you'll be there." She grins.

I grin back at her.

When I get home from work that night, Mom is sitting at the piano with her back to me. She's crying.

I hear it from the moment I step through the doorway, and it gets louder as I pull myself toward her, one foot in front of the other, already on autopilot—the mechanical panic that sets in when something is wrong and I need to be there for my mother. The door is slammed shut behind me, and I drop my backpack off on the ground, discarded somewhere on the way to the piano.

"What happened?" is the first thing I say.

"Nothing." She won't look at me. I set a hand on her shoulder, try to get her to turn to me. "It's . . . I'm fine."

"You're not, Mom. What—"

"I said I'm fine!"

Mom hasn't raised her voice like this in a long time. We look at each other in the aftermath of her outburst, and I know we're both thinking about the night with Lucas, when I demanded answers I never quite got.

I think about what Lucas said on the phone. *Your mom's not doing well.*

I take my hand back slowly.

"It's nothing, Gael," she repeats, quieter this time. She places her hands back on the piano keys like she's going to play, still avoiding my eyes, but she doesn't press down. Her hands just hover there, waiting. Thinking.

I grab my backpack off the floor and set it on the couch. She still hasn't offered an explanation or an apology. Something is definitely up, but I can't pry. If I do—

I don't know. I don't like it when she gets like this. I know she won't tell me what happened, and I can't make her, but I can't leave her alone either. I sit on the couch and pull out my laptop. She still won't look at me.

We sit like that for a while, and I don't leave until I know for sure she's feeling a little better.

Later, when I'm sitting up in bed with yarn splayed around me as I crochet, Mom comes to my room. She knocks, the sound hesitant, almost sheepish, and opens the door.

"Can I sit with you?" she asks, shuffling in.

I shrug, looking down at my project. The blanket I'm still working on looks like little more than a slab of red and orange yarn right now. I haven't been working on it much lately, too busy with school and work and friends. But now, I make a loop. I pull. A weight settles next to me on the bed, but we don't speak.

It's like this after she's had an episode. I don't think she knows what to say. There's not really much *to* say. The explanation is: She's mentally ill. She can't always control it. She's sorry anyway.

"I'm sorry I yelled," she says. "I shouldn't have."

I nod. "It's okay."

That's it. She apologizes; I forgive her. She doesn't offer an explanation; I don't ask for one. We make up. We don't talk about it. We don't say what we're both thinking.

So I make another loop. And I pull.

On Thursday, I get to the football field ten minutes before the game starts. The bleachers are already packed with students and family. I text the group chat to let everyone know I'm here, but while I'm waiting for a response, I get a message from Declan.

declan: Hey!!! Over here!!

When I look up, I spot him waving from his seat with the rest of the band. His uniform is black and white with dark-blue accents, and the hat he wears is so big it's almost comical, the feather at the back sticking straight up. I wave back and can just see the grin on his face before the boy next to him says something, drawing his attention away.

I look back at my phone.

gael: nice hat

declan: Thanks!! We all have to wear them, but I'd like to think I look the best in it. :P

Before I can respond, Jacqueline's voice comes from behind me. "Hey! You made it!"

I turn to see her and Annie making their way through the stands to me. Jacqueline carries a huge bucket of popcorn, while Annie holds a drink carrier with four sodas. Annie nods toward the stands. "Jeremiah went ahead and got us seats."

I follow them to the bleachers, and we squeeze our way through the throngs of people to our seats.

declan: Are you ready to experience High School Football™?

gael: depends

declan: It'll be fun!

gael: is there anything i need to expect from this

declan: To be BLOWN AWAY by our amazing halftime show.

  :)

declan: And to find the actual game lackluster at best.

declan: Highschool football is not that exciting.

gael: im not sure ANY football is

declan: Good point!

Jacqueline nudges my shoulder. "Whatchya doing?"

I look up from my phone. "Declan's texting me."

She glances across the bleachers to where Declan is seated. "Instead of paying attention to the game? Classic."

"Do you guys come to these a lot?"

She shrugs. "We end up going at least a few times a season to support the band, but if they weren't performing, we definitely wouldn't go. Sometimes my girlfriend, Maggie, comes too, even though she's not at GHS, but she couldn't make it tonight."

I nod. "About Maggie . . . have y'all talked about what happened with her application decisions?" Jacqueline hasn't mentioned anything about Maggie since the events in Environmental Science.

"Kind of? Not totally. *I've* been trying to, at least. She just gets really weird every time I bring it up, and I hate feeling like I'm pushing her to talk about something she doesn't want to talk about, so I always end up dropping it." She sighs. "It's . . . kind of a mess."

"Damn. I'm sorry."

"Such is life." There's a gust of wind, and she pulls her jacket a little tighter around herself.

"Well, if it helps, I'm here to talk whenever you need."

A small, thankful smile. She bumps my shoulder with hers. "Thanks, Gael. And same to you, you know."

I smile and bump her shoulder back.

We go on like that, mostly sitting around, talking in between glances at the actual football game, me and Declan still texting. I'm sure it's clear to the people around us that we aren't really paying any attention to the field, at least not until halftime hits, and then Jacqueline is sitting up straight, her expression lighting up, and she fusses at Annie and Jeremiah and me to look. "They're about to start!"

The crowd hushes as a voice comes over the loudspeaker, announcing the Glenwood High School Marching Band, and then soft, quiet percussion starts as the color guard approaches the band members.

They beckon the band forward, leading them farther onto the field, then herding them into a large circle. As the percussion builds, the color guard enters the crowd of band members, coming into the middle of the circle and commanding their movements. The percussion gets louder—the color guard pulls someone into them, then lifts the band member into the air as everyone else circles around them. When they lower the person back down, the sound softens again, and the band members spread out, now finding their instruments on the ground and beginning to play.

It's hard to tell who's who in their matching uniforms, but after a moment, I'm able to spot Declan in what I guess is the mellophone section. He shuffles backward with the rest of the group until they're in a slithering line, while the color guard twirls white rifles. I can't take my eyes away. I can't imagine memorizing all those movements while *also* playing an instrument, and the color guard seems more like a dance troupe at some points, a few people doing flips, much to the crowd's excitement.

Near the end of the show, Declan is pulled out of his section by the color guard, his mellophone yanked from him and replaced with one of the rifles, and he follows their movements, twirling and spinning just as quickly as they do. As the music swells, he throws the rifle into the air, and there's one breathless moment before he catches it.

I don't realize I've stood, my cheers loudest in the crowd's, until Annie lets out a delighted laugh next to me.

"I'm glad you're enjoying it so far," she shouts, grinning.

I sit back down sheepishly, but I try not to let myself feel too embarrassed. Declan is worth cheering for.

After the game, Declan meets up with us near the entrance to the football field, looking exhausted and happy and frazzled. We all compliment the performance, Jacqueline and Annie pulling him into hugs. Only after we're done talking about the game do we broach the topic of food.

"Chipotle?" Jeremiah proposes.

"Yes, please," I say. Everyone else agrees, and we decide we'll meet up there in fifteen minutes. Jeremiah, Annie, and

Jacqueline head to Annie's car, and since Mom dropped me off—she needed the car for a recital tonight—I go with Declan.

"So, what'd you think?" Declan asks, as we're walking to his car.

"About the game or the band?"

"Both. Either."

A boy a few feet away from us, also in a band uniform, shrieks in laughter at something his friend said. The parking lot hasn't quite cleared out yet, although it's thinning by the minute. "Good," I say. "I know I already told you, but y'all did really well."

He beams. "We've been working really hard this season. I mean, we always do, but I think we could actually make it to finals this December."

"For?"

"Nationals! We always make it to semifinals, but you have to make top fifteen in the country for finals, and we haven't gotten there yet. . . . But we're feeling pretty good about it this time."

"I think you guys could do it," I say. "I mean, take that with a grain of salt because this is the first band show I've ever seen, but . . ."

"You think?" He looks at me, hope written plainly on his face. It's hard to believe anything other than that they'll win when he looks at me like that.

I smile. "Definitely."

We walk toward his car for a moment more in silence, letting our conversation sit between us. I'm distracted, still thinking about the show and my cheering and the way Declan just looked at me—so it takes me a moment to recognize who's sitting in the car idling a few spaces down from us.

I freeze.

Lucas is sitting in the driver's seat, scanning the parking lot with his fingers tapping the steering wheel.

"Oh my God" is all I think to say. When Lucas's eyes land on me, his face lights up. As he opens the door, I push past Declan and sprint to his car.

He follows. "What's wrong?"

"My fucking *dad* is here."

"What? What's he doing here?"

"I don't *know.*" I tug at the passenger-side door, trying to will Declan to unlock the car faster, but while he's fumbling in his backpack for his keys, Lucas catches up.

"Gael!"

He's jogging up to us, face pulled into an amiable smile as if the last time we talked I didn't tell him to get out of my life. Some of the crowd that's left looks to us, drawn by his shout. "Did you get my call?"

"What are you doing here?" I demand.

Instead of answering me, his eyes flick to Declan standing to the side, keys in hand. Lucas reaches his hand out for Declan to shake. "Hey, I'm Lucas. You're a friend of Gael's?"

And because he's Declan, he shakes Lucas's hand and introduces himself, all with a polite smile in place.

"*Lucas,*" I interrupt. "*What* are you doing here?!"

He turns to me, expression pulled down briefly into something like hurt. It's quickly written over, replaced with calm neutrality. "I came to pick you up. Ana said you were going to a game tonight, and since you didn't have the car, I figured I could give you a ride back to the apartment—"

"You figured," I repeat, incredulous. The situation finally registers, and I'm hit by the absurdity of it all, of Lucas, here in the GHS parking lot in front of Declan's car, because he just *figured* it would be a cool idea to come see me unexpectedly, to invade my world, shove his way back in. And what's worse: I can't just hang up on him and ignore his texts.

I manage to keep my anger in check long enough to ask Declan, "Can you give us a sec?" because the last thing I want is to explode at my dad in front of him. He nods, eyebrows furrowed, and gets into his car.

I trudge back to Lucas's car with him but don't get in. My anger is simmering just below the surface, threatening to overwhelm me any second, and I know that people are staring, their eyes burning into my back, but I can't bring myself to care right now.

I start, "I'm not going home with you."

He doesn't seem bothered by what I'm saying, his expression still even. I keep going.

"I'm not gonna let you take me back to the apartment like that's normal. I don't want you to pick me up, and I don't want you to call me all the time just to 'see how I'm doing,' and I don't want you popping by Glenwood at all because I *don't want you* in my life!"

By the end, I'm shouting. My hands shake.

Lucas sighs. "Listen, I know that I messed up with you and your mother—"

"*Messed up*?"

"—and I know that you're still mad at me for what happened. And I get it—I do. I broke your trust. I hurt you. I hurt your mother. But I'm here now, and I'm trying to make it up to you. I'm trying to show you that I've changed. I'm a different person than when you were fourteen, Gael, and I want to be here for you and Ana. And the truth is . . ." He pauses, as if what he's about to say is something painful. "With your mom's depression, she needs someone else with her while—"

"Maybe you should've thought of that before you cheated on her and left *me* alone to keep her from killing herself!"

That shuts him up.

"I've been with her for three years without you," I say. "We *don't* need your help *now*."

The look he gives me is stricken. But I watch his hurt turn to anger, to frustration. He's been annoyingly calm this whole time—I see as it starts breaking down.

"This isn't something you can just tough out to spite me," he says. "Your mother needs a larger support system—your aunt Isabella isn't around to help, so she *needs* me back in her life. No matter what you think, you're not equipped to help her when she actually goes downhill, and you can't keep shutting me out."

"You don't get to tell me I can't help her when *you're* the one who put me in this position."

"You're missing the point." He throws his arms out. "You can be angry about the past all you want, but that doesn't change the fact that I'm here, today, right now, *begging* you to let me help again."

We look at each other. I'm breathing like I just ran a mile, my hands shaking. Lucas lowers his arms, takes a deep breath, and puts his hands in his pockets.

"Look," he says. "I was hoping coming here in person would help change your mind. I know when we talked on the phone last, you were . . . unreceptive. But this has gone on for too long. Your mom needs someone that can be there for her who *isn't* her kid. I know you two are close, but it's always going to be different with you. She's always gonna hold back."

I think about the times that I've seen her cry. About watching her play piano.

"It doesn't have to be something huge right now," he says, softer. "What's the harm in letting me drive you home?"

"Just . . . no." I turn around and walk back to Declan's car.

He calls after me, but I jump in the passenger seat and slam the door behind me, muffling Lucas's voice. And without saying anything, Declan peels out of the parking lot.

"I'm sorry that happened," Declan says, once we're on the road and away from GHS.

"Me too," I mumble.

"What did he want?"

I shrug. "He thinks Mom's not doing good and that she needs him there, which is pretty funny considering *he's* the one who . . ." I take a deep breath. "Never mind. It's not worth talking about. Let's just head to Chipotle."

"You're sure? 'Cause I wouldn't blame you if you wanted to head home after that. . . ."

I look at him, and he glances from the road back to me. My

gratitude for him hits me all at once, and I want to ask *How did I get you in my life?* because I still don't understand how I could deserve someone like Declan. How I got so lucky.

"It's okay," I say. "I think I just want to take my mind off it."

He nods. "We can do that."

I'm overwhelmed by him—by how much he means to me, by the fact that I can ask this of him. When we come to a stop at a red light, I unbuckle my seatbelt and envelop him in a hug. It's a little awkward with both of us sitting down, but he hugs back, and I bury my face in his shoulder. We part when the light turns green, but it still doesn't feel like enough.

"Thank you," I say.

"Anytime." He smiles.

At Chipotle, I try my best to act normal, to not let Lucas ruin this for me, too. And I think I almost succeed—I get close to putting him out of my mind, to laughing with everyone, to shutting it all out for an hour. But it's there, underneath everything—*What's the harm in letting me drive you home* and Mom raising her voice at me the other day and Lucas saying he wants to help again.

A part of me knows Lucas is right. I can't do this by myself.

But I also can't just let him back in. It doesn't matter what he does now. Eventually, he's going to hurt us, and we can't go through that again. Mom can't go through that again.

So I can't let him in. I can't let him wreck our lives a second time.

I *won't*.

Fifteen

I DON'T TELL MOM WHAT happened with Lucas that night, but I try to bring it up before Plus the next day.

She's in her room, lying in bed with the covers pulled as far up as they'll go, just her head peeking out while she watches something on her computer. I plop down on her bed. "What are you watching?"

"*How It's Made,*" she says.

"Oh." I peer around to see her laptop screen and watch it with her for a few minutes, trying not to make it so obvious that I have something important on my mind. Only when the show has moved from talking about rice cookers to folding chairs does Mom press Pause.

"Do you have any plans tonight?" she asks.

"I have Plus. Why?"

"I was thinking about ordering pizza, but I won't if you're getting food with your friends."

"Nah, I'll probably head straight home after the meeting."

She nods. "How was the game, by the way? I didn't get a chance to ask you when I got home."

This is my opening. "Actually . . ."

From her bedside table, her phone rings. I see the name lighting up the screen before she can answer.

Lucas.

Because of *course* it is.

The words I was going to say die in my throat.

"Hello?"

I can just barely hear Lucas's muffled voice on the other end of the line. *"Hey, Ana."*

I get up from the bed. I feel sick.

"Gael," Mom calls after me, and I stop at the doorway, turning around to offer her a halfhearted smile.

The concerned look she gives me doesn't lessen, even when I say, "I'm gonna go take a shower."

I don't wait for a response before I leave, shutting the door behind me.

This week's Plus meeting is about bisexuality and pansexuality, the differences and similarities between them, and why some people might prefer one label over the other. Dakota, who's pan, leads the meeting. I spend most of the time listening to everyone else, but at one point, we stray off that topic and talk about queer awakenings instead.

"Did you guys ever watch *Teen Titans*?" one girl says. "I had the *biggest* crush on Raven."

That leads people to talk about some of their earliest crushes. After a few minutes, Annie raises her hand.

"I feel kind of like the odd one out most of the time," she says. "I didn't really start wondering if I was queer until last year, and I'm still not sure what term fits. Most of my life I just sort of assumed I was straight, and I think I might've had crushes on guys when I was younger, but I'm not really sure if those were actual crushes or if I was just trying to fit in?" She looks down. "I've liked mostly girls the past few years, but I don't know if that makes my earlier feelings less real, you know?"

A person to Annie's left raises their hand. Dakota gestures for them to speak.

"I definitely get that," they say. "And I don't know about you, but for me, being genderfluid also kind of complicates it. Like, I didn't realize I wasn't cis until a few months ago, but most of the time it's like 'Oh, if you didn't know since you were, like, a toddler, then you're just faking it.' And then throw sexuality into it, it's way more complex. Like, what does it mean that I thought I was just cis and straight up until a few months ago? It just feels like I should've noticed earlier."

"I think it's important to remember that there are tons of people who don't realize their sexuality or gender until much further in their life," Nicole says. "I know it feels kind of like everyone else has everything all figured out, but I promise there are plenty of people who don't come out until later. Not understanding everything right now doesn't mean you never will, or that you're any less queer. It's not a race."

While the discussion continues, I think about sexual

awakenings. Do straight people have those? Is there a moment I was meant to have thought "wow, I'm attracted to girls"? Would that have been *before* realizing my gender, or after? I've heard about some straight trans guys identifying as lesbians before realizing their actual gender, but I've never struggled with that, never even entertained the idea of possibly being a lesbian before I came out as a boy. And if I've never had that thought, what does that mean about who I'm attracted to?

I rack my brain, trying to find a moment when I was a child where I realized I liked a boy or a girl or anyone at all. But I never really had crushes growing up. Like with friends, I just never seemed to find anyone I clicked with. Once, in seventh grade, I was sleeping over at Brianna's house, and we got to talking about crushes. At one point, she told me that she thought this boy in our social studies class liked me and asked if I thought he was cute. I remember saying yes, but like with Annie, was that an actual moment of attraction, or did I just feel like I *needed* to say yes?

Thinking about middle school reminds me of Declan, what he told me about coming out to his parents and how he was outed at school. I look at him. He hasn't spoken during the meeting so far, but he's engaged, his knees pulled up to his chest and his arms wrapped around them. I study his profile—long eyelashes and a round face and brown eyes focused on whoever's speaking. I look at his lips. They're closed, but they part when he looks at me and mouths *what?*

I shake my head and look away, my face hot. But I'm still thinking about his lips.

* * *

While I'm in my room that night, Declan texts me.

> **declan:** Is it weird that I think it might've been Zuko who
>   made me realize I'm gay?
> **declan:** Like, as a kid he was probably my first fictional
>   crush.
> **declan:** And definitely not the kind of fictional crush where I
>   could be like "I just think he's neat."
> **declan:** Like, it was INTENSE, lmao.
> **gael:** zuko?
> **declan:** From Avatar: The Last Airbender!
> **gael:** ???
> **declan:** Have you not heard of ATLA?
> **declan:** Gael.
> **gael:** yes
> **declan:** Who are you.
> **gael:** someone who hasnt heard of atla apparently
> **declan:** This is unbelievable.
> **declan:** I'm making you watch it with me as soon as I can, oh
>   my GOD.
> **gael:** to answer your question it probably isnt weird
> **gael:** even though idk who zuko is
> **gael:** what made you think of that
> **declan:** Our conversation at Plus about fictional crushes.
> **declan:** I couldn't remember who my ACTUAL first fictional
>   crush was.
> **gael:** too many to pick from?

declan: Honestly, yes.

declan: I fall in love easily.

declan: What about you?

gael: what about me

declan: Who was your first fictional crush?

I look at that message for a long moment before I decide to just call him.

"Is this becoming the norm for us?" Declan says in place of a greeting. It sounds like he's smiling.

"No," I huff. I flop back onto my bed, facing the ceiling. "I just don't like typing, so this is easier."

"Convenient excuse."

"I can hang up if you're going to be annoying about it."

"No, no, it's fine, I'll stop."

I grin, but it fades when Declan says, "So . . . fictional crushes? Did you call about that?"

"Kind of," I admit. "I don't know. I've never had one. At least . . . I don't think I have, I guess?"

"What do you mean you guess?"

"I mean, I've just never really thought about it until recently. I didn't have much reason to think about crushes when I was a kid." I roll onto my side so I'm not facing the door and pick at a thread on my comforter. "I didn't really connect with anyone at my old school, and then stuff with my parents happened, and I started my transition. . . . It just didn't seem like there was time to think about that."

"I guess that means you've never dated anyone?"

171

"Nope. Have you?"

"Yeah." A pause. "This guy Terry during freshman year, but we were only together for a few months before we decided we were better as friends. And then sophomore year, there was this guy Corbin. He was a year older. We dated for almost all of sophomore year before he broke it off."

"I'm sorry."

"Don't be. I mean, I'm not gonna lie, the thing with Corbin seriously sucked, but I don't really think about him anymore, and the thing with Terry was mutual. We still talk sometimes, actually."

"What happened with Corbin? If you don't mind talking about it, I mean."

He sighs. "He was an asshole, to put it bluntly. Things seemed to be good at first, and I really liked him. But, after a while, I noticed that he almost turned into a different person with his friends. They were all white—he was too—and all gay, and they'd always make these *comments* about his dating history. He'd only ever been with white guys before, and his friends made such a weird thing about it, like it was so adventurous and exciting for him to date me just because I'm Black. And no matter what they said, he'd just laugh along with it. Some of his friends even went to Plus, and they'd put on this whole act during group discussions, nodding along whenever someone talked about racism in the queer community and how we need to call it out more, completely unaware that *they're* the kind of people who need to be called out. But whenever I tried to talk to Corbin about it, he'd just be like, 'Oh, but they're good people, and they're oppressed too, so they would never do something like that' as if they're incapable of being racist just because they aren't straight."

"I'm sorry," I say. "I know that's not much, but . . . you didn't deserve that."

"It's okay. I mean, it isn't, but it's over now, and he and his friends graduated, so at least I don't have to see them around school anymore."

"You dated for almost the whole year, right? What made you stay together?"

"To be honest? I still don't totally know." He pauses, and when he speaks again, his voice is quiet, a little vulnerable. "I think maybe I felt like, on some level, my feelings weren't as important as his or his friends. I convinced myself it wasn't actually a big deal. It wasn't even until we broke up that I realized the extent of how much he'd hurt me."

"Did your friends know about what had been happening?"

"Some of it. But I didn't tell them everything until after we broke up. I didn't want to worry them. I wanted to be the one to help *them*, you know? Not the other way around."

"They're your friends," I say. "You're allowed to ask them for help when you're struggling with something."

"I know, but . . . at the time, I didn't want to be a burden."

"You're *not* a burden," I say, and even I'm surprised by how forcefully it comes out. I pick at a thread on my comforter. "And . . . I know I didn't know you when this was all happening, but you weren't a burden back then, either. Your feelings mattered, and you deserved to feel like you could talk to someone about them."

I can hear the smile in his voice, small and soft. "Thanks, Gael."

After that, we're silent for a moment. I'm not sure what to say, mostly because my brain is filling in some of the gaps in my knowledge about Declan with all this new information. I'd like to think I know him well, but there's still so much *more*.

I think back to what Annie said about knowing Declan through everything, and even though I know it wasn't all fun—even though I know middle school was hard on him—despite all of that, I'm sad that I've missed it. I want to keep knowing him.

"Did you know there's a word for requited love?" Declan asks.

I pull my blankets over myself even tighter. "You mean other than just 'requited love'?"

"'Redamancy.'"

"That's a word?"

"Yeah. If I had to pick a favorite word, it would be that."

I smile to myself. Of course. What else would Declan love, if not the act of loving back?

We get off topic after that. I spend the next hour trying not to fall asleep as we discuss AP Lit and parents and marching band and anything we want to, and it isn't until I've woken up from a very brief nap that we finally decide to hang up.

When I finally go to sleep, I'm still thinking about Declan and redamancy.

Declan picks me up Monday morning, and we arrive at GHS a full hour before classes begin and start setting up, the world slowly coming into focus as the sun rises. It takes us ten minutes to get the table, coffee, and pastries all laid out, but it's another

174

ten before any cars pull into the parking lot.

Two girls get out, looking disgruntled, and as they approach, Declan shifts into his customer service facade. One of the girls notices our table and nudges the other, pulling her toward us.

"Good morning," Declan chirps, sounding far too perky for six thirty in the morning. "Y'all interested in buying some coffee?"

"We're raising funds for a local organization," I say. "It's a collection of free programs at the youth center to help teenagers in the city."

"Oh, cool." The girl looks between the prices on the poster board and the coffee containers. She buys a cup and two muffins, while her friend just gets a muffin. Declan waves as they set off, and I see the moment his facade falls away.

"Our first sale," I say.

"I didn't know you wanted to talk to the customers," Declan says, blinking at me.

My face heats. "I wasn't planning on it, but . . . I don't know. That's just what Nicole says when people ask. I mean, she usually also mentions the LGBT thing, but . . ."

He nods. "Still. Maybe *you* should be in charge of the sales."

"I wouldn't go that far," I say, and he laughs.

We sell six more coffees before Jacqueline gets to school, yawning as she approaches us. She pulls her pink sweater tighter around herself. "*Why* must it be so cold in the mornings if it's just gonna be hot as balls in the afternoon?"

"Perhaps a warm cup of joe would help with that?" Declan wiggles his eyebrows as I gesture toward our selection.

"A muffin also wouldn't hurt," I add.

"How's that supposed to keep me warm?" she asks, but she buys one along with her coffee anyway and grabs a seat on the curb.

We sell another ten cups and a few more pastries before Jeremiah and Annie show up too, Jeremiah grumbling at Declan's bright "Good morning!" while Annie just smiles. They both buy coffee and sit down with Jacqueline, sipping their drinks and watching as Declan and I sell to the students amassing near our table, drawn over by the smell of coffee. And even though it must be uncomfortable to sit on the ground, and they have no obligation to be here, they stay with us until classes start.

A little less than half of the students ask what the fundraiser is for, and each time, I explain it to them. The words come out smoother as the morning goes on, the explanation a little more in-depth, until I find I'm not just reciting what Nicole says. I'm glad that I'm the one talking. That I can do this for Plus. It feels good to use my voice.

Sixteen

annie: Could u guys read what ive written for my essay and
maybe give me feedback??? I cant tell if what ive written
is working or not

jacqueline: Of course!! :))

annie: Sent prompt_1_essay.docx

annie: Tell me what u think!!

jacqueline: Ahhhh oh my gosh Ann!!!!!! Sorry this took me
a second to read but it's so good!! I wish u could write MY
essays for me :(

jeremiah: She might if you pay her enough

gael: i agree with jacqueline

jeremiah: A man of many words as always

gael: yep

annie: Ahh thanks yall :') I appreciate it <3 anything I can do
to improve it??

declan: Hello, sorry, I was at band practice and just saw this. Ann, I really liked it too! But I think you could work on the opening a bit more because it feels like the weakest part of the essay right now. You could maybe try cutting the first two paragraphs and see if that's a stronger beginning? But other than that, it's really good!

annie: Hmm that's tru . . . Ok thank u!! :) What about you guys? How are apps?

jeremiah: Ugh

declan: Yeah, me too. :/ Have any of y'all submitted yours yet?

jacqueline: Not yet but getting close!

gael: im applying regular decision, so no

jeremiah: I cant wait until all of this is over. But until then I can drown my college sorrows by hanging out with yall

jeremiah: Speaking of . . . .

jeremiah: Guess who's throwing a Halloween party this Friday

jeremiah: And guess who's legally required to attend if they love me and want to stay my friends

annie: Im guessing its us

jeremiah: Ding ding! We have a winner. Its at my place and starts at 8.

jacqueline: Is there a reason it's this Friday instead of closer to Halloween?

jeremiah: Cuz Im impatient

jeremiah: And Declan might not be able to come if we do it closer to Halloween cuz of his familys plans

178

declan: Aww, thanks, Jer. :)

annie: Do we get to dress up?

jeremiah: Oh Ann you sweet summer child not only do you GET to dress up

jeremiah: It's also mandatory

gael: just like attendance?

jeremiah: Correct!

"What's so funny?" Mom stops as she's passing me on her way to the kitchen, trying to get a look at my screen.

I lock my phone quickly. "Nothing."

She raises an eyebrow, already grinning. "You were smiling a lot for just 'nothing.'"

"I was not."

She laughs, and heads back to the kitchen. "If you say so. I won't force you to tell me."

"There's nothing *to* tell," I insist, but it's more for show than anything. She must be in a good mood today to laugh and smile and joke with me. When she isn't doing well, she doesn't seem to register anything that's going on outside of her head.

It's Wednesday afternoon, and since I don't have work tonight, I'm watching *Bake Off* while Mom's set up at the kitchen table getting work done. She's just started grading papers when her phone rings.

For a second, I think it's going to be Lucas—but she answers the call with a "Hey, Isa," and I'm quietly relieved. I've been trying not to think too much about how she and Lucas have been in contact. Maybe I should just be thankful that he hasn't called

179

or texted me since he showed up at the football game, that I'm allowed this moment of relative peace after everything—but it just makes me even more anxious because I know he's *going* to show up again. It's just a matter of *when*.

And with Mom . . . it's all a guessing game. She seems to be doing good right now—but there's no telling how long it'll last. I can't predict her moods, and I can't do much of anything to help her.

What I *can* do, though, is help Nicole out with Plus. We made around $200 on Monday and another $150 today, so we're on track to reach our goal. I also signed up to run the table with Declan again for the next two times, but on top of that, Nicole's enlisted me to help out with the gala in a little more than a month. I'm in charge of the volunteer slots—making the signup sheets, following up with people, that kind of thing. I've already started sending out emails to others who've shown interest in helping the night of the gala, and I'm surprised by how much I actually *don't* hate it.

Privately, Declan messages me.

> **declan:** Do you think you're going to Jeremiah's thing?
> **gael:** not sure yet
> **gael:** even tho attendance is apparently mandatory
> **declan:** Lol
> **declan:** Well, you should go! If you're available and want to, I mean.
> **declan:** It'll be a lot more fun if you're there. :)
> **gael:** do you know whos going?

declan: Our group + some of Jeremiah's other friends.

declan: I think, like, 15 people in total.

Fifteen.

For someone like Declan, that isn't a lot. That's probably the perfect amount for a party like this, actually, but just the thought of being around that many people at one time makes me frown.

But I know he wants me to come, and as long as I have people there I know well, it should probably be okay. I think.

I hope.

gael: ill think about it

gael: no promises tho

declan: :D!

I don't actually make the decision to go until the night of.

"So, what's the plan?" Jacqueline asks as Declan, Annie, and I walk through the youth center parking lot after Plus.

"I'm gonna take Gael home," Declan says. "Then meet you at Jeremiah's at eight?"

Annie nods. "Sounds good. See you guys!"

Jacqueline and Annie head to their cars while I go with Declan. "Actually . . . about the party . . ."

He grins, and I know he knows what I'm getting at. I narrow my eyes. "What?"

"Nothing, nothing." He waves me on. "Continue."

"Well *now* I'm not sure, since you're all smiley—"

He laughs. "I'm just happy!"

"You don't even know for sure what I was going to say!"

"Fine, fine, I won't smile." He smooths his expression out, but it's only a few seconds before the grin is back.

This time, I laugh too, shaking my head. "Whatever. I'll go to the party."

"Yes!" He slings an arm around my shoulder, pulling me into him.

But I still need to get back to talk to Mom about my last-minute decision, so he drops me off at the apartment. Mom's working in the living room, and I tell her about the party and ask if I could take the car tonight, and she's so excited that I'm going to a *party* with all my new *friends* that she doesn't seem to care about the car thing.

Jeremiah's place is twenty minutes from my apartment, so it's a little after eight by the time I get there. His house isn't huge, but everything in it looks and feels expensive, with the kind of minimalism that only rich people can aim for. I try not to stare at the second-floor balcony overlooking the foyer. Already I feel out of my element.

Annie greets me at the door. "Gael! I didn't know you were coming?"

"Me neither, until an hour ago," I say. She nods, the antennae on her headband bobbing with the movement. Her hair is pulled back into a high, braided ponytail. I can't tell what she's supposed to be until she turns to lead me farther into the house and I see the symmetrical wings attached to her back. It's a pretty basic costume, but it's more than what I've got.

I only feel worse about not remembering to dress up when I get into the living room and see everyone in costume. Jacqueline's sitting on the couch, wearing black cat ears and intense eyeliner, while her girlfriend Maggie sits on the couch arm next to her. The whiskers drawn on Jacqueline's cheeks move when she turns to smile at me, waving me over.

"Hey!" she says over the music. "What's up?"

"Not much. Just got here." I try desperately not to feel so out of place. Everyone looks perfectly at ease in the living room, laughing about something I can't catch, sitting anywhere they can find. I don't see Jeremiah or Declan in the group, only kids I don't recognize.

Annie puts a hand on my shoulder, unknowingly grounding me.

"You okay?" she asks, keeping her voice down. She's only a few inches taller than me, but I always feel small next to her. "You don't look so good. You want me to get you some water?"

"Um." I look toward the kitchen. "Yeah, thank you."

While she's gone, Jacqueline pushes herself off the couch, dragging her girlfriend with her. "Have you met Maggie?"

"I don't think so," Maggie answers for me. She's slightly taller than Jacqueline, with long black hair shaved on one side and dark makeup. She might be dressed as a casual Wednesday Addams. "Gael, right? It's good to finally meet you."

"You, too." This is my first time seeing her outside of Instagram posts or the occasional Snapchat story. Jacqueline only gets to see her a few times a week since Maggie goes to a different school and we've all been so busy since senior year started. At least, that's what the official excuse is. But privately, Declan's said that he's not sure how much longer they'll be together, and I get where he's coming from. I've noticed that Jacqueline doesn't really talk much about Maggie anymore. It seems like the two of them still haven't figured out the college stuff.

Annie returns with a plastic cup in each hand. She offers one to me, and I mumble a thanks. I ask the group, "Has anyone seen Declan?"

"I think he's upstairs with Jeremiah." Jacqueline points toward the hallway. I nod my thanks, wave an awkward goodbye, and head upstairs.

I find them in what looks like a guest bedroom. It's sparsely furnished, and Declan is standing in front of the window, his back to the doorway. Jeremiah sees me, but he doesn't say anything, and I realize a second later that it's because Declan's talking. It's too quiet for me to hear the words, but from the way his head is ducked, it looks important.

"Dec," Jeremiah says, once he's stopped talking. Declan doesn't respond immediately, so Jeremiah taps his shoulder.

"What?"

He nods toward me, and Declan turns around. His face brightens when he sees me. "Hey!"

"Sorry, um, I don't mean to interrupt anything . . ." I say, looking down.

"No worries, you aren't," Jeremiah says. He's dressed as a cowboy, wearing a T-shirt and blue jeans but with the added cowboy hat and worn boots.

Declan's dressed as a vampire, in a white ruffled shirt with a dark red vest, his hair pulled into a bun at the nape of his neck, but when he speaks, I can see that he's missing fangs. "I'm glad you made it."

"I told you I would."

He smiles, flashing dimples. Jeremiah claps Declan on the shoulder as he scoots past us.

"I'm gonna head down and make sure no one's getting into trouble." He gives Declan a look I can't parse before disappearing downstairs.

"What was that about?" I ask, eyebrows furrowed.

"What do you mean?"

I gesture toward the room. "It looked like you two were having a pretty serious conversation. Everything okay?"

"Oh, that." He rubs the back of his neck, avoiding my eye. "Yeah, all good. It wasn't anything, really. We were just talking about . . . stuff."

"Very specific."

He kind-of smiles, but he still seems embarrassed. Even though I'm confused, I don't want to make him uncomfortable by questioning him more, so instead, I start toward the stairs. "Let's go see what everyone else's up to."

Downstairs, Annie is standing to the side, her arms crossed loosely over her chest. Jeremiah's leaning against her, an arm thrown around her shoulder despite being shorter. Declan and I join them, making a half circle.

"What're you supposed to be, little missy?" Jeremiah asks Annie in a horribly fake southern accent.

She rolls her eyes. "I'm a butterfly, obviously. And what are *you*? A farmer?"

"Cowboy," he corrects, grinning. To me, he asks, "What about you, Gael?"

"Sorry, I forgot. . . ." I put my hands in my hoodie pockets, my face warm.

Declan nudges my arm with his. "What's that one Agatha Christie quote about people always wearing masks? You're basically in costume, by her logic."

"No human on the planet would get that reference except you," Jeremiah says.

"Yeah, it's not like she's one of the most famous authors of all time or anything," Annie says.

He turns to her, putting a hand on his heart. "Et tu, Ann?"

While they keep debating Agatha Christie, Declan says, "I'm getting something to eat. Come with me?"

In the kitchen, the counters are covered with bowls and plates of chips and pretzels, along with four large pizzas. An array of soda bottles lines the counter, one close to the edge and waiting to be knocked off by an unknowing passerby. I scoot it further back onto the counter while I wait for Declan to stack three slices of pizza on a paper plate.

"I thought there was usually alcohol at these types of things," I say, more to myself than to him. At the curious look I get, I gesture toward the living room. "You know, high school party, parents are gone. . . ."

He sets his plate on the counter and pours Coke into a plastic cup. "Probably," he admits. "But you know us."

"None of you drink?"

"I mean, sometimes, if it's just us. But with a big group, nah. Too much chaos. It wouldn't be any fun."

I nod. I can hear Jacqueline laughing in the living room, that high-pitched, unadulterated laugh she does when she's lost in the moment and not worried about appearances. I can just make out pieces of conversation. It sounds like they're playing a party game.

"Do you?" Declan asks. It takes me a beat to remember what we were talking about.

I run a finger over my eyebrow as subtly as I can. "Just once. My mom left wine sitting out one time, and I was fourteen and home alone. But never with a group of people. I'm not big on . . . parties." I shift and pick up my cup, but I don't drink anything. I catch the way Declan's eyes flicker to the living room, full of people.

"Yeah, I sort of got that." He looks at his pizza.

"Although," I lean forward almost unnoticeably, "it's not nearly as bad as I thought it would be."

He smiles. "That's the highest compliment one could receive from you."

I shift, and my arm brushes against his. I don't know if he noticed, or if it's just me that's suddenly so aware of our proximity. I bring my cup to my lips to keep myself busy, but our arms only press against each other more. Declan's eyes follow the cup. When I lower it, he's still looking at my mouth.

My face is burning. I clear my throat. "We should probably, um, get back to everyone else."

He blinks. "Yeah, totally. Lead the way."

We go back to the living room, but I'm still thinking about his eyes on me.

By nine thirty, everyone who's coming has already arrived, and I'm getting tired. Jeremiah put on *Halloweentown* (because, according to him, it's a classic) and I sat next to Declan and Annie on the floor, half participating in the group's conversation, half watching the movie. It's been fun, being here; Jeremiah's friends are funny, Maggie seems nice enough, and Annie and Jacqueline are having a good time. But, still, after an hour and a half, I'm in need of some time alone to recharge. At the end of the movie, Declan and Annie excuse themselves to get more food, so I get up to head outside.

On my way out, I pass the kitchen, where Annie's refilling her drink while Declan says something to her, his eyebrows furrowed and his arms crossed. When he sees me, I gesture toward the pool area to let him know where I'll be, and he nods, giving me a small, uncomfortable smile. Something is definitely going on with him—he's been like this on and off tonight, completely fine one moment, weirdly quiet the next. But I haven't found a good moment to ask about it yet.

Outside, I sit at the edge of the pool, slide my shoes off, and dip my feet in. Jeremiah's pool probably hasn't been used since school started up again, and it's a little cooler than normal tonight, but the cold water feels good. On the other side of the pool, I watch Jeremiah's cat, a small brown tabby, prowling around in the dark.

"Hey."

I turn around and see Declan. "Hi," I say.

He pauses before taking a seat next to me. He slips his shoes and socks off and leaves them somewhere behind us. He shudders when his feet break the surface of the water. "Jesus *Christ*, that's cold! How are you enjoying this?"

I shrug. "You get used to it."

Inside, the party is still going, the music muffled through the patio door. Declan is unnaturally quiet. When I turn to look at him, his eyes are trained on the water, watching the ripples.

I ask, "Are you okay?"

"Yeah, why?"

"You've just seemed . . . kind of off tonight."

He shrugs, as if he hasn't switched between his usual good mood and uncharacteristic solemnity all night. I can't help thinking about the conversation I walked in on earlier, the way his head was ducked, his voice so quiet I couldn't hear him.

"I'm not trying to," he says. "Are *you* okay?"

"You've asked me that two other times."

"And you've lied every time, so I'm gonna keep asking."

I roll my eyes. "'Fine' isn't a lie. I'm just tired."

"Mm-hmm," he agrees sarcastically.

"And what about you?" I demand. "You can't call me out on that when you just did the same thing to me."

He opens his mouth, then closes it. "Okay, fine, you got me there."

We sit in silence for a moment. Earlier in the night, his bun started coming loose, so now his curls frame his face. He also ditched the red vest, so he's just in the white ruffled shirt and tight black jeans. They look good on him.

"You're supposed to be a vampire," I say. At the look he gives me, I nod toward his costume. "Right? Or was it something else?"

"Jeremiah just sort of threw something at me, but I think that was the intent, yeah."

"Ah. I see."

I take my feet out of the pool and fold my legs so I'm sitting crisscrossed. My jeans will be damp where my feet are tucked under me, but I don't care. Declan takes a breath like he's going to say something, but he pauses.

I look at him. "What's up?"

He avoids my eye, instead staring at the water. "So, speaking of Jeremiah . . ."

He pauses, and I don't know why, but I suddenly feel nervous, which doesn't make any sense, but I think about the look Jeremiah gave Declan before going downstairs, and it makes my stomach twist.

"The conversation you walked in on—it wasn't anything bad," Declan says. "We were just talking about crushes. Annie said I could tell you and Jeremiah that there have been some developments in the romance department for her."

"With that girl she went bowling with?"

He shakes his head. "Oh, nah, they sort of mutually ghosted each other after the second date. No, she's got feelings for Jacqueline."

I blink. "Oh. Huh. I guess that makes sense."

"Right? I thought she and Annie were gonna get together ages ago, but then Maggie asked Jacqueline out, so I didn't think about it again."

"Is she gonna do anything about her feelings?"

He shrugs. "I think she's just waiting right now to see if they'll go away."

I nod, and we fall back into silence. Jeremiah's cat has started chewing on a bush.

"Do you like anyone?" he asks suddenly.

"What, like, romantically?"

"Yeah."

"Not any more than you do."

He lets out something between a laugh and a sigh. "That's a lot, then."

From the corner of my eye, I watch him. He looks anxious. This is what I've been noticing all night—this weird nervousness. But rather than ask about it, I say, "So, you like someone?"

"Well, yeah. I thought it was pretty obvious."

"How would it be obvious?"

"I don't know. I just figured it was, since everybody else seems to have noticed." He pauses. "Except you, I guess."

I can't help it—I ask, "Who is it?"

He doesn't answer for a long moment, and my heartbeat is loud in my ears.

"You'll have to guess," he finally says. When I look at him, he's smiling, the smallest tug of his lips. He bumps his shoulder against mine.

"I can just ask Jacqueline." I don't say that the reason I don't want to guess is because then I might get it right. "*She'll* tell me without making me work for it."

"I'm not so sure about that."

Jeremiah's cat makes her way around the pool and up to Declan. She rubs against his side, meowing for his attention. "This is Zelda," he introduces, petting under her chin.

"Oh, like the character?" I reach my hand out gently. Zelda bumps her head against it.

"Yeah, like the character."

Zelda purrs loudly when I scratch behind her ear, Declan still scratching under her chin.

"Where are Jeremiah's parents?" I ask. Zelda sits between Declan and me, forcing us to scoot a little apart to make room for her. I hadn't noticed how little space there was between us until now.

"His dad's on a business trip," Declan says.

"What about his mom?"

He looks down. "She passed away a few years ago."

"Oh." Zelda nudges my hand again.

Declan's silent for a moment. "Yeah, it was . . . pretty rough. Still is."

"Did you know her well?" I ask gently.

He nods. "Jeremiah and I grew up together, so she was like a second mom to me. His family was always there for me when I needed them, and vice versa. When I came out in eighth grade and my dad didn't take it well, I spent a lot of time over here, trying to get some space from him, and Mrs. Reid was always so understanding. . . ." He looks at me. "Did I ever tell you about all the stuff that went down after I was outed at school?"

I shake my head.

"It was . . . well, obviously it sucked. I was dealing with kids at school suddenly knowing I was gay, and at the same time, my dad wasn't handling my coming out well. He told me I was too young to know my sexuality, and that I shouldn't go around saying things like that at my age, and that I should start trying to 'blend in' at school more so the comments would stop. . . ." He takes a deep breath. "We argued about it a lot for a few months. Mom did the best she could when we got like that, but it was hard on her. I know she wanted to support me, but she also didn't want me talking back to my dad or escalating things, and it put her in a weird place. She didn't agree with my dad, and she knew I needed her acceptance, but they were also supposed to be, like, a unified front during arguments, you know?

"Anyway, one night, my dad and I got in a huge, blowout fight over it—the worst fight I've ever gotten in with my parents. I don't even remember how it started, but it became about the stuff at school and my coming out, like it always did those days, and Dad was telling me that I was at fault for the bullying and that I needed to stop fighting so hard for something that he was convinced was just a phase, and I just . . . exploded. I told him that I was never going to be straight, and if he didn't want to accept that, then I didn't want to live under his roof anymore."

"Jesus," I say.

"Yeah, tell me about it." He laughs quietly, running a hand through his curls. "It's so weird to think about now, since obviously he's grown a lot and our relationship is much better, but things were *bad* back then. After I stormed off to my room, my mom tried to talk to me about it, but I couldn't get over how she'd hurt me, too, by not standing up for me during my fights with Dad, and I just . . . I felt like I couldn't be there. So, I called Jeremiah and snuck out. Jeremiah and his mom picked me up, and I spent the night there."

"I'm assuming you got in trouble for that."

"Oh, big time. I was grounded for three months, and it's still the one and only time I've ever been seriously in trouble." He grins, but it fades quickly. He looks down at his hands. "I don't think Jeremiah's mom knew just how much that meant to me, letting me stay over that night. Jeremiah and I didn't *tell* her that I'd snuck out of the house—we tried to play it off like everything was fine—but it was obvious that I'd been crying. And, still, she didn't push me for answers. I really appreciated that."

I'm silent, taking his story in. I think about the first time I went over to his house—how nice his parents were, how normal it seemed between him and his dad. "I can't imagine you in a fight with your parents," I say.

He snorts. "Yeah. Me neither, sometimes. It feels like a lifetime ago."

I put my arm around him and pull him into a side hug. "Thank you for telling me all that. It . . . it means a lot."

He hugs me back, a hand resting on my waist, and I try not to make it obvious how the touch surprises me. We sit there like that, watching the water.

"You know you're allowed to ask for help, Dec," I say gently. "It doesn't always have to be *you* helping everyone else."

"Yeah, I know. It's a work in progress." Then he pauses. "You've never called me that before."

I blink. "Oh. Um. Yeah. I guess I haven't."

"No, no, don't worry—it's fine. I liked it."

Our eyes meet, and we both seem to realize that his arm is still around me. He moves away a little, but our shoulders still brush.

"We should, uh, probably go inside," I say.

"Yeah, probably."

But neither of us moves. When I look at him again, he's already looking back.

Then, he smiles. "About earlier . . . you never guessed."

"Okay. . . ." I unfold my legs and pull my knees up to my chest. "Does he go to our school?"

"Yep."

So we're playing *this* game. "Is he in our grade?"

"Yep."

"Do I know him?"

He nods. I go through a mental list of guys in our grade, ones that I imagine he might be interested in, but I can't think of many. The name tastes bitter in my mouth, but I guess anyway: "Jeremiah?"

"He's straight," he says. "Not to mention he's like my brother. We used to take baths together when we were kids." He wrinkles his nose. "It's kind of hard to have a crush on someone after that."

"So, *not* Jeremiah." I hate it, but for some reason, that relieves me. I think of other boys we both know, plucking names from the list, but they're all wrong. "Why can't you just tell me?"

"You can ask Jacqueline if you give up."

"You're annoying," I mumble.

"Any other guesses?"

"Are you gonna tell me if I keep going?"

"Maybe."

I don't like that *maybe*. I don't like this game at all, if I'm honest. Every name I guess leaves a bitter taste in my mouth, and the image of him kissing any boy from our school makes my stomach curl like it did when I thought about how fondly he looks at Jeremiah. But curiosity eats at me, and I know I'm going to keep guessing.

Zelda gets tired of waiting for us to pay her attention again and skulks off to the patio door. Declan watches her scratch at the door before asking, "Do you give up?"

"Not if you're gonna look so smug about it."

He laughs. "I'm not trying to look smug. It's just fun sitting out here with you." He scoots a little closer again, bumping our shoulders together. He's warm. "Things with you don't have to be exciting. They can just . . . be."

"Yeah?" I shift closer too, only a little. If he notices, he doesn't comment on it.

"Yeah," he agrees quietly.

I think about his hand on my waist, his warmth, how he refuses to flat-out tell me who he likes. I think about redamancy and the way he always picks up when I call and those first few days we were getting to know each other.

The thought enters my head, loud and sudden and impossible: Is it me? Is it possible that *I'm* who he likes?

The music inside switches off abruptly.

For a second, neither of us moves or says anything, like we're holding our breaths for the music to return. When it doesn't, he again mumbles, "We should probably go inside."

"Okay," I say, but I don't stand. Declan doesn't either. We sit at the edge of the pool, closer than I think is probably normal, and the thought I had keeps nagging at me. I doubt it—it couldn't be true—but . . . I want to ask. I want to know the answer.

"About who you like . . ." I whisper.

He turns to me at the same time that I turn. Our noses are almost touching, and I can't tell if we'd always been this close or if he's leaning in. "I'll tell you if you don't have any more guesses."

I do, but my mouth glues itself shut. My tongue is heavy with my guess. Instead, I just nod. His breath is warm on my face, his cheeks flushed. It's endearing, I notice somewhere in the back of my mind. It's cute.

And then Declan leans in and kisses me.

When people talk about first kisses, they act like it all comes natural. *Feels* natural. Like you'll just know intuitively which way to turn your head, or how to kiss back, or what to do with your hands, or what to do when your brain stops short-circuiting and you realize with sudden, horrifying clarity that your best friend is kissing you and you don't know what you're supposed to do, or how you're supposed to feel, or what the fuck that even means.

And when people talk about first kisses, they certainly don't mention how your best friend will pull back after what must've been only a few seconds but felt like hours; or how he'll stare at you, waiting for you to say something; or how your whole body will go warm with an anxious heat that's been chasing you all night, until your chest constricts tight enough to make it hard to breathe; or how you won't know what to say, or how you'll know what you might say if you were someone else, someone better, someone braver, but you can't say it now because your mouth is clamped so tightly shut that you don't think it'll ever open again.

And they don't mention that you'll see your best friend's face fall when he realizes you're not going to say anything.

Yeah. They don't talk about that.

Declan stands up abruptly, grabbing his socks and shoes.

"I'm sorry," he's saying. "I—I should go."

And I watch his back as he retreats inside, disappearing in the crowd.

Seventeen

I REPLAY THE KISS OVER and over in my head while I'm driving home, and while I'm getting ready for bed, and while I'm lying down and trying and failing to fall asleep.

Maybe if I play the scene again and again in my head, it won't have been *me* he kissed; it won't have been his lips against mine, or his breath on my cheek, or my actions—or lack thereof—that made his voice shake when he apologized and ran back inside. Maybe it won't be real.

Because it couldn't have been me. I don't get things like that. I don't have other people like me. I don't have other people find me attractive enough to kiss me, or get upset when I panic and don't kiss them back.

I *don't get that.*

I want to talk to Nicole about it. I probably *need* to talk to Nicole about it. But when I start typing a text, I can't get myself to type the words.

Declan kissed me.

I get as far as *Declan* before my chest constricts again and I don't feel like myself.

It's a while before I fall asleep.

In the morning, Mom is throwing up.

I can't tell if it's from sickness or anxiety. I wake up to the sound of her vomiting, and my first instinct is to jump out of bed, panic already settling in, and rush to her, but she waves me away halfheartedly when she realizes I'm standing in the bathroom doorway.

"Sorry," she mumbles. "I didn't mean to wake you."

"It's fine." I help her up and we move to the couch. She leans her head on my lap. I don't realize she's crying until I feel tears on my thigh. "Mom . . ." I run a hand through her hair, careful of the tangles.

"I'm sorry," she hiccups. "I'm sorry. I'm sorry."

"It's really okay, I can just go back to sleep—"

But that just makes her cry harder. This isn't about just waking me up. That can't be why she's shaking so bad, why she's sitting up and pushing away from me and burying her face in her hands like a child, why she just cries harder when I try to comfort her with my arms around her shoulder.

"I don't know what to do," she says.

"About what?"

She just shakes her head, and it makes something settle in my stomach, a heavy weight.

I don't know what to do. I was too young, the first time she was at her lowest, to really understand the symptoms of her depression, the signs of an episode, the suicidal thoughts—so I don't know for sure that this is the kind of stuff she was saying back then. But I imagine if she was saying anything at all—if she hadn't simply retreated into herself, back to silence—then it was probably something like *I don't know what to do.*

Lucas's voice rings in my head. *I know you two are close, but it's always going to be different with you. She's always gonna hold back.*

I take a deep breath. Inhale for six seconds, exhale for eight.

"It's okay," I tell her. "It's okay, Mom. I'm here. It's gonna be fine. I'm here. You're gonna be fine."

And I don't know that it helps her. But I keep saying it anyway.

I work most Saturdays, and today, as shitty as it already is, isn't an exception.

I almost try to see if someone else can cover my shift so I can stay at home with Mom (and avoid Declan, because I know he's working today and I have no clue what I'm going to say to him when I see him), but after a half hour of crying and sitting on the couch together and not speaking, she gets up, takes a shower, and comes back to make breakfast. After that, she seems to be back to normal, or at least back to *pretending* things are normal. She still doesn't look great, but she sits in the living room and gets some grading done, and when I tell her that I have work tonight, she looks at me like she doesn't understand why I felt the need to let her know so far in advance.

It's still the most scared I've been in a while, but this is a good sign, all things considered. So I go to work.

Declan isn't there when I arrive, and I wonder, briefly, if he got someone to cover his shift last minute—but his car pulls into the parking lot a few minutes later. When he gets inside, he doesn't look at me on his way to clock in.

I keep my head down. The anxiety that's flooded my system makes it hard to breathe.

Nicole notices. "Hey," she says, putting a gentle hand on my shoulder. "Everything okay?"

"Um," I say. "Yeah, no, I'm all good. Just kind of . . ." I wave my hands around my head as if that can convey what I'm feeling.

Her eyebrows furrow. "Did something happen?"

I think about telling her what happened with Declan, but the idea of talking about it, saying the words out loud—it's still too much. So, instead, I go with a half truth. "My mom."

Her expression smooths into one of understanding. "I'm here if you wanna talk about it."

I look down at my shoes. "Maybe later."

It's not hard waking up Monday morning, mostly because I didn't get much sleep to begin with.

Declan didn't text me all weekend, and I just assumed he wasn't picking me up for school, so Mom drove me. Even though she drops me off earlier than I asked, Declan's there, the Plus fundraising table already set up.

As I'm getting out of the car, Mom rolls the window down and calls, "Good morning! You must be Declan!"

"Good morning, Ms. Adams." Declan waves back at her,

smiling gently. They exchange a few more words I'm trying not to focus on before Mom finally says goodbye and drives off, leaving us in silence.

Declan doesn't look at me until we've been waiting for fifteen minutes for students to wander over to our table. Even then, it's only a quick glance before his gaze returns to the parking lot. "People are taking longer to show up today," he comments.

I shrug. "Yeah, I guess."

A part of me wants to kick myself for not saying something else, something that could lead to an actual conversation—or at least an exchange that isn't so painfully awkward. But the rest of me is glad for the silence. I don't know how I'm meant to act, what I'm supposed to say.

When Jeremiah shows up thirty minutes later, he doesn't seem to notice the weirdness. Or, if he does, he does a good job hiding it.

He drops his backpack to the ground and, between yawns, says, "I don't know *how* you guys wake up early enough for this."

"Not all of us go to bed at three a.m. every night," Declan says. Jeremiah pours himself a cup of coffee and hands me three dollars. I slide it into the lockbox.

"I don't go to bed at three a.m. *every* night."

Declan shakes his head, grinning faintly, and it hits me how much I wish it was *me* causing that smile.

That night, I'm sitting at the kitchen table, scribbling an answer to a discussion question for AP Lit in a desperate attempt at distracting myself, when my phone buzzes.

declan: Hey. Can we talk?

I stare at my phone screen for a second. Then I take a deep breath and type *sure*.

He doesn't waste time calling me. I wait for my phone to ring twice before I pick up.

"Hey," Declan says. There's a forced casualness to it. "Sorry for calling so late."

"Don't worry about it. I wasn't gonna go to sleep for another few hours anyway."

"Yeah, should've figured that." There's the sound of fabric rustling over the other line and then nothing. I wonder where he is in his house right now. I wonder what he's going to say.

Before he can get anything out, I say, "I'm not angry."

There's a pause. "You aren't?"

I stand up from the kitchen table and head to my room. "No. I mean—I'm not. I thought maybe you thought I was, and I just didn't want you to think that. So, no. I'm not mad."

"You probably should be," he mumbles.

"Why?"

"I mean, I read the situation wrong. I . . . I didn't ask before I did it if it was all right, and I didn't even say anything about it afterward, and . . . it was gross of me."

I close my bedroom door. My crocheting supplies sit in a basket next to my bed, and I get out the blanket I've been working on, sit up against the headboard, and start where I left off.

"I don't think 'gross' is the word I'd use," I say.

204

Declan hesitates. "What word *would* you use?" he asks carefully.

I use my shoulder to press the phone to my ear as I crochet. The movement is more muscle memory than actual thought, which is how I'm able to work on a row with my heart thudding loudly in my ears, my fingertips warm with nerves. "Maybe . . . surprising. Quick." I pause, then add as an afterthought, "Not that I actually have anything to compare it to."

The response is immediate. Declan sputters, "That was— are you serious? That was your first kiss?"

"I told you I've never dated anyone before."

"Well, *yeah*, but that doesn't necessarily mean . . . I guess I just thought . . ."

"Thought what?"

"I don't know. That someone like you would've had someone to kiss already."

My face heats. "Nope. First time."

He groans. "Now I *really* feel like a dick."

"Don't. I already told you I'm not mad."

"But you should be."

Outside, police sirens blare past my apartment. The yarn I'm using is soft, the expensive kind. My mom bought me a bunch of it for my birthday this year.

I start tentatively, "So . . . you're gay."

There's confusion in his voice when he answers, "Yeah?"

"And, I mean, you obviously know I'm trans."

"Yeah? What about it?" Again, he doesn't seem to get it.

"That doesn't bother you? That I'm trans?"

There's a lot more I want to say about that. *That other people—grosser people, worse people—think of me as a girl? That I don't have the parts that everyone says you need to have to be a man? That I still get misgendered sometimes, that I have to bind to have a flat chest, that my license's gender marker doesn't reflect who I really am, that other gay people might not get it, that they might call you fake—*

There are a million caveats. Stories from Nicole swirl in my head, past partners and strangers on the internet and ex-friends alike all spouting the same transphobic bullshit at her. *No lesbian will want to date you. No one will want to have sex with you. No one will want to love you.* I parrot it in my own head, waiting for Declan to change his mind, to say, *Oh, silly me, I forgot. Never mind! Feelings revoked.*

Because I don't get this. I don't—I don't know. I don't deserve this. *This body* doesn't deserve this.

But Declan just says, sounding once again confused, "Why would that bother me? Gael, you're a boy. I'm gay. I *like boys*. And I like *you*."

"Oh." It comes out more like a breath than a word, relief that the worst hasn't been said. And also a little because I'm not used to him saying he likes me.

We're both quiet again. Loop, pull.

Declan kissed me, I think. *Declan kissed me, and Declan likes me. Declan likes me.*

"You don't have to feel bad if you don't like me back," he says.

"No, that's not—"

"It's okay—"

"I just didn't know what to do," I say loudly, trying to speak

206

over him. "When you kissed me. I . . . panicked. But not because I don't like you."

"Oh." He pauses. There's a bit of hope in his voice when he says, "So . . . does that mean that you *do* like me?"

I think about what Nicole said, about knowing the difference, and I think about how I felt in the moment right before he kissed me. I know I've never liked someone the way I like him, and that I think about him all the time. I want to ask if he thinks about me the same way, if the way I feel is the same as how he feels—but I don't know that I could handle the answer. That I can handle being an object of someone else's affection. That I can handle someone thinking of me—and my body—as worth wanting.

What I say is, "I mean—I think so. Yes. I— Maybe."

"Maybe?"

"I'm sorry, it's not—"

"No, no." He kind of laughs, and it alleviates some of my guilt. "Don't apologize."

"It's not that I don't *like* you," I say, desperate now to make him understand, to say what I mean, to articulate how it feels for once. "I just—I don't know that I can do . . . dating. I mean, you saw how I reacted when you kissed me. I don't know if I can . . . give you that."

Because I can give him those other parts of me. Small, almost unnoticeable touches. Staying up late to talk to each other. Being open in a way I haven't before. But the moment it went further—I freaked out.

But I don't know if that's because of how I feel about Declan, or because of how I feel about myself. Or if those things can even be separated.

"Kissing?" he asks.

"Really anything . . . physical. Or more physical than we've been. It's like . . . So, you know about gender dysphoria? It's like that, kind of. Or, it's tied to that. It's just that . . . I don't think of myself or my body as something that can be . . . liked."

"Gael—"

"It's not as bad as you're imagining," I interrupt. "I mean, it's not *fun*, but it's just how it is with me. Until I met you, I'd never had a reason to think about relationships or what that means for me because I spent the first three years of high school just trying to get by unnoticed, and a future where I dated anyone was . . . just, like, a fantasy. Something I knew would probably happen but didn't want, or couldn't imagine. Did you know that Jacqueline asked once if I was straight? I just told her yes, but it wasn't a yes because I've ever been attracted to girls, it was a yes because it's never seemed like there'll be a future where anyone wants me or—who I am. I just assumed that if anyone *did*, it would be a girl, the way that kids assume they're straight but without thinking about an alternative. Because . . . people don't *like* me, Declan. People *can't*." I choke on the words. "Not like that."

"I do," he says softly. "*I* like you like that."

"And that's fucking terrifying," I admit.

He sucks in a breath. "Yeah. If it makes you feel any better, I'm pretty scared too."

It doesn't, but I smile a little.

There's another silence. Then, gently, he says, "We could . . . be scared together?"

And I think I want that. I mean, I know that I don't want to lose what we have. But . . .

"I can't give you anything right now," I tell him, hating the words but knowing I have to say them. "It might be weeks or months or years before I'm comfortable with . . . anything."

"But you *do* like me," he says.

I nod. Then say out loud, "Yeah." And it's a relief to say that. *God*, is it a relief.

"Then we don't need to change anything," he says. "We don't need to call ourselves a couple or do anything you aren't already comfortable with. We can just . . . do what we've been doing."

"But don't you want more?"

"I mean, yeah. But I'm also happy as we are. I like hanging out with you. I like how we've been."

I think about redamancy. Is it really enough, to keep on as we are? Is it really enough for him, just knowing that I like him back? Maybe he's only saying that because he's Declan, and he's too good to push me.

Or . . . maybe not.

"Okay," I say. "Yeah."

"Yeah?"

I hear the smile in his voice this time, and even though guilt still bubbles in my stomach, it makes me smile too. "Yeah. We can do that."

Eighteen

HEARING MY MOM SING WAS a rare occurrence. She'd never really liked her voice; she said it wasn't her strong suit. But sometimes, back when I was little, she would sing for me so I could fall asleep, or as she tried to teach me piano, or when she thought nobody would hear. She sang in the shower, hummed as she cooked, whistled jingles from commercials when she thought I wasn't listening. For so long, her life orbited around music, and in turn, so did mine.

Then her mental health plummeted. She got worse. And worse. And I got used to her silence, until it was like she'd never played piano or sang for me at all.

But something switched when Lucas left.

A week after he was gone, I woke to my mother's voice, to her deft fingers pressing into the piano keys, to the sound of my childhood reinvented. I pulled myself out of bed and stood with my back against my closed door, listening to my mom.

Not for the first time, my chest ached with the memory of what my life used to be, of what it could have been if Lucas hadn't—if Mom wasn't—if *I* weren't—

Her voice cracked on the last line of the song, and the piano cut off suddenly—then there was the clatter of keys, discordant and heavy and resentful. I could hear her crying, faint through the wall.

I'm sorry, I thought, but I couldn't move, couldn't get my legs to push me toward the living room to comfort her. At fourteen, I still couldn't fully handle this—this responsibility. This maturity. I was lost and confused and didn't know what to do when Mom cried except disappear back in my room and pray that was the right choice and let my anger toward Lucas grow and grow and grow.

Even now, I don't think there's any sound worse than my mother crying.

After lunch on Tuesday, Declan and I walk to AP Lit together like usual. Things at lunch were fine; we joked around, talked about the tests we have coming up, discussed the movies coming out soon. Normal things. I could almost forget that Jeremiah's party happened at all.

But walking to class, it hits me that this is the first time that Declan and I have been alone since Friday night. Not that we're really *alone* in the hallway, but with Jacqueline, Jeremiah, and Annie off to their own classes, there's no buffer, no backup, no way to *not* draw parallels between now and the last time it was just the two of us. I keep thinking about his hand on my waist and his lips on mine and how he sounded on the phone last night. I tried to go to sleep after our conversation, but I couldn't get my mind to quiet down. I lay there for what might have been hours, replaying everything we said. Not even in a bad way, really. I just couldn't stop thinking about it.

I can't stop thinking about it now, either, as we enter the classroom and take our usual seats.

"Are you working tomorrow night?" he asks.

"Um." I don't know why—it's an easy question—but I suddenly feel put on the spot. "Yeah. Why?"

"Just wondering. I'm not sure why, but Lisa scheduled me for less hours than usual this week. Not that I'm complaining." He grins, and maybe I'm just reading into it, but it seems a little bit off from his usual carefree smile, and I wonder if he's feeling as weird as I am right now.

I don't understand why I'm so hesitant. We ended our conversation last night on a good note, knowing we're both on the same page. I felt a million times better about everything that happened after we talked, and I was hopeful that we'd be able to go back to normal today.

But, somehow, there's still this *thing* between us, still something that makes everything weird. And I realize suddenly that I don't know how to act now, how to pretend that what happened *didn't* happen. Is it even possible to return to normal, now that I know he likes me? How can I pretend that I don't? How can *he* pretend that I didn't basically tell him we can't date?

Guilt forms a knot in my stomach. I try to smile back, but I know he can tell it isn't genuine.

The bell rings a moment later, and we don't talk for the rest of class.

After work on Wednesday, Nicole and I go to Cook Out, at my request. This isn't the kind of conversation I can shove into a fifteen-minute car ride home.

"So," Nicole says, settling into the booth across from me with her milkshake and fries. "Something's going on with you."

I can't resist blowing my straw wrapper at her, and while she's rolling it up into a ball to chuck back at me, I say, "Something's always going on with me. That's nothing new."

"Your mom?"

I flinch, and her expression softens. Before she can say something about it, I say, "Not my mom. Well, not . . . entirely."

"But she's still a part of it?"

She's *always* a part of it, but I don't say that. "Yeah."

Nicole pauses to dip a fry in her milkshake. "So, what's *actually* bothering you?" And when I just look at my quesadilla, she says, "It's just us, Gael."

Her voice is gentle when she reminds me. Fond. That's the part that gets me—her fondness. Her support. Her love, something familial.

I sigh, my shoulders dropping. "It's . . . stuff with Declan. That I haven't told you about."

She sits up straighter. "What kind of stuff?"

I tell her what happened.

It's a weird story to tell. I try to be detached as I speak because I know if I don't, I'll start down an anxiety spiral. Not

213

that I haven't already done that a few times since the party, but I try to keep the outward panicking to a minimum.

Once she's all caught up, Nicole leans back in her seat and says, "So, just to summarize, you and Declan both like each other . . . but you're not doing anything about it?"

I nod. "What do you think this means?" I say. "Like, with my sexuality?"

"Well . . ." She sighs. "I can't make any real call for you, but from what I know about you, and from what you've told me about your feelings . . . it sounds an awful lot like you're only interested in guys. Or at least this *one* guy." She lowers her voice, providing us some sense of privacy. "And, honestly, I see a lot of my old self in the things you've been saying."

"Really?"

"Oh, yeah. Especially with the body stuff. This was before we were really friends, but when I was a sophomore in high school, I was dating this girl—and I hadn't come out to anyone or started transitioning at this point, you know, so she was straight—and I wouldn't do anything past kissing while we dated. And it wasn't that I wasn't attracted to her or interested in sex. It was just that even the *thought* of her seeing my body or touching me like that was enough to send me running. Eventually, I got over it, but not until after we'd broken up and I'd started transitioning."

"But that was about sex," I say. "My thing is—basically anything related to . . . I don't know. Dating. Getting close. I mean, I couldn't even kiss him without freaking out. . . ."

What I mean goes unsaid: *Isn't it pathetic that I can't even get to that point? Isn't that unfair to Declan, to not even let us kiss when we both like each other? Isn't this weird of me? Aren't I overreacting?*

She reaches across the table and holds my hand. "You're not doing anything wrong by taking things slow."

"*Slow* isn't even the word for it."

"Okay, then you're not doing anything wrong by waiting until you're sure you're comfortable." She squeezes my hand. "Gael, wouldn't you rather enjoy your time with Declan?"

"But it's not fair to him to make him wait—"

"And it's not fair to *you* to make yourself do something that causes you distress and anxiety just to make him happy. And I know for a *fact* he would never want to force you into that position. He agreed to letting things sit, didn't he?"

I stare at my food. "Yeah."

"Then you don't need to beat yourself up about it." She lets go of my hand and scoots her container of fries my way. "Want some?"

I nod, and while I'm dipping fries in my milkshake, I think over what she said.

When I'm done eating, I push my container forward. "How do I make myself *not* afraid of all this?"

"Well, first, what are you specifically afraid *of*?"

I think about it for a moment. "I guess . . . there's two parts to it."

"One of them is the physical stuff, right?"

I nod. "But I also think . . . liking someone, and knowing they like me back, is . . . It makes me feel really vulnerable."

She tilts her head. "Yeah, that makes sense. Relationships

definitely require a lot of vulnerability and being honest about your feelings. But what's so wrong with that?"

I can't find the words to explain how scary that sounds to me. Nicole knows I'm introverted and a bit of a loner, obviously, but she's the only person I've never had issues sharing personal stuff with. She's been in my life for so long, I don't worry that I'll scare her away or that she'll suddenly leave, so she doesn't see this part of me—the part that hides everything, that made me ghost my friends in middle school, that makes it so opening up feels like bleeding.

So, instead, I shake my head. "I don't know. I'm not making any sense."

"It's okay."

I smile a little, and she takes a sip of her milkshake. We sit in comfortable silence, and after a moment, I ask, "How do you think I'll know when I'm ready to . . . *start* a relationship?"

She shrugs. "Honestly? I'm not sure. If it were the exact same situation as mine, I might be able to tell you, but since yours is a little different . . . maybe you could try out smaller things."

"Smaller than . . . kissing?"

"Yeah! You know, hugging, holding hands. Maybe go out on a really casual date—something that can help you feel out your reactions to everything. Right now, you know what your reaction to kissing is, and you know what your reaction to strictly platonic stuff is. Take some time to check all the other things, too. There's more to dating than just physical intimacy, you know."

"I know that," I mumble, avoiding her eye. But I make a note of that idea. It's at least a better plan than "wait around until I wake up one day completely comfortable with everything."

Nicole asks, "So, in the meantime . . . how have things been with you two so far?"

"Awkward," I admit. "I feel like I've forgotten how to act around him."

She smiles a little. "Ah. I think that's normal. I'd be surprised if there wasn't at least a *little* weirdness every now and then. When McKayla and I were still trying to figure things out, it was . . ." She waves her hand around. "You have no idea."

I smile. "Worse than with me and Declan?"

"Oh, *way* worse."

I laugh, just a little, and some of the tension I've been holding is released with it. Even if things with Declan are weird, I still have Nicole here.

If nothing else, I always have Nicole.

At lunch on Thursday, Declan slams his tray of lunch food down on the table before declaring, "Guess who *finally* got Jeremiah to agree to come to Plus!"

Jacqueline, Annie, and I are already at the table. "I'm guessing it was you," Jacqueline says, raising an eyebrow.

Jeremiah comes up behind Declan and sits down. "He didn't get me to agree to go to Plus. I *only* agreed to go to the gala," Jeremiah corrects.

"And I'm counting that as a win." Declan flicks a piece of corn at him. While Jeremiah starts to retaliate with some of his own, Declan continues loudly, "*Anyway,* I'm letting you guys know in advance so that more people will hold him responsible when he freaks out and decides to bail last minute."

"I'm not gonna 'freak out.' When have I ever done that?"

Declan raises an eyebrow. "Do you genuinely want an answer to that? Because you know I can put you on blast here in front of God and everyone if that's really what you're requesting."

Jeremiah glares.

"Do you think you'd be interested in volunteering to help with the gala?" I ask, leaning a little over Declan to see Jeremiah better.

"I probably won't be able to," he says, grimacing. "Sorry, man. Things are super busy right now with school and college applications and stuff, and it's just gonna get worse the next few weeks—"

"Yeah, 'cause your schedule is so packed," Jacqueline interjects. He sticks his tongue out at her.

"That's fine, I just thought I'd ask," I say.

"Gael's, like, *the* volunteer person for Plus." Jacqueline stabs a green bean with her plastic spork and waves it around as she speaks. "All official and fancy, making sure everything's taken care of."

"Not really. I just like helping out," I say.

Annie snorts. "Now you sound like Declan."

"He must be rubbing off on you," Jeremiah says.

Against my better judgment, I glance at Declan. He's tensed up, like he's preparing for this conversation to turn sour, and he doesn't look my way.

A knot forms in my stomach. I look back down at my food and don't say anything.

* * *

Saturday night, as I'm getting ready to go to sleep, I go to Mom's room. She's sitting up in her bed, her computer on her lap as she types.

"I gotta have my shot tonight," I tell her.

"Oh, shoot. I forgot." She finishes whatever she'd been typing, closes the laptop, and gets up. I'm holding the small bottle of testosterone, a disinfectant pad, a Band-Aid, and a disposable needle. I sit down on the edge of the bed, setting the supplies next to me.

It's a quick process that I'm already used to. When I first started T, I'd have to close my eyes or stare at the TV, distracting myself while I waited for the inevitable pain from the needle jab. I don't know why I was always so freaked out by that part. I think sometimes the idea of getting hurt was worse than the hurt itself. But I'm pretty all right about it now.

When it's over and I'm smoothing the bandage on, Mom disposes of the used needle and asks, "Is there something bothering you, honey?"

It's a sudden question. But I guess I've been quieter than usual tonight.

"I'm fine," I tell her.

Mom gives me a look, some mixture between disappointment and sympathy. I know she understands the impulse to lie, which is maybe why she doesn't ask me to elaborate.

"Well," she says. "If you want to talk about it . . ." She trails off, the invitation clear.

I nod. Then pause, before saying, "Have you ever wondered

about . . . I don't know, my sexuality?"

I'm still sitting on the edge of the bed, and now that she's done cleaning up, she takes a seat next to me, the bed shifting under her weight.

"A little when you first came out," she admits.

"What did you think?"

"Well, before I really did any research," she says, "I guess I thought maybe you liked girls."

"And now?" I prod.

"What about now?" she asks.

I don't say anything. She sets a hand on my knee. "Is there someone you like?"

I nod. She nods too and waits.

Finally, I say, "It's a boy." Then, "I mean, I don't know *what* I am."

"Have you ever liked a girl?" she asks, not unkindly.

"No." The answer is immediate and honest.

"Then, it's possible you might be gay. You know it's okay if you are, right?"

There's an implicit end to that: *You're allowed to be two things. You can be both trans and gay. It's all right.*

And I *do* know that, logically. But it's so hard to remember, sometimes, when Nicole's the only other person I really know who resembles me; when I've never seen who I am or might be on TV or in books or in movies; when I hear horror stories online about the way trans gay people are treated by cis gay people. It's hard enough being transgender. Being not-straight on top of it is a whole other layer entirely.

Some part of me wants to resist accepting that as my identity. There's some distant voice in my head saying that to be a man, I have to love women, I have to be masculine and all that it traditionally entails, including heterosexuality. I have to conform as much as I can.

And what happens if I don't conform? If I break every rule silently set for trans men, for trans people? If I realize that even in this community, I don't fit the "acceptable" mold, the one that will garner me the most respect from transphobes and homophobes alike?

What happens then?

This is the same route of thinking that caused me to ask Declan if he still liked me even knowing I'm trans. And Declan had been so reassuring. He had been so immediately certain. It didn't matter to him. *Doesn't* matter to him.

Does it matter to me?

Should it?

I don't know.

But it doesn't matter to my mom. And this should be the least of my worries. This shouldn't be hard, shouldn't be emotional. When you've already come out as trans, coming out as anything else should feel like nothing in comparison. So why do I start crying?

"Sweetie," she says, pulling me into a hug. I haven't cried like this since before I started T; I used to cry all the time at the smallest things, but being on testosterone has made it harder to let the tears out.

It doesn't stop me now, though, and I'm hiccupping the way

Mom does, another thing I got from her. She lets me cry into her shoulder.

"Sweetie," she says again, this time into my hair. "Gael, dear, I love you so much. So much."

"I don't know why I'm crying," I admit. It's punctuated by more hiccupping. I hug her back tightly, holding on to her. I feel like a child.

After a few moments, when I've calmed down, she pulls away but leaves her arm over my shoulder. We sit for a moment, not speaking.

I confess suddenly, "Declan kissed me."

I can tell she's surprised, even as she tries to hide it. "He did?"

"At Jeremiah's Halloween party."

"You *did* seem kind of distracted when you came home that night," she muses, more to herself than to me. "What did you tell him?"

"That I like him too," I say. "But that I can't . . . handle a relationship right now. Not yet."

I don't elaborate, and she doesn't push me after that, only assuring me she's here if I want to talk.

If there's anyone that would understand the need for space and time to think, it would be Mom.

Nineteen

OUR FINAL COFFEE SALE AT GHS is the first week of November. Things with Declan have been more or less the same, our conversations a little stilted. It feels like the first few days we talked, awkward and uncertain, and I still feel like that when I show up that morning.

When our first customer appears, I fumble for the card reader, and when Declan's arm brushes against mine, he flinches away like I've burned him. My chest tightens, and I wish, desperately, that I had asked someone else to do this. I'm sure the student can tell the shift in mood when Declan's "Thanks so much!" is a little less sincere than usual.

"Hey," Declan says, once the person has gone inside the school. "Are you okay?"

I put my hands in the front pockets of my hoodie and turn to look at him. "Yeah, I'm fine. Why?"

We've managed to keep eye contact so far—this is probably

223

the longest we've been able to do that since Jeremiah's party—but now he glances away. "You just seem . . . down."

"Oh. No, I'm okay."

"Okay. Good." He taps the lockbox in our silence.

It's only after we've sold another handful of cups that I get up the courage to say something else. "How's your family doing?"

"They're fine," he says. "My parents made me join them for trick-or-treating, so that was all right. Ellie went as Moana for the second year in a row."

"What about your brothers? Did they dress up?"

"Joshua wore a Ghostface mask, but my mom made him keep it off most of the night because it freaks Ellie out. Jordan was a pirate."

I nod. It's another moment before I ask, "So, how's Jordan been?"

He lets out a small sigh. "He's okay, kind of. He hasn't been having too many panic attacks lately, so that's good, but . . . school's been rough on him. His school's administration isn't being very accommodating, so he's having a hard time staying, like, focused and stuff."

"Shit. I'm sorry."

"Yeah. It's . . . yeah."

I want to say something to let him know he can talk about this with me, that he doesn't have to pretend things are fine. I want to comfort him, to hear what he's thinking, to be let in, the way that he let me in when he drove me home after Plus, or when I found him during AP Lit, or the night of Jeremiah's party. I want to hug him. Hold him.

But someone approaches from the parking lot before I can

find the words, and the moment is lost.

I realize, as Declan greets them with a wide, fake smile, that there's nothing I can say to make things between us normal again. Not all the way. Not how I want them to be.

The gala is quickly sneaking up on us. We only have two more weeks to fundraise, and even though we're on track for our goal, the next week is a whirlwind. When I'm not following up with volunteers to confirm they can cover what they signed up for, trying to write my college application essay, staying on top of schoolwork, or waiting tables at Joey's, I'm trying not to notice the distance between Declan and me. I don't know how to bring us back to where we were. How to fix this.

So, instead, I bury myself in gala preparation. Contacting other volunteers hasn't eaten up all my time—it's mostly texting or emailing people to confirm they understand what their responsibilities are and following up with them the day of their event—so I talk to Nicole and offer to take over getting the performances in order. We're hoping to have acts by local slam poets and musicians. She's told me about a few poets she likes, so I'm in charge of emailing them to see if they would be interested in performing, along with the bands Dakota and Nicole decided on together. I'm surprised by how much I *don't* hate the idea of getting in contact with these complete strangers. It's almost fun, actually. It feels like I'm someone . . . I don't know, important. Useful. Someone who can help make a change.

The gala is a good distraction from the Declan stuff for the time being. But that doesn't last too long when Jeremiah brings it up.

We're both in the cafeteria before school starts. It's one of the rare times when our other friends haven't gotten here yet, leaving the two of us to grab breakfast. The first thing he says to me when I sit down is: "So, you and Declan are going through some things."

I don't meet his eyes. "I guess."

"He told me what happened."

"Oh." That shouldn't surprise me. After all, I told Nicole *and* my mom about it, and I know Declan and Jeremiah are close. But still, I'm caught off guard.

"Yeah." He nods and sits down. I take a sip of my orange juice, waiting for him to say something, and the silence we sit in is surprisingly tense. I don't know why I feel so weird around him—we're friends, after all. This shouldn't be a big deal.

But . . . he's Declan's friend first. And now that I know that Declan's told him what happened, I can't help worrying that his opinion of me has changed. I mean, it's not like I broke Declan's heart or anything, but if it were Nicole in this position, I'm sure *I'd* have complicated feelings about the person she liked.

He finally says, "Declan *really* likes you."

I look at him, but I can't think of anything to say to that that doesn't feel inadequate.

When I don't respond, he continues, grinning faintly, "Like, he *never* shuts up about you. He's just so bad at hiding it. Even if he hadn't let me know he was gonna tell you at my party—"

"He told you that?"

"Yeah. Before you got there, he told me he wasn't leaving the party without letting you know how he feels."

"So, when I found you guys talking . . ."

He nods. "Yep."

I think back to the look Jeremiah gave Declan before he left us alone upstairs. ". . . Oh."

Jeremiah laughs. "Dude, how did you seriously not pick up on it?"

My face heats. "It's not like I didn't notice that he acts different around me," I say, and it comes out more defensively than I mean it to. "It's just . . ."

I think about when I was guessing who Declan's crush is, how long it took me to even consider myself as an option. How impossible it feels that anyone could like me, even now.

"I don't like to get my hopes up," I say. "I'm not exactly used to people being into me. So, I guess I just never . . . let myself consider that there was a chance he might like me."

He nods. "Yeah. I get that. But, man, you don't have to worry about that at all. I've never seen him like this with anyone."

"Like what?"

"Annoying, for one." He grins, but it doesn't stick for long. His expression deflates to something more serious. "I don't really know how to say it, but he just thinks you're the best, you know? He gets really . . ." He waves a hand around vaguely. "Affected. By, like, *everything*."

"Oh."

We're silent again. My phone lights up with a text from Jacqueline to our group chat, something about not wanting to go to school today.

Before I can lose my nerve, I admit, "I was jealous of you."

Jeremiah looks at me, and even though he doesn't seem to be judging, it still makes me burn a little with shame. I continue,

"Before Declan said he likes me, I thought he had a thing for you. He said he didn't, but . . . you guys are so close, so . . ."

"So, you were jealous of me?"

I nod.

"Oh, man." Jeremiah grins. "You probably already know this, but you had exactly *zero* reason to be jealous. Even if he wasn't like my brother, he was basically in love with you the moment you two started talking."

I stiffen at the use of *in love*, but I don't refute it, either.

"I know that now," I say. "But it was hard when I first started getting to know you guys, because he talks about you so much, and it just seemed like you were . . ."

Everything I'm not. But I can't bring myself to admit that out loud. I don't think I'd even been able to admit it to *myself* until now. It's not just that the two of them are close—it's that Jeremiah is so different from me. He feels so much more like the kind of guy that Declan *should* have a crush on. He's funny and sarcastic and confident and—a small part of me can't help pointing out—*cis*. If it were Jeremiah that Declan had feelings for, people wouldn't question his validity as a gay man. They wouldn't ask how Declan could possibly like him.

And, maybe more than that, I doubt that someone like Jeremiah would have all the hang-ups that I do, this fear that I carry around with me. Do other people need this much time? Am I alone in feeling like this?

"It just seemed like you would be a good fit" is what I land on instead.

Jeremiah thinks about that. "Yeah, I guess I can see how that would be hard, coming into the friend group when we're so close."

Some underclassmen pass us, laughing way too loudly for eight in the morning. I take another sip of my orange juice before asking, "How much did Declan tell you about our conversation?"

"He said you talked about how you both like each other, and that you decided to stay friends."

"Did he mention why?"

Jeremiah shrugs. "Nah. He said it was personal stuff, so I didn't push it."

Both our phones buzz with another text from the group chat, this time Annie asking if anyone's at school already. Jeremiah sends *me and Gael are in the cafeteria* in answer before putting his phone away and crossing his arms.

"Can I say something?" he asks.

My anxiety kicks up, but I nod.

"It's not my business," he starts, "and I don't know *everything* that's been going on between you two, but . . . I get where you're coming from, I do. Shit's scary, and it's easy to get bogged down in how terrifying it is to put yourself out there. But it's also really, really worth it, and I know you and Declan mean a lot to each other, so . . ." He runs a hand through his hair. "I just want you to know that you don't have to force yourself to date him if you really don't want to. But if you *do* like him and want to be together . . . don't get in your own way, you know?"

I'm not sure how to respond to that. All I can really manage is a nod.

"Okay. Cool. I just wanted to get that out there," Jeremiah says, and we fall silent.

Thankfully, we don't have to sit there just the two of us for much longer. Annie finds us a minute later, setting her backpack on the table and sitting down next to me.

"Good morning," she greets cheerily. She takes her coat off, looking between us. "Something up?"

"Nothing," I say too quickly. If she catches it, she doesn't push, instead going on to talk about her morning. Jacqueline arrives a few minutes after, then Declan, and the group falls into our normal banter until we head to class.

And Jeremiah doesn't bring the subject up again.

The week before the gala, Nicole offers me a ride home after work and parks at a gas station a few miles from Joey's.

She goes inside, and I wait in the passenger seat with my phone out. Declan texts the group chat with a link to another playlist he made, and I'm scrolling through the track list when the driver's door opens and Nicole climbs back in.

She hands me a Snickers bar. "Here. You look like you've had a rough day. Thought it might cheer you up."

"Aw, thanks." I take it from her, turning the bar over in my hands a couple of times.

My phone buzzes with another message. I flip it over and set it in the cup holder before shoving the Snickers bar into my hoodie's pocket. I don't have much of an appetite right now.

"Something up?" she asks.

"Nothing I haven't already told you," I say, but I know that's not what she's asking. I can tell just from the look she gives me that she wants to know about my parents—about the "situation at home."

Home situation. Plus situation. Declan situation. There's always a *situation*.

Nicole doesn't push me, though. She just turns back around in her seat, buckles, and leaves the parking lot.

"How are things with Plus?" I ask.

"They're a little better. The coffee sales have been helping, and with the gala coming up, things don't seem so bad."

"That's good."

"It is. And I don't know if I've told you this, but I'm really proud of you."

I laugh a little. "What?"

"Yeah, I'm serious! When you found out that Plus needed help, you were so quick to volunteer, and you've gone above and beyond helping with the gala. I mean, you really didn't have to take on the entertainment stuff, too." She smiles. "I'm happy to see you get so into something, you know?"

"I just didn't want to sit around while you were trying to keep the group going. Not when there was something I could do about it."

"Actually, about that . . ." Nicole comes to a stop at a red light. "I'm meeting with a potential sponsor the day after the gala. Dakota was supposed to go with me, but they had to cancel, and I can *technically* go by myself, but since you're so passionate about helping Plus . . . well, it certainly won't hurt to bring that kind of energy to the meeting."

I look at her. "Wait, you're serious?"

"Only if you're available, obviously. It's not a huge deal if you can't, but I'd like you to be there."

"Sure. I mean, yeah, I can do that."

She grins, and I can't help smiling back. "Great! I'll let you know more details when we get closer to the date. For now, we gotta focus on making sure the gala doesn't flop."

"Noted."

But I'm still thinking about what she said, about how I've found something to be passionate about, and I can't help feeling excited for the meeting. It's nice to be needed like this. And more than that, I really like what I do with Plus. It's work, yeah, but it doesn't feel like the same kind of work I do at Joey's or for school. It's more fulfilling.

When I get home that night, I check the majors offered by the universities I'm applying to, starting with MTSU. The website has their majors organized by colleges—Liberal Arts, Education, Business, Media and Entertainment, Behavioral and Health Sciences . . . I click on each, expanding to reveal all the options, all the paths I could take. Then I google what degree you need to work at a nonprofit. There are a million different answers, but a few say something along the lines of a bachelor's in business or communications, maybe with a master's in nonprofit management. I expand MTSU's list of majors under Business again and click on each, reading through their requirements, their faculty, their courses.

I try to imagine myself majoring in business. And even though the image is fuzzy and kind of intimidating and a little unreal, I can see myself there, graduating, going on to work with places like Plus. For the first time, it doesn't feel like an impossible future.

Twenty

THE WEEKEND BEFORE THE GALA, Jacqueline convinces us all to go dress shopping, which means I spend two hours following them around and watching Annie and Jacqueline sort through racks upon racks of options. Jeremiah is surprisingly diligent when it comes to helping them shop, carrying clothes for them when they need it.

"How many dresses do you think that is?" Declan asks as we watch Annie dig through a mass of black fabric. Draped across her arm is a pile of other dresses, and Jeremiah's carrying yet another pile. Jacqueline's only carrying a couple that she's picked out.

"Gotta be in the twenties," I say.

"She'll probably only try on one."

"Are you an expert on Annie's shopping quirks?"

"Yep. I'm just observant like that." He surprises me when he bumps his shoulder into mine. Things have been okay-ish with us since my talk with Jeremiah. I've been thinking about what Jeremiah said, about not getting in my own way, and I've tried to take his advice. Declan and I still aren't back to where we were before the party, but our conversations are a little more natural, and I don't feel quite as awkward when we're alone. I'm starting to accept that, for now, this is how things are, and it's going to have to be enough.

That doesn't mean I don't miss being close to him, though, and my skin burns where we touched. But instead of saying *Please keep doing that*, I ask, "You went to the gala last year, right? How was it?"

He shifts his weight from one foot to the other, and it makes him lean a little away from me. I immediately miss the closeness. "It was pretty fun. Kind of like prom, but fewer drunk teenagers and less awkward dancing and weird lights."

A few feet from us, Jacqueline is on her tiptoes trying to get a shirt down from a high rack, while Annie and Jeremiah just watch, both of them looking amused. "Have you ever been to prom? Or, like, a big school dance?" Declan asks.

I give him a look. "You even have to ask?"

He smiles. "I just wanted to make sure. You have a habit of surprising me."

"When have I *ever* surprised you?" I ask, but then I see the look that passes across his face, an expression like he wants to say something but can't, and I know he's thinking about our conversation on the phone, when I admitted I liked him.

He flicks his eyes back to Annie, where she's given in and helped Jacqueline get the shirt down. I can't make out their conversation, but Jacqueline laughs at something Annie said, and Annie blushes.

"Pretty often," Declan says. "Like, just the other day I found out that you actually *listen* to the playlists I send you."

"And you weren't expecting that?"

"Not beyond a cursory play-through, or when I get dibs on deejaying in the car. I think everyone else just looks at them once then forgets about them."

It suddenly feels important that he understands why I do that—why I make it a priority when no one else does, why I listen to his favorite songs. Why he's the only one I do this for.

But I can't find the right words, so I say, "I'm not everyone else," and hope he understands what I mean.

He glances over at me. "Yeah," he agrees. "You aren't."

Now that Annie's gotten the shirt down for her, Jacqueline holds it up to her chest, trying to judge if it's the right size. She seems to think it works, laying it across her arm with the other outfits she has picked out. Along with two dresses, she's also got a blue button-down and a formal pair of pants. Annie's moved on to another rack, sorting through each of the options, and I think about her crush on Jacqueline. Since the Halloween party, I haven't been super plugged-in to what's going on with my friends' love lives, but from what I've gathered, it seems like Jacqueline and Maggie are in a fight right now—Jacqueline hasn't even mentioned inviting her to go to the gala with us. I wonder how Annie feels about that.

"How have things been at home?" Declan asks.

"They're . . . kind of okay. My dad hasn't called me since

the last time I saw him, thank God. My mom is . . . well, she's not the worst she's been, but I don't know. I don't get to see her much because she's been busy with work, and I've spent most of my time helping out with the gala, so . . ."

"Right." He nods. "I'm assuming that means you're going?"

"'Course," I say. "Why do you ask?"

He ducks his head down a little, scratching his cheek. "If you weren't, I was going to ask if you wanted to hang out instead."

"You aren't planning on going?"

"Well—I mean, I'm not sure yet. . . ." He glances away. "It's fun, but I've been before, and I know you're not big on parties, so I just thought, you know, if *you* weren't going, we could go to eat or hang out at my place. It's not the same as getting all dressed up, but . . ."

Before I can respond, Annie comes over, holding up two dresses, one short and simple and the other long and more formal. "Can I get y'all's opinion on which one fits the gala's vibe?"

"They're both good, but the longer one probably fits a little better," I say, and Declan nods his agreement.

Annie beams, thanks us for our input, and goes back to the rack of dresses she'd been looking through.

"They barely need us here," Declan says, and I snort. He smiles, showing off his dimples, and I don't mean to stare, but I suddenly feel like I can't stop looking at him. Even when things are off between us, I realize, I want to be around him.

"Let's do something after the gala," I finally say. "That way we get to do both."

"Yeah." Declan's smile is small. "We can do that."

When I get home from shopping, I'm on my way to my room when I hear my mom's voice through her door.

"I'm sorry, Isa, it's been—"

I pause in the hallway, straining to catch what she's saying.

"I was gonna say *difficult*," she says. "No, I heard your voice-mail, it's just . . ."

Mom doesn't speak for a while, and I can just barely hear the vague sounds of Aunt Isabella on the other line.

"I think he's okay right now. He's had a lot going on, but it mostly seems for the better. He's involved in this after-school program, and he's been looking into colleges for next year. We've also been getting things for his surgery in order, so his first consultation visit will hopefully be in the next few months. . . . No, I don't think so. . . . Lucas hasn't been by the house in a while. After last time, I think he got the message that Gael still isn't ready to talk to him, so he's been keeping his distance again. . . . Trust me, I've already discussed with him about showing up out of nowhere. He's gonna be at Gael's graduation, though, so if you're planning on making it, I need you to promise now that you won't make a scene. . . ."

I head to my room after that, tired of eavesdropping. Ten minutes later, Mom pokes her head into my room. "Hey, honey, how was shopping?"

"It was all right," I say.

She smiles, and it's a real one. Mom seems to have gotten her energy back the past few days. "I'm ordering pizza for dinner," she says. "Anything specific you want?"

"Nah."

"Cheese it is then."

She starts to close the door, but I stop her. "Hey, Mom?"

"Hm?"

"How've you been?"

She blinks as if surprised by the question, before offering a small smile. "I've been fine, sweetie."

I nod. There's more I want to ask, but she seems so normal right now, so *okay*, that I don't want to push it. So I leave it at that, and she closes the door behind herself.

I don't know how long this burst of life will last. She's been so—precarious lately. Crying some mornings, smiling others. Back and forth. But sometimes the bouts last longer, like this good mood the past week.

I still think about what Lucas said. About needing his help. *This isn't something you can just tough out to spite me.* But that's what we've *been* doing—toughing it out. We can do this on our own.

We don't need his help. We don't need him to ruin our lives again.

I just hope Mom's good mood lasts.

The last Friday before the gala, Nicole pulls me aside at the beginning of Plus.

"About our meeting this Sunday," she starts, keeping her voice low. Around us, kids are sitting on the floor or standing near the whiteboard, some doodling, others looking at their phones. Jacqueline isn't here yet, so Annie and Declan are standing near the entrance, talking. I see Declan glance over at me, but I look back to Nicole before he can meet my eye.

"Is everything all right?" I ask.

"No. Or, yes, but . . ." She fidgets. "Well. I was wondering how comfortable you are with . . . meeting the sponsor by yourself?"

I stare at her. "Oh."

"It's okay if you can't," she rushes to say. "The problem is, McKayla had a family emergency come up so she's going to drive to San Antonio, but I really don't want her driving fourteen hours all by herself so I told her that if she can wait until after the gala we could leave first thing in the morning, but she has to be there as soon as possible so we *really* don't want to leave Monday and I can't reschedule with Ms. Jackson because this is the only time that worked for both of us—"

I put a hand on her shoulder to stop her. "Whoa, Nicole, it's okay! I can meet with Ms. Jackson by myself."

She blinks at me. "Really? You're sure?"

"Not . . . one *hundred* percent," I admit, "but it's obviously important, so I can manage."

"Oh, thank you." She sighs in relief and pulls me into a tight hug. "You just saved my *life*, oh my God."

I pull away, smiling. "That's what I do."

"So, you're meeting with Priscilla Jackson at the Holly Café in Glenwood at ten a.m. this Sunday—"

"Nicole, don't worry about it. I already know." She's given me the rundown about this before. Ms. Jackson is with a local law firm, and if Plus gets them as a sponsor, it could be a big deal. The hope is that it will fill the gap Plus's previous sponsor left.

She sighs deeply. "I know. I'm sorry. I've just been so frazzled lately."

"Let's just focus on the gala tomorrow. Things'll work out."

"Yeah. I guess you're right." She pauses, then reaches over to mess up my hair. "When'd you get to be the mature one, huh?"

I duck under her, evading her attack. "I've always been the mature one."

While she continues teasing me, I feel Declan's eyes on us. When I look over, Annie's saying something to him, but he's looking at Nicole and me. For the first time in weeks, he doesn't turn away. Instead, he lets our eyes lock, and he smiles gently.

I smile back.

The next day I go to the gala venue early to help Nicole set up, and most of the people who attend Plus meetings are there, too, setting up chairs and straightening decorations, blue and white and gold and glittering. Nicole and Dakota reached out to a lot of places for the gala's venue, but the Gazebo Inn, a historic hotel in downtown Glenwood, offered their ballroom for the night. And apparently the hotel is run by an older lesbian couple who told Dakota in their meeting that they wish they had a community like Plus when they were young.

An hour before the gala starts, I head back to my apartment to get changed. I'm dressed and in the living room, waiting for Declan to pick me up, when Mom comes out of her room and demands a photo of me.

"Mom, you really don't have to do that—"

"No, no protesting!" She's already got her phone in hand,

waving it around as she speaks, and she motions for me to get up from the couch. "This is an important night. You might not have another event as fancy as this."

"Senior prom is still a thing," I tell her, even though that feels a million years away.

A look crosses her face that I can't pinpoint. Or, I *can*, but it's so different from her previous energy and excitement about the dance that it takes me a second to understand that, no, that really *is* a grief-stricken expression that flickers across her face before she smooths it over into a smile and raises her camera. "Smile!"

I do. I don't think it comes out very genuine, though. I only have one "formal" outfit, and that's what I'm wearing now, the tie a little too long for me and the shirt big at the shoulders. I feel like a kid playing dress-up in my parent's clothes, and I'm sure I look like it too.

But Mom doesn't seem to get that memo. After more photos than necessary, she locks her phone and holds it to her chest, just looking at me with a smile that I know means she's going to cry any second now.

"Mom," I say, and she pulls me into a hug before I can ask anything.

"You'll be okay, won't you?" she says into my hair. "I mean— you're growing up so much. You're graduating so *soon*. You'll be okay, won't you?"

"What's this about?"

She doesn't answer me for a long moment, just holding me there. "Nothing," she says finally. "It's just—it's nothing, dear. Just your mom getting emotional." She pulls away but still holds me at arms' length, smoothing down the wrinkles on my shoulders and fixing my tie.

I let her fuss over my appearance until there's a knock at the door. She lets me step out of her reach so I can let Declan in, but I get the feeling that if she could've, she would've kept me there forever.

Declan looks much better dressed up than I do, that's for certain, with clothes that actually fit him well and his hair pulled into a half ponytail. He steps inside to exchange niceties with Mom while I realize that I left my wallet in my room. When I'm back and ready to leave, Mom pulls me into one last hug.

"I'll be okay," I answer her, a little late, but she seems happy at the confirmation. It's important that she hears my question, though, so I make sure she's pulled away from the hug and looking at me when I ask: "Will you?"

The question throws her off. She blinks. Then her expression melts, and she looks like she might cry again.

"I'll be fine, Gael," she says softly. "You have fun tonight, okay?"

There's a feeling in my stomach, like there's something I'm missing, or something I need to do before I go. But I don't know what it is, and she's walking me to the door and offering Declan a hug, and Declan's pulling me out of the apartment, and I just see my mom's face a last time before she closes the door, that smile-that-isn't-really-a-smile.

But I don't say anything about it.

I just follow Declan to his car.

Twenty-One

THE DRIVE TO THE HOTEL is surprisingly okay, especially considering this is one of the very few times Declan and I have been fully alone together since the night of Jeremiah's party. I'm jittery, and I keep running my finger over my eyebrow, trying to do *something* with all this energy.

While stopped at a red light, Declan glances over at me. "Are you nervous?"

I grimace. "Is it that obvious?"

"A little." But he smiles. "Don't worry. I know everyone's worked really hard on this—*you've* worked really hard on this. It's gonna be great."

"I didn't do *that* much," I mumble, but I still relax a little at his assurance.

At the gala, most people are huddled around the catering tables, shuffling their feet in the middle of the room, or setting up camp at one of the many dining tables taking up the majority of the space. Near the stage are the tables for items people will be bidding on. Half are prize baskets pulled together from donations received from local businesses, like a date night package or a spa package. Along with the prize baskets, some local artists donated handmade items to auction off, so things like colorful art glass, jewelry and pendants, and a few framed pieces of art are also on display.

Declan and I find a table, and I eye the kids a few feet away from us swaying to the music. There's a small dance floor in front of the stage.

"Are there usually this many people dancing?" I ask. The band is just loud enough that I can use it as an excuse to lean into him. "I thought this was explicitly *not* a dance."

He turns a little, and our faces are suddenly very close. "Why? You wanna go join them?"

"Not what I meant," I say quickly.

He laughs. "Somehow, I'm not surprised."

The song's verse transitions into a smooth, bubbly chorus. I look at the people around us and, without glancing at Declan, try to make it as casual as possible when I shift and our hands brush. I might've imagined it, but I think Declan holds his hand there, pressing his knuckles to mine for a second longer. It makes my stomach squirm in a good way, knowing he's not only caught on, but that he's all right with it. My skin tingles where we touch.

It almost makes me brave enough to *actually* hold his hand, instead of just this sly back-and-forth we have right now—except, just then, Jacqueline, Annie, and Jeremiah arrive and spot us from the entrance.

"You both look so good!" Jacqueline exclaims as they walk to our table.

"You're one to talk," Declan says, grinning. "Look at you!"

She strikes a pose, showing off her dark blue suit and black heels. Annie's wearing the dress that she asked my opinion on, and it's a light gold in sharp contrast to Jacqueline's blue. Jeremiah wears a white button-down, his tie matching Annie's dress.

While Declan and Jacqueline talk, Annie and Jeremiah go with me to get food. As we're filling up our plates, I ask Jeremiah, "How are you feeling so far?"

"Pretty good," he says. "This is definitely better than Glenwood's GSA, I can say that."

I laugh a little. Annie reaches past me to grab some utensils as we move down the line, and I nudge her good-naturedly. She nudges back, smiling.

I feel bubbly, almost, with both nerves and excitement. It's felt like so long since we first started getting ready for the gala, I'm a little in awe that it's happening. That first Plus meeting I went to, where I was so nervous that I couldn't even raise my hand during discussion, feels like years ago. Now, I have a place here. I'm someone who can make a change, who can help put on something as big and grand and exciting as this. I have *friends* now, friends that I met through Plus. And even though I'm still uncertain about all the things with Declan, I can't help feeling a little excited about that, too.

I've been thinking a lot about what Nicole said, and I've

realized that, if there's any place or time to actually, tangibly try out her advice, it would probably be here, tonight, at the most LGBTQIA+-safe space I could imagine. If I don't manage to get the courage tonight, I don't know if I ever will. So, I need to do something before the night's up. Even if it's as small as holding Declan's hand. Even if I decide that I still can't handle anything romantic yet.

While I'm at the catering tables, I make one plate for myself and one for Declan. When I start making the second one, Jeremiah raises an eyebrow but thankfully doesn't comment. We return to the table with our food, and I slide into my seat next to Declan and put the second plate in front of him.

"What's this?" Declan asks, eyebrow raised.

"I just thought that, since I was already up there, I would get you some food, too. I tried to get what I know you like."

He looks back and forth from the plate to me, then smiles, wide and genuine. "You didn't have to do that."

I shrug, hoping I come off as more nonchalant than I feel. "I know, but I wanted to."

The way he looks at me then is almost overwhelmingly fond, and when I feel my cheeks starting to heat, I have to glance away.

"Well, thank you," he says, and under the table, he brushes his hand against mine. I don't reach to hold it, but I don't move away, either. We sit there, our hands pressed together, touching ever so slightly, and it's nice. It's more than nice.

When everyone seems to be settling in, Dakota and Nicole come onstage. Nicole looks stunning in a blue maxi dress, her hair in curls down her back, a wide smile on her face, while Dakota wears a black suit and tie, notecards in hand.

"Welcome, everyone," Dakota says, "to Plus's sixth annual gala!"

Claps from the audience. Next to me, Declan's eyes are trained on the stage, a small smile in place. Nicole and Dakota introduce themselves, and Dakota launches into a story about the group's conception. After that, it's Nicole's turn to speak.

"Plus has been a light in a very dark tunnel for many people, myself included," she says. "It's shown so many queer kids that they deserve a space to feel comfortable, a space to explore themselves and build community. For many of us, it's the only time we're able to be who we truly are.

"I got involved with Plus when it first started. I was still in high school, and I wasn't out to anyone yet, not even myself. But my best friend didn't want to check it out alone, so of course I went with her when she asked. I thought it was kind of silly at first, something that I wouldn't be super into. Obviously, I was *very* wrong." That gets a few laughs from the audience.

"It was there, with that community, that I learned who I am. It was there that I began to allow myself the possibility that I wasn't who I'd been told to be—and more than that, that it was *okay* if I wasn't. It was beautiful, even." She smiles softly. "Plus gave me some of the courage I needed to acknowledge my identity. To celebrate it. To tell myself and my loved ones and the world: I don't want to hide anymore.

"And that's what we've been doing every year since. Providing that space. Letting kids know that they don't have to hide, that they're worth more. And, with your support, we can continue providing that for LGBTQIA+ youth in Glenwood for many more years to come."

The crowd applauds. As Nicole exits the stage, she catches my eye and smiles. I smile back.

Around eleven o'clock, we finally head out, and I think I can say that the gala was a success. Way more potential donors showed up than I imagined would. The slam poets and the band were both fantastic, and although I didn't really know what to expect with the auction, it seemed to go well, if Nicole's relief at the end of the night was anything to go by. My friends and I stayed after to help clean up, so we're leaving later than I thought we would, but I can't say I mind.

As much fun as we've had, I think everyone but me just wants to head home. Normally, I would be just as exhausted, but tonight, I'm buzzing with nerves and excitement and anticipation—and not just because an event I helped put together was a success.

I didn't do anything at the gala with Declan. I just . . . couldn't. The timing wasn't right, or I didn't want to distract him, or there were still too many people around, or . . . any other number of excuses that kept me from just reaching out.

But I'm not giving up. I promised myself I'd try something tonight, no matter what, and even if I've been unable to so far, I still have the drive home to make this count.

I can do this.

I *want* to do this.

I think that as Jeremiah and Annie leave together, and then again as we walk Jacqueline to her car and she hugs both of us goodbye, and a final time as we're heading back to Declan's car in comfortable silence. *I can do this. I want to do this.*

We pull out of the parking lot, another playlist Declan made already on shuffle, and he glances at me. "Tired?"

"Not really," I admit. "You?"

"Me neither," he says.

I check his phone for the time—11:05. Not too late, but late enough that most restaurants are already closed. Except, of course, one place.

"Do you want to go to Cook Out?" I ask.

"Yeah." He grins. "Let's go."

"Shit, it's cold," I say, as Declan and I get out of his car in the Cook Out parking lot. The November weather is fine when the sun's out, but not so much at night once the temperature has dropped, and I forgot to grab my jacket before I left the house.

"Hold on one sec." Declan reaches into the back seat and pulls out a hoodie. He locks the car before holding it out to me. "You left this in here last weekend after we went shopping," he says.

"Ah." I take it from him. "That explains why I couldn't find it yesterday. Thank you."

"No prob. I just left it in here since I figured, you know." He shrugs. "We spend a lot of time in my car, anyway." A beat. "That came out . . . weird. I just mean—"

"I know what you mean," I say, smiling.

He nods, smiling too.

For a moment, we just look at each other. The hoodie is cold from sitting out in his car, but I curl my fingers around it. I don't think I've ever left something of mine in a friend's car before or at their house or—anything like that. Just this. Just with him.

And it's a silly thought, it doesn't mean anything, it's not even something that matters, but—my whole chest aches with how much I suddenly want to be touching Declan. Even just holding his hand, like I couldn't earlier. Even something small.

I stand there for another second, still holding the hoodie, still thinking of touching him, before I follow him inside.

Twenty-Two

COOK OUT IS PACKED. OVER the numbers being called through a megaphone, Declan and I order, then find a booth at the back of the restaurant. He slumps into the seat across from me and sighs dramatically.

"What's up?" I ask, not able to keep the amusement out of my voice.

"Life," he says.

"Life," I repeat.

"Yeah, you know." He sits up again and leans forward with his elbows on the table. I lean forward too. "Being at the gala got me thinking about high school dances and prom and things, and . . . I don't know. Every time I go to something like this, it makes me feel both older and younger than I am."

I take a moment to think about that. "Then why go?"

"It's not a *bad* feeling. It's just . . . things like school dances are supposed to be the archetypal high school *thing*, next to football games and group projects and skipping class, right?"

"In movies," I agree.

"So, when you're finally *at* one, it's like . . . you've reached the peak of teenagerdom, but also it's just something kind of *okay*, instead of this huge, awesome thing that makes you suddenly more normal than you were before."

Declan's number is called. He gets up to get his food, and while he's gone, I think about what he said.

When he gets back, I say, "I didn't realize you were worried about being normal."

He unwraps his straw. "I'm not, usually. But doesn't everyone wanna feel like they're doing this whole high school thing 'right,' even just sometimes?"

My number is called before I can respond. I get my food and sit back down across from him, but before I can continue where we left off, he asks, "What'd you get?"

"Three quesadillas and a strawberry milkshake."

He starts to reach for my food before stopping with his hand hovering near the container, smiling as he silently waits for permission. I roll my eyes jokingly before pushing my container closer to him, and he tears off a piece of a quesadilla.

"Anyway, I don't mean that there's *actually* one right way to do things," he says. "I know that the whole teen fantasy thing is a bunch of bullshit when you actually get down to it. But it's hard not to feel sometimes like we're . . ." He pauses. Shrugs. "You know. Missing out."

"I know," I say. And I do.

"That's part of why I love Plus so much," he says. "Even if

that teen fantasy doesn't exist, we can at least feel like it does for a couple hours. We can even take whoever we want as our date to the gala without feeling unsafe. What a concept!"

He punctuates the statement with a sip of my milkshake. I take a sip of his as payment, and he doesn't even bat an eye.

"You really like it there," I say, not a question so much as an observation.

"Don't you?"

"'Course," I say. "It's fun. And it's basically the only time I get to talk about . . ." I gesture toward myself vaguely.

"Me too. I mean, not *exactly* that, but you know. I'm glad you have that. Honestly, I was really happy when you started going."

"Why?"

He gives me a look like I should know the answer, and I guess I do. But I kind of want to hear it out loud. I sip my milkshake and just look at him, waiting.

"*Fine*, if you're gonna make me say it," he gives in, but he doesn't actually sound upset, only a little embarrassed. "When you showed up that first time, it surprised me 'cause I didn't realize there were other people at GHS who knew about Plus. But then, it was like . . . I started noticing you everywhere."

"We share a class," I say.

"I know that!"

I laugh.

He's grinning when he says, "Shut up, I'm just saying—after that first time, you were suddenly everywhere. But in a good way. I liked seeing you all the time. You were . . . interesting."

"What a distinctly neutral way to describe someone."

"Okay, fine, you were interesting and also I was into you, is that less neutral?"

For a second, I expect the blatant admission to make me squirm, or feel uncomfortable or overwhelmed. But other than the heat in my cheeks, it just makes me smile a little. "That works."

"Good." He nudges my foot under the table. "So . . . I was pretty happy that you started going all the time. Even happier when we started actually becoming friends."

"I was happy about that too," I admit. I gently nudge his foot back, and we end up with our ankles pressed together.

"I'm sorry I've been so weird," I say quietly, still not looking at him.

"Weird about what?"

"You. Us."

He takes a breath. "You don't need to apologize."

"But I want to."

"Gael."

I wish suddenly that we weren't here. That we were somewhere private, or maybe just that the restaurant was empty. That way, I could reach across the table and grab his hand and hold it for once, and not be afraid—of other people's reactions *or* my own.

"I *do* like you," I say. I try to keep my voice down, but it's lost in the restaurant's noise anyway. "I like being with you and talking to you and hanging out and texting and calling you late at night and—"

"Then we don't need anything else," he says.

"But I *want* something else."

He pauses. "You do?"

I nod, but I still can't look him in the eye. "I don't know . . .

254

how I'm going to react yet. But I want to find out. And the only way to figure this out is if I try."

"And you like me enough to try?"

"More than enough."

He sucks in a breath. "Oh."

I finally look at him. There's a soft, honest smile on his face that melts some of my anxiety. "Do *you* want to try?" I ask.

"Yeah." His smile widens. "I'd like that."

It's a little after midnight by the time we leave. Once we're back in Declan's car, I take my tie off, put my hoodie on, and text my mom. *Declan and I stopped to get something to eat, but I'm on my way home now.* The text reads as delivered.

"Hey," Declan says.

"Hey," I say back. I lock my phone and put it in my hoodie pocket, which is when I realize I left the chocolate bar that Nicole bought me there. I pull it out and set it in one of the cup holders. I'm so distracted that I don't notice that Declan's reaching for my hand until he's holding it. "I— Oh."

"Is this okay?"

I think about it for a second, then lace my fingers with his. "Very okay."

He smiles and squeezes my hand.

Unfortunately, he still has to drive. We let go while he backs out of the parking lot, but once we're on the road headed for my apartment, I reach for his hand again.

Mom hasn't responded to my message. That wouldn't normally be weird—she goes to bed pretty early, and I wasn't really expecting a response anyway. But the message doesn't just read as delivered anymore. It says she read it two minutes ago. I send another message: *almost home. are you up?*

We pull into the apartment's parking lot, and Declan parks. For a moment, we just sit there, the music he put on playing between us. When I check, I see that it's a song by The National.

"I had fun tonight," he says. He shifts so he can look at me better from his seat.

"Yeah, me too." I reach for the candy bar. "Want some?"

"Sure." We sit quietly until the song ends, passing the candy bar between us until we've finished it.

"I should probably head inside," I say. Another song starts up.

"Probably," Declan agrees.

Neither of us moves.

"Could we—"

"I think—"

We speak over each other. Declan waves for me to go. "You first."

"I was gonna ask if we could—" I look at the candy wrapper, my face burning. "I don't know. Try kissing again."

"Oh. Are you sure? I mean, not that I wouldn't *want* to, but I don't want to make you feel like you're obligated to—"

"You're not," I rush to say. "I just think . . . maybe it'll be different this time, if I know it's happening. It won't catch me off guard."

I look at him. There's no light except from the streetlamps, but I can still make out the curl that's fallen loose from his half ponytail, the way his mouth is parted just a little, the furrowed eyebrows that smooth slowly out of worry as he looks at me,

256

searching for confirmation that I'm absolutely sure.

It feels like we've never been more alone than now.

He nods. "Yeah. Okay."

I shift in my seat so I'm facing him better, my heart pounding. I reach for him, then press my lips to his in a poor imitation of a kiss.

I miss the first time and catch the corner of his mouth instead, and it isn't until he turns slightly that I meet my mark. It's longer than our first kiss but not by much, and when we pull away, I'm left feeling somehow fuller and emptier than I had before. It's satisfying, but I still want to do it again.

We don't say anything for what might be forever. He looks at me and I look back. I get then what Jeremiah meant about Declan, about how *affected* he is by everything, about how even Jeremiah's never seen him like this. Declan's looking at me like I hung the moon. I think I'm probably looking at him the same way.

He breaks the silence.

"Good?" he asks.

I nod. Once, then again, and again. "Yeah. That was—that was really good."

He laughs. I hadn't meant it to be funny, but I laugh, too.

I'm about to ask him if we can try it a third time when my phone buzzes.

A text from Mom. It just says *I love you.*

My whole body goes cold. I don't know what she means by this text, and panic clasps its hands around my throat.

"I—" I start to say as I rush to call her, and as it rings, I unbuckle and get out of the car, distantly aware of Declan asking me what's going on. The phone is still ringing, ringing, ringing.

"Gael?" Declan starts to follow me. "Is everything okay?"

Mom doesn't answer. I call again and tell him, the words rushing out, "Yeah, yeah, no—I'm sorry, I think there's something with my mom, I'm gonna check on her. Thanks for tonight, drive safe—"

I think he responds, but I'm already breaking into a sprint. I'm entering the building and she still isn't picking up, and I'm trying to tell myself that freaking out isn't going to help me, that the best way to handle this is to calm down and look at the facts. But it's so hard to do that when I'm imagining the worst.

And then I'm fumbling for my keys and unlocking the door and hearing the worst noise I've ever heard—so much crying—and I call for her and try to find where she is and I hear the crying get louder and yank the bathroom door open and she's sitting there and she's crying and she's got an empty pill bottle next to her and I'm yelling and I think I say something—but I don't know what because what do you say other than *What the fuck what did you do*—and she's still just weeping—and I am too and I'm grabbing my phone and dialing 911 and trying to get her to *throw them up please just throw them up please you can't do this Mom please* and she's saying she's sorry she's so sorry she's sorry and she loves me and she's kneeling over the bathtub with her fingers down her throat—

And I don't remember much of what happens right after that. Maybe I could, if I tried hard enough. But I don't think I want to.

Twenty-Three

LUCAS DRIVES ME HOME FROM the hospital the next morning.

It's Sunday. I rode in the ambulance with my mom and didn't get any sleep the whole night. I stayed at the hospital, even when they confirmed she'd be okay. *Physically, at least. Has she been seeing a therapist? A psychiatrist?*

I told the doctors that I couldn't remember her going to therapy since before my parents split up, but she still sees a psychiatrist every few months. She used to say that therapy just made her feel worse most of the time, and she could get by with just the psychiatrist prescribing meds. I guess she was wrong.

Lucas showed up around two a.m. I hadn't wanted to call him. It was only when a nurse asked me if I had any relatives who could pick me up that I thought about him. Until then, it felt like there was no one in the world but Mom and me. No one to turn to. No one who could make this any less horrible.

Declan had been calling and texting me, worried about me rushing off, but I didn't respond to any of the messages. I still haven't. I don't know what to say.

Lucas didn't hug me when he got here, but he put his hand on my shoulder and left it there for what might've been hours. I kept hearing him speaking under his breath. "Oh, Jesus. Christ. Shit." And at one point: "Not again."

Except he was too late. We'd already reached "again."

We didn't leave the hospital until six a.m. There was a lot of talking. Planning. Figuring things out. What to do with Mom. Where to go from here. I'm there for all of it, but I don't register anything we're saying, not fully.

Lucas and I drive back to the apartment in silence. Once inside, he stops in the kitchen and just stands in front of the fridge for a moment, staring at it with his hands on the door.

"We should eat," he says, and then, after another pause, "I think I'm gonna make pancakes."

I don't say anything, but he doesn't seem to notice.

I don't know how to calm myself, how to stop feeling like I'm in someone else's body right now. I want to scrub off the memory of Mom getting her stomach pumped, Mom on the floor crying, Mom's *I love you*. I go to take a shower. I think it'll help. I hope it will.

I turn the faucet and let the water run but don't get undressed. I stare at the water, the steam as it rises, listen to the sound of crashing against the inside of the tub, and while I'm looking, I swear it sounds like Mom's hiccups when she cries.

The panic hits me.

I turn the water off and stumble into my room, the only part of the apartment that hasn't been touched by yesterday, and, not for the first time today, I break down.

I sit on the floor. Knees pulled up to my chest, head bowed. I take deep breaths. Try to steady them: four in, six out, or is it six in, four out? I try to remember what Mom used to sing to me when I couldn't go to sleep, except I can't remember the words exactly, and I can hear Lucas in the kitchen puttering around, trying for some sense of normalcy, something to do. I imagine that he isn't making anything—that he's just standing there; that he found no point; that, like me, he hoped and tried and couldn't. I imagine him standing at the stove, flipping it on and off again, or filling up pots with hot water and dumping them right back out. I think about pointlessness. I think about calling Nicole.

My phone sits on my bedside table, plugged in. Once I can breathe again and the tears have stopped coming, I pull myself off the floor and reach for it. I have so many unread messages from Declan and the group chat. The group chat's messages are inane, something about the gala—which, I realize, was last night, and not a month ago, not years ago, the way it feels. I look at the preview for one of Declan's messages. *I'm going to bed, all right? I hope everything works out with your mom and please call me when*— but it gets cut off there, and I don't open it.

I really did try to respond when he first texted me last night. I read his messages, but the words made my stomach sick, the reminder of what happened, everything so real, too real. I was in the parking lot when Mom was sitting on the bathroom floor, planning to take her life. I was so close, so *fucking close*

261

to being there for her—to stopping her—to talking her down.

But instead of going inside, I stayed out in the car. I sat and talked and kissed Declan while my mom needed me the most she's ever needed me in my life. I can't think about what I'd do if I'd stayed in that car a minute longer, if I hadn't texted her as we were leaving Cook Out, if I'd kissed Declan again like I'd wanted to.

She could've died because I was too caught up in my own bullshit to notice her getting worse. How many signs had she given me? How many times did I find her crying for no reason, sick from stress, distant and unlike herself? She'd all but told me she was planning to hurt herself as I was leaving for the gala. She'd asked me if I'd "be okay." She was tearing up. That should've been enough to tip me off.

I should've noticed. I should've stayed home. And if I weren't so focused on myself, I *would've* stayed home.

My mom shouldn't be in a hospital right now.

So, I can't text Declan back.

I just can't.

I burrow under my comforter and fall asleep and don't wake until two p.m.

When I get up, I see I have five missed calls, three texts, and one voicemail. Two of the missed calls are from an unknown number, but everything else is from Nicole.

nicole: how are things going with the meeting?? thank u so much again for ur help xoxo

nicole: i just got a call from ms jackson saying u didn't show?? is everything alright???

nicole: gael????

Fuck.

Fuck.

I sit there, looking at the texts, the panic and the guilt rushing in. I don't listen to the voicemail. I can't. I can't hear Nicole's confusion, her panic cast in amber on my phone. She was probably freaking out, trying to smooth things over with Ms. Jackson while I was entirely unconscious. Between everything that happened, I didn't once think about the meeting—the meeting that could save Plus. I fully stood Ms. Jackson up. Will she be available for another meeting with Nicole? Will she even *want* to sponsor Plus after all this?

I can't even respond to Nicole. I can't handle her disappointment or her pity or her understanding—I don't deserve it. I cost Plus a sponsor. All the hard work for the gala—all the coffee sales and the calling volunteers and emailing performers—all the things I've done for Plus, and I couldn't do this one, the most important. If Ms. Jackson doesn't want to sponsor us after all this, I'll be the reason Plus goes under.

I turn my phone off, and the only thing I can think is: fuck, fuck, *fuck.*

Twenty-Four

I SKIP SCHOOL THE NEXT day. I want to sleep in the whole day—sleep until things are back to normal again, until Mom is out of the hospital and back home, until Lucas is gone. But I keep waking up, on and off between bad dreams that I can't really remember by the time I wake up but that leave me feeling panicked anyway. At ten a.m., I finally decide to just get up and do something else to occupy my time.

Mostly, I watch *Bake Off* in bed while crocheting and try not to leave my room. Leaving my room means seeing Lucas, and seeing Lucas means he's going to talk to me. I know that I can't completely avoid him, but that doesn't mean I'm not going to put it off for as long as possible.

I try not to check my phone.

> **declan:** Hey. How are you doing?
> **declan:** I got notes from AP Lit for you.

declan: Gael?

declan: You'd let me know if I did something wrong, right?

nicole: gael, please respond. im worried about u.

nicole: declan told me u werent at school

nicole: pls at least let me know ur ok?

Lucas is making dinner. He's staying on the couch. I told him originally that he could have my room, but he just waved me off, saying that wasn't necessary. So, now the living room is his makeshift bedroom, with his bags on the floor next to the coffee table and bedsheets spread out on the couch.

He hasn't really tried to talk to me today, but as he sets water to boil, he gets going with his signature small talk. "Winter break is coming up in a month," he says. "Are you excited?"

"I guess."

"Have you sent in any college applications yet?"

I shrug. The answer, of course, is no; college is not high up on the list of things I want to think—let alone talk—about right now. I know I won't be able to meet any of the early action deadlines coming up. I've accepted that I'm gonna have to apply during the regular period.

The water's boiling. Lucas pours in enough pasta for both of us, his mouth pulled into a frown. He looks lost. I don't usually see him like this. With Lucas, I've only ever seen the love, the explosion. Never the aftermath. Mom's always the one looking lost and distant. It's kind of disorienting to see it on him for a change.

"Your voice sounds deeper," he says suddenly. I raise an eyebrow at the weird change in topic, and he continues, trying to get me to say something, "You're still taking your shots, right?"

"Yeah. Every two weeks."

"Ana still do it for you?"

He left before I started T. I guess Mom told him at some point about our system, but I kind of hate that she did. I wish she hadn't let him in on that part of my life.

I don't want him to know anything about us. Anything about me.

So, I just nod.

He looks down at the pot. "I called your aunt," he says. "Just to let her know what's going on."

"Oh."

"She can't get here until next week."

"You think Mom will still be in the hospital then?"

He thinks about it. Quietly, he says, "I'm not sure, Gael."

The boiling water is loud in our silence.

My phone buzzes with the two-minute reminder of Nicole's last text. I stare at the screen, debating for a moment, before going to my messages. To Nicole, I type *im sorry*, then delete it and write, *im okay*, then delete that and just stare at the gray bubbles, solitary and alone. Then my screen lights up with an incoming call: *nicole fletcher*.

"Excuse me," I mumble to Lucas, heading to my room and closing my door.

I don't want to worry Nicole, but I failed her—failed Plus— so intensely. I don't know if I can handle her telling me I cost them a sponsor and now all our hard work will have been for nothing.

I stare at the screen. Then, before I can tell myself not to, I press Answer.

"*Gael*," she says, relief in her voice. "Why have you been ignoring me? What *happened*?"

My eyes water. I barely manage to get out "I'm sorry" before I burst into tears.

And I tell her everything.

When I'm done, she says, sounding close to tears herself, "I'm so glad she's okay, Gael. I'm so sorry."

I look at the ground. "Me too."

"And you already know what I'm going to say, right?" When I don't respond, she continues, "Your mother's life is more important than Plus, Gael. I'm not mad you forgot about the meeting. We can find another sponsor."

"But you were already just barely getting by. . . ."

She sighs a little. "That's true, but that's not your fault."

I'm not sure what to say to that. We're silent for a moment.

"So . . . what happens now?" she asks. "With your mom, I mean?"

"They're keeping her in a psych hospital. Not sure yet for how long. We're allowed to visit her this weekend." My dad and I haven't heard from her since she was admitted. I don't know if she's not allowed to call us, or if maybe she just hasn't wanted to talk, but either way, I'm not feeling great about waiting so long to see her.

"What are you going to do while she's there?"

"Lucas is staying with me."

There's a long pause. Then, hesitantly, "Gael . . ."

"I know," I say. "But he's my dad, and I'm still a minor, and it's what Mom wanted, anyway. She doesn't want me staying here alone."

"I hate that I'm not there right now to be with you. I should be back soon, but . . ."

"Don't worry about me," I say. Then, "Thank you. For everything."

"Of course. You know I'm always here for you."

We talk a little longer after that. Once we hang up, I lie in bed with the comforter wrapped around me. I don't fall asleep, but I wish I would.

On Tuesday, I have two choices: go to school and face Declan or stay at home and deal with Lucas's incessant attempts to talk to me.

It's a difficult choice, but I choose school.

In Environmental Science, I sit next to Jacqueline like usual, and at first, she doesn't act like anything's wrong. I'm starting to think maybe no one but Declan's noticed my absence until halfway through the period, when she says, looking at her textbook as she finds answers for our busywork, "Soooo, what'd you and Declan end up doing Saturday?"

Anxiety immediately prickles at my fingertips. "What do you mean?"

"Like, after the gala and everything?"

I focus on my textbook's page. At the top right corner, a

previous owner scribbled a small tornado and then a stick figure seemingly running from it. I feel a little like the drawing when I shrug, trying to keep my voice as normal as possible and not betray just how much I don't want to keep talking about this as I say, "Just went to Cook Out."

"It must've been hell by then," she says. "Saturday nights are rough."

I shrug again.

Jacqueline shifts slightly in her seat. "Anything else happen?"

"Not really. We got milkshakes."

I can tell she's a little disappointed by my answer, but she doesn't push for any more details.

I wonder if Declan told her about our kiss and my rushing off, and if he did, if he's told her how I haven't texted him back, or how I've been MIA ever since. Some part of me hopes he hasn't. My silence in the group chat isn't that unusual, so if he hasn't mentioned anything, then maybe, at least when I'm at school, things could be . . . normal.

Lunchtime rolls around.

I still don't know if Declan's told anyone anything, but even if he hasn't, it would be pretty much impossible to miss the way he stares at me when I sit down at our table, lunch tray in hand. I meet his eye for exactly one second before I feel like I might throw up and quickly look away.

"Feeling better?" Annie asks.

Her question causes a different panic. "What?"

"You weren't here yesterday," she says. "Were you sick?"

Right. I wasn't here yesterday. Of course they would assume I was sick.

I need to calm down. Breathe.

"Um, yeah. I guess I just needed a day at home." I try to smile reassuringly.

I can feel Declan looking at me. "So you're feeling better now?"

He doesn't say it like he's angry, even though he has the right to be. He just sounds worried.

And that should relieve me. It should make me happy that he's talking to me like everything's normal. That he's not angry. But it doesn't. It just sort of makes me want to cry.

I still can't look at him, so I say to the table behind Annie, "Yeah, I'm doing fine now."

If I've ever told a larger lie than that, I can't remember it.

That afternoon, I get home to Lucas going through old photo albums in the living room.

"Oh, hey." He looks up while I close the door, slipping my shoes off at the entrance.

"Um, what are you doing?" I ask.

"Looking through some photos." He's got three different albums open, spread out on the floor in front of him. There's a small pile of photos next to him, taken out of the albums.

"Yeah, but why?"

He turns a page. "I, uh, realized that I don't have a lot of these with me, so I figured I could scan them to my computer while I'm here. Plus, it's, you know . . . something to do." He says the last part sheepishly, like he's embarrassed that he's not at work right now. He's taking a few days off while things get settled. "Oh, look—this is from the bakery's opening day."

He points to the page. I think about ignoring him and going straight to my room, but curiosity overrules my desire to be alone. I've honestly never looked through these albums. I knew Mom had them, but she never went through them in front of me, and I never thought to get them out.

I set my backpack down near the sofa and crouch on the ground near him. The first one shows the outside of the bakery, a younger Lucas in front of it with his arms outstretched and a wide grin on his face, the sign reading BAILEY'S shiny and new. The next photo is of my parents inside the bakery, Mom's hair in a high ponytail and the corners of her eyes crinkling up from smiling; Lucas's hair is grown out and his teeth are white. Below that is a photo of Lucas and me in front of the shop. He's bending down to be at my level, his arm around my shoulder and cheek pressed to my head. He looks happy. The small version of me is laughing.

I keep looking at it. When Lucas goes to turn the page, I almost ask him to stop and let me stare a little longer.

The following three pages are dedicated to the bakery—photos of pastries and cakes Lucas made, the receipt for the first order they ever put in, a copy of the recipe for Lucas's pecan pie. After that, it's more photos of our family and the inside of the shop, three people who I hardly recognize set to a backdrop that I've mostly tried to forget. Not because I didn't like it there—but because I liked it so much that after it closed down

271

and everything went to shit with my parents, thinking about that space was too painful to handle. Better to just try to forget it, if I could.

We keep looking through the photos, and I give in and sit down. Photos of the beach trip we took when I was six; of Aunt Isabella when she came to visit a few Christmases in a row; of Lucas's side of the family visiting for Easter, me in a pink church dress playing with cousins I don't remember meeting; of my seventh birthday, the cake homemade and my smile wide; of Lucas lifting me onto his shoulders as we walk down a street I don't recognize. And then, when we get to other albums, photos backward in time—Mom and Lucas as teenagers, at a dance, with their friends, graduating high school, getting engaged, going camping, the first apartment they got together, their wedding. In every picture, my parents look so happy. It almost makes it hard to believe that these are the same people that I saw fighting for so many years.

That's the weird thing about these albums. They don't preserve the bad stuff, and I get it—who would want to keep those moments? But the problem, then, is that it leaves so much out about our lives together. Guts the whole truth. Now we're left with an album of incomplete memories. A half-told story.

"You remember when Ana taught you how to ride a bike?" Lucas says, while still looking at the album. We're on a page full of photos from a vacation to Florida.

"Yeah, I do. Why?"

"You fell and scraped your knee pretty much as soon as she let you go." He turns the page, like we'll find a photo of my bloody knee in here. "You were pretty upset about it."

"I was eight," I say. "Of course I was upset."

"Were you really eight by then?"

I nod.

His eyebrows shoot up. "That'll be ten years ago in April." He thinks about it for a second. "That was the same year you broke your leg, wasn't it?"

"Same one."

"And the year that you got a part in your school's play."

"It wasn't a real part," I protest. "I had, like, *maybe* one line."

"Still, it was a big deal." He looks back at the album, now showing a candid taken of Mom at a restaurant, a large birthday cake in front of her and her attention focused on someone to her right. The photo's dated as her twenty-first birthday. "Was that year really as busy for you as it feels like it was? It seems like a lot happened then."

"It was the last year before you guys started fighting."

I can feel the way that hits him. I'm not even really saying it to hurt; it's just what happened. That was the last year we were happy as a family. I mean, I guess it was probably building up before that for my parents, but that was the last year it could sit quietly bubbling under the surface, ignored and out of reach. It was the last year I remember things feeling normal.

Lucas is scrambling for something else, I can tell. He turns the page, seems to find nothing, and turns the page again.

After a minute of not speaking, he asks, "When do you think you knew you were trans?"

"Oh." I wasn't expecting him to ask about that. I shrug. "I

think I always felt like something was off, but I thought everyone felt like that, so I ignored it. It got harder to ignore as I got older. And then it got so bad that, I, you know. Figured it out."

"After all the stuff with your mother and me got worse?"

"After," I agree. "But you guys didn't have anything to do with—"

"No, I know, I wasn't trying to imply that. . . ." He looks down. "I just want to understand better, how all this has been on you."

I stay quiet, and he doesn't say anything else for so long that I think the conversation's ended. Then he says, "I was so scared for you, when you first transitioned."

I don't know how to respond.

"I can't imagine how scary that must've been when you were first figuring it all out. And after you came out and started high school—I was so worried all the time about you. I know I can't protect you from everything, but it was just so hard not to feel like that when . . ."

"When people suck?"

I mean it genuinely, but he laughs. "Yeah, when people suck." He pauses. "And then I was so worried—and it was right around when I moved out—I . . . I just never acknowledged it. I never asked you about it. But I don't want you to think I didn't know it was scary. I worried about it all the time."

"I don't need you to pity me," I say.

"What? No, I don't," he insists. "It's not about pity. It's . . . Gael, I'm your *dad*. I care about you, and I'd be naïve not to worry for your safety when I know how much harder it is in the world for trans people. I'm not coming from a place of pity. I just . . . I love you."

His southern accent, which he hides most days, creeps in whenever he's getting emotional. I look at him—the handful of wrinkles he has and the thick eyebrows I got from him, furrowed. And I realize that, as much as I wish I hadn't, I've missed him. The thought makes me sad. Then it just makes me frustrated.

"Why didn't you call us for so long?" I ask.

He blinks. "What?"

"You just dropped off the face of the earth after my birthday. *Months* of nothing."

"I thought you didn't want me to call you."

"I didn't want to *talk* to you, but that's not the same thing," I say, and I'm surprised by how much I mean it. "Of course I wanted you to call. You're my dad, even if you're an asshole. I wanted you to try to make up for every shitty thing you've done—I wanted you to show interest in my life and apologize to Mom and stop being so condescending like you weren't the one who messed everything up."

I don't say the last part to hurt him, but he flinches anyway. I keep going.

"I wanted to know that you cared, and then you wouldn't show that to me. And you wonder why I still don't like being around you? What've you done since you cheated on Mom to show that you're a better person now? What at *all* have you done? Meanwhile, did you know I have friends now, for the first time in my whole life? Or that I'm getting top surgery once

I turn eighteen? Do you know anything about me or my life or how much I've grown? Anything at all?"

"You won't *let* me know, Gael," he says. "How can I know you when you won't let me in?"

I hate that he's right about that. I hate that this conversation has turned back around to me. I hate that I don't let people in. I hate that once I *did* let someone in, it led to my mom almost dying.

I hate that every single thing right now is wrong—that I can't get anything right—that Lucas is here, that Mom isn't, that I've been ignoring Declan and that Declan's just letting me. I hate that what Lucas said makes my eyes sting.

I hate that the only thing I can do is stand up and storm off to my room, unable to offer a real answer.

"Gael," he calls after me, but I don't know what to say.

And I hate it.

Twenty-Five

THE NEXT DAY, I SKIP school again. I don't have any new texts when I wake up, so I go back and reread the ones Declan sent me. He doesn't sound angry in any of them, even though he'd have every right to be. Part of me wishes he were.

Why can't he just be mad at me for avoiding him? Why can't he yell at me, blow up my phone, type in all caps, or call incessantly? I wish he would just call me an asshole. His patience is somehow worse. I *know* my silence is hurting him—there's no way it isn't.

I spent so much of high school by myself: eating lunch alone, riding the bus alone, doing homework alone, sitting at home on Friday nights alone. I mean, I had Mom, and I had Nicole, but there was so much silence. And the weird part is that I didn't even *realize* it was silence; it was just how life was.

But I filled it all with people—with talking, with laughing, with Plus discussions and going to Cook Out and Declan's hand in mine—and only now that it's gone do I realize how quiet everything is.

I figure if there's ever a time it's okay for me to miss a few days of school, it's now, so I skip Thursday too, sleeping in and avoiding conversation with Lucas by locking myself in my room. But I do have work that night. For a hundred reasons—I can't handle pretending everything's fine, I'd rather stay at home and sleep for another twelve hours, I don't want to see Declan—I *really* don't want to go. And for a hundred other reasons—I need the money, I can't get anyone to cover my shift this late, I *want* to see Declan—I go anyway.

Nicole got back from San Antonio last night, which is why I'm not surprised to see her when I get to Joey's. She gives me a small side hug, like she wants to comfort me but doesn't want to make it too big of a deal.

"How's everything?" she asks. She follows me as I make my way to the back to clock in and get into my apron.

"Same old," I tell her. I slide my apron on. "Help me tie this?"

She smiles. "Only 'cause you asked before I could offer. Turn around."

She ties it a little too tight, but I don't complain.

"How's McKayla?" I ask.

"She's okay. She's staying in Texas for the next few weeks, and I couldn't really afford to miss any more classes, so . . ." She gestures toward herself. "Here I am. We can talk more about that and your 'same old' if you come with me to get ice cream after work, though." She smiles.

I think about the fight Lucas and I got into Tuesday afternoon, the unanswered texts from Declan, how we haven't heard from Mom since she was admitted.

"Yeah, we can do that," I tell her.

The entire shift, I keep looking at Declan. There's something about him talking to strangers that looks natural in a way that I highly doubt I ever do. Maybe because he's more extroverted than me, it's easier for him to interact with customers, smiling and bustling around with their orders, cracking jokes with them and making their day brighter. Most of our regulars know him by name, and I can't help being in awe of how he moves in the world.

At one point, he passes by me with a tray of food, and I rush to get out of the way, mumbling apologies. He just offers a half smile and keeps going.

I miss him. I want to tell him that.

But instead, I ignore him. I return with drinks to the table I'm waiting on and glance at him from across the room and hope he knows what that means, what I can't say out loud, what I wish I could give him but can't.

Later that night, Nicole, sitting across from me and nursing two scoops of red velvet ice cream, asks, "Sooo . . . how's having your dad staying with you?"

I have a scoop of mango ice cream in a bowl, covered in rainbow sprinkles. While answering, I press the sprinkles into my ice cream, making indents. "Rough."

"Ouch. That bad?"

"Pretty bad. We got into an argument Tuesday. Mostly over the fact that he ghosted me and my mom for a few months earlier this year."

"And how'd that conversation end up going?"

"Eh, you know." I press the sprinkles further into my ice cream. "Me telling him to stop acting like he knows me when he doesn't because he's never tried, and him saying that I've never *let* him try."

She takes a bite of her ice cream. "And what do you think about that last part?"

I look at my bowl. "I think that I'm never gonna be able to let people in and not end up paying for it."

"*Gael.*"

"Come on, Nicole, you saw what happened literally *while* I was . . ." My fingers tighten around the plastic spoon. "I'm the worst."

"You're not."

"My mom almost died because of me."

Nicole reaches across the table and finds my hand, taking it away from the spoon. There are red lines on my palm from where I was holding on too tight, and she covers them with her own hand, squeezing mine comfortingly.

"None of your mom's actions are your fault," she tells me gently. "And neither are they Declan's."

"I don't think—"

"I didn't think you did," she says. "I just mean, don't blame your relationship with him for all this. Your mom is sick, and she needs help, and, Gael, I know you love her enough to try, but you can't help her all on your own. You can't be responsible for every bad feeling your mother has. I understand how difficult this is for you, trust me, I do, but I don't want you to throw away what you have with Declan because of this."

I look down at the table. "This sucks."

"Yeah," she agrees softly. "It does."

I squeeze her hand once before letting go. "I don't know how to talk to Declan again like everything's normal."

"You don't *have* to talk to him like everything's normal," she says. "Things *aren't* normal right now. You just need to talk to him like he means something to you, and I know he does. Also, be honest with him. That's a big one."

"You're too smart for your own good, you know that?"

"Damn right I am." She smiles. Then the smile fades a little. "I'm assuming you're not coming to Plus tomorrow?"

I shake my head. "I'm sorry."

"Don't be. I can't blame you."

"No, I mean . . . about Ms. Jackson. Are you guys going to be able to, you know . . . stay open?"

"We'll be fine, Gael."

"But—"

"We *will*," she insists. "We'll find a way. We always do."

I go to school Friday.

Everything is uncomfortably normal, the way it was on Tuesday. None of my friends bring up my continued absences, but Jacqueline's smile when I take my seat in Environmental Science is a little gentler than normal. I'm positive Declan has told them what's up with us by now.

In AP Lit, I almost say something to him. It's before class has started, so kids are wandering around, talking or staring at their phones. Declan and I sit next to each other like usual, but we don't speak, and I look over at him. He's looking at his phone, his feet up on the empty chair in front of him. Every now and then, something he's looking at makes him smile or frown or raise an eyebrow. I want, all of a sudden, to say something.

I want to say: *I'm sorry.* I want to say: *You deserve better.* I want to say: *I like you so much it hurts.* I want to say: *My mom almost did something terrible.*

Really, I think, if I get down to it, what I want isn't just to tell him that she did something—I want to tell him *everything.* I want to tell him what I saw. How I felt when I was running up to my apartment, when I was unlocking the door, when I was grabbing my phone to call 911, when I was struggling to speak and then speaking too quickly to the operator, who was so calm and composed on the other line. I want to tell him how it felt to tell the operator that my mother had tried to kill herself, that I needed help, here's our address, *please hurry I don't know how many she took.* I want to tell him how it felt to sit alone in that hospital waiting room for so many hours, how that was probably the loneliest I've ever been in my whole life, and I want to tell him how every time I'm in that bathroom it makes me hurt like I've never hurt before.

I want to tell him how scared I was to lose my mom. How scared I am to lose *him.*

He shifts in his seat, taking his feet off the chair in front of him, and catches my eye. I turn away quickly, but not quickly enough to completely avoid his gaze. My face burns, but whether that's from shame or the tears I suddenly feel, I'm not sure.

Twenty-Six

SATURDAY MORNING, I ASK LUCAS, "Who did you cheat on Mom with?"

He stiffens immediately. It's eight a.m. In a few hours, we'll visit Mom at the hospital, but for now we're in the kitchen, the coffee pot crackling as Lucas makes himself a cup.

He lets out a long sigh, suddenly looking so much older than he is, and runs a hand over his forehead. "Do you really want to know?" he asks.

From where I'm leaning on the counter, I nod. I woke up this morning feeling like I needed to do something drastic, or at least find one answer to the millions of questions I have about why things turned out the way they have. I can't talk to Declan and I can't make my mom better, but I can at least ask for answers. Search for—I don't know. Closure, maybe.

"It was . . ." Lucas pauses. Then, "I don't think you'd remember her. She lived in our building."

I don't know what I expected, but that surprises me. "You

283

cheated on Mom with our neighbor?"

He presses his lips together, then sighs again, heavier this time. "I'm not sure that it's good for us to have this conversation. I mean, last time we talked about—"

"Bullshit."

"Gael—"

"A lot of things aren't 'good for us,' but that doesn't stop either of us from doing them. That's never stopped *you*."

"This is exactly what I'm talking about." Here it is: the old version of Lucas, the one that I know. A Lucas who gets riled up, frustrated with my attitude, and wants to assert his authority. Not the Lucas that tells me how much he worries for me or how badly he wants to be in my life. "We can't talk about this because it's not appropriate for you to know, number one, and number two, you aren't mature enough to hear the truth without . . . without acting like *this*."

"Like what? Angry? Don't I have the right to be angry?"

"*Of course* you have the right to be angry!"

"Then *let* me be," I say.

He looks at me for a long time, eyes calculating, searching for something in my expression to tip him off, maybe. The coffee pot yawns again, almost finished.

When it looks like he's still going to say no, I add, "I deserve to know. You . . . both of you kept things from me. For *years*. I had to find everything out on my own. Neither of you told me Mom was depressed or suicidal, and you didn't say *anything* about the bakery having trouble until it was already closing. This wasn't the first time you broke my trust."

"Is that what this is about? Your mother?"

"That's always what this is about."

He pauses. When he speaks again, it's quieter, the frustration in his voice gone and replaced by something defeated. "How was I supposed to tell you your mom was depressed? That's not something you can easily explain to a kid. Would you have wanted me to sit you down one day and tell you your own mother tried to kill herself? That she was hurting so bad that she'd rather die than live? That she didn't love you enough to try to stay?"

"That's not what this is about," I say. "You know Mom can't just *choose* to not be depressed. She can't help it. It has nothing to do with whether or not she loves us."

"That's . . ." He huffs and runs his hands over his head, then down his face. "That's not what I meant. I just mean that that's what it would've looked like to a kid. Shit, Gael, it *still* looks like that to me."

I lean back against the counter and cross my ankles.

"It was never about how much she loved us," I finally say, more of a mumble. But my voice is steady this time. "She loves me now and she loved me then. She loved *you*, before everything happened. I think she still does sometimes."

"I'm not good for her."

"No. You're not."

He doesn't say anything for a moment, just staring at the coffee pot.

"If it wasn't about love," Lucas starts, "then why . . . why did she do it? Now, and back then? Shouldn't the thought of us have kept her from trying to take her own life? Didn't she think of us at all when she was attempting with the intention, the *real* intention, of not coming back? Of *her* leaving *us*?"

I don't know my dad very well anymore, but I think I get why he's struggling so much with this. I understand Mom's impulses more than he does because he's never experienced it, never been in that kind of place. I've never been depressed enough to want to truly kill myself, but back when my gender dysphoria was almost too bad to handle, I would wake up some days thinking I couldn't go any longer living like that. It felt impossible to bear. Even when I knew I didn't want to leave the people I love, it felt impossible.

"I don't know," I answer. "It's hard to explain if you've never felt it."

The coffee maker sputters one last time before it's quiet for good. Lucas looks down. He mumbles, "Sounds familiar."

I get the feeling that we're talking about the affair again now. I lean further into the counter and wait for Lucas to continue. I'm afraid that if I interrupt, he'll stop and never pick back up.

"About what you were saying earlier . . ." Lucas says. "I shouldn't have . . . You have to understand, Gael, I was struggling, too. Ana's depression . . . it hurt me. And you, even though you didn't get what was going on. You still knew something was wrong, didn't you? Don't you have moments when you realize memories like that aren't normal? *Experiences* like that?"

He's talking about the ones where he and Mom are fighting, where Mom is screaming and crying and banging on his chest with his hands encircling her wrists, where she doesn't say anything at all and just sits, vacantly. The ones where she refuses to move, where I come home to see her seated in front of the TV cradling a pillow, not speaking and not looking up at me.

The memories he's talking about are all the bad ones, the ones he refused to acknowledge for years, that never made it into the photo albums, that I think might live in me for the rest of my life.

"Yeah." I uncross my ankles and pull myself up onto the counter's ledge. If Mom were here, she'd give me a knowing look and tell me to get off.

"It doesn't excuse it," Lucas says.

"No, it doesn't."

"But it's the reason," he says quietly. "At the time, in my head, it was what I thought I needed. To survive with her like that. Getting worse so quickly."

Neither of us says anything.

In the silence, I think about how I so desperately wanted to tell Declan everything yesterday. And I think about the pile of photos Lucas had taken from the albums, stacked up so he could scan them for safekeeping. And how happy I looked as a kid in all those pictures.

"Do you realize," I start to say, but those words get stuck in my throat and I've got to cough them up again. "I mean—you guys . . . A lot of what you guys did messed me up."

Lucas looks at me. Eyes wide. I try to continue.

"I know that no parents are perfect and that everyone has problems, but . . . Don't you think it hurt me, growing up seeing

287

stuff like I did? From Mom *and* you? And just thinking that's normal and all right, thinking that getting close to someone is supposed to hurt 'cause you never know when they're gonna try to hurt themselves or leave you or both, and . . ." I trail off and look down, at my legs dangling off the floor and my fingers curled around the counter's edge.

I know my parents tried with me. I know they were supportive about my transition, that they care about my well-being, that they just want what's best—but it's hard to ignore how many of my issues all tie back to them.

"Is that really how you feel?" he asks.

This conversation suddenly feels pointless. I think that might be the closest I'll ever come to truly getting across what I want him to know, and even that didn't do much.

I push myself off the counter onto the floor and start toward my room. "Never mind. I don't know why I brought it up—"

"Gael." My dad puts a hand on my shoulder to stop me, and before I've even fully turned around to face him, he's pulling me into a hug.

To my own surprise, I hug him back. Lightly.

"I'm sorry," he says into my shoulder. "I should've been there. When Ana was struggling . . . you shouldn't have had to deal with that alone. And I never meant to mess you up. We wanted so *badly* to do right by you. That's why we stayed together for as long as we did, you know? Because we thought getting a divorce would just scar you more and we could tough it out, and then I *couldn't* tough it out, and I screwed everything up . . . and it was all a mess, all of it. . . ."

It sounds like he might be crying.

He pulls away. "How long have you been feeling like this?"

"Which part?" I say.

"Like you can't get close to someone in case they leave. Or like it's supposed to hurt to care about people."

I'm suddenly embarrassed. I guess I knew logically—from movies and other people and talks with Nicole—that caring about someone isn't supposed to feel horrible. Letting another person in isn't *meant* to be a kind of bleeding. But having someone else—and my dad no less—point out so blatantly that I've been going about relationships the wrong way makes embarrassment churn in my stomach.

"I don't know," I say, crossing my arms over my chest. "I guess forever."

"You know it's not true, right? You know that you don't have to be afraid of getting hurt every time you care about someone?"

"But don't I, though?" I say, more defensively than I mean to. "Isn't that how life works—you meet people and you're happy for a while but then you hurt them, or they hurt you, or they leave, and you're left alone again, and you gotta do it all over with someone else?"

"Not always." He shakes his head. "Not always, Gael. And you know what? Even if it happens every time—even if you get the emotional shit kicked out of you with every relationship you start and end—it's a *hell* of a lot better than being alone."

I think about how quiet everything is now without my friends. I think about how it felt, sitting across from Declan at Cook Out and opening up to him about being trans and watching *Star Wars* with him. I think about Annie checking in on me at the Halloween party; about Jacqueline's laugh when she isn't worried about impressing anyone, loud and open and sincere; about Jeremiah talking with me before class.

I think about Declan's face in class yesterday. How I wanted to say something, and how bad it hurt that I couldn't. How I used to sit silently every day—how I used to hurt like that without knowing it was hurting.

I don't know what to say to Lucas. Mostly because I realize he might be right.

So, instead, I nod toward the coffee maker. "Your coffee's probably cold."

Lucas reaches for the pot and goes about getting his cup, shaking his head to himself. But he doesn't look smug that I had no real response to what he said. Just pensive.

Family members are allowed to visit the psych hospital on Saturdays, so Lucas and I head over. During the car ride, Lucas is silent except to tell me, as we're pulling into the hospital parking lot, "Your mom is stronger than you know."

She proves him right when she still smiles at us, still reaches across the table to grasp my hand with a soft warmth that's been her trademark for as long as I can remember. The table is cold, a dark-gray color. Other patients sit at similar tables across from their loved ones, some crying, others speaking in low voices, and others even laughing and telling stories. The room feels heavy with emotion, the air thick with the weight of where we are.

Lucas moves like he's gonna set a hand on my shoulder but stops halfway there. The hand lowers, forming into a loose fist on the table.

"How is everything at home?" Mom asks, looking between us.

"Things are okay," Lucas says. "We're holding up. How've you been? How is it here?"

"It's okay," Mom says. "It could be worse. It could definitely be worse. Everyone's been so nice. And they've upped my meds, and that's been helping so far."

I glance at Lucas. He's pressing his lips together. I wonder if he's also thinking about all the pills she shoveled into her mouth.

"I think I'll be ready to go home soon." Mom brushes a strand of hair behind her ear. Her hair is in a braid, pieces falling out and into her face, no doubt done this morning when she got up. "People are usually only here a week before they feel safe enough to come home again, and I've felt a lot better since being here."

"You can check yourself out when you want, right?" Lucas asks.

"Right." Then she glances between us. "And you've been staying at the apartment all week?"

"Yep."

She nods. "Good. Okay. That's good."

It occurs to me suddenly that Mom doesn't want me left home alone. Not because I can't take care of myself—I've proven capable of much more in the past three years—but because she's afraid of how it'll affect me, living without someone else, with her gone.

I don't have the same kind of problems Mom does. There's nothing sinking under my skin or convincing me there's no point in living. Instead, my problems clamp my mouth shut, keep me rooted in place with fear, make me shut everyone out. I won't try to kill myself like she did, and she knows that. I don't want to die. But—and I think this is what she's afraid of—I think they could still do something to me, these things that keep my mouth shut. I won't cave in like her, but given the chance, I might . . . erode.

Maybe that's why Lucas is staying with me. To keep me from eroding. Redemption, maybe, for failing his wife all those years ago.

"Gael," Mom says. She offers me a smile. "How've things been at school?"

I sit up a little straighter in my seat, now that the conversation's on me. "They've been all right. Just school."

"How are your friends?"

"Fine, I think." I glance away from her. "I've, um, not really been talking to them much."

She frowns and opens her mouth, but she seems to change her mind. She closes it again, then says, quietly, "I'm sorry."

I know she's not talking about my friends right now. I give her a smile and reach across the table to touch her hand. "I know, Mom. I am too."

That night, I can't sleep, so I open my phone and stare at the texts Declan sent. I look at the letters, the gray bubbles encasing them, the times they were sent and the minutes between messages. I stare at them for so long that I memorize them.

I never responded to any of them.

It hits me all at once just how much I've messed up with him this week. How much he hasn't deserved my silence. I think about what Lucas said—*It's a hell of a lot better than being alone*—and what Nicole said—*You just need to talk to him like he means something to you, and I know he does*—and what Declan said—*We could be scared together*—and I think about this thing that keeps my mouth shut, that won't let me talk openly, that makes it so I never know how to get across what I mean, and I think about how I wanted the other day to tell him everything. I wanted to let him know me.

And I realize that I don't want to be quiet anymore.

gael: are you still up?

Twenty-Seven

I'M AT DECLAN'S HOUSE BEFORE I can even fully decide what I'm going to say.

I park on the street and sit in my car for what feels like forever, trying to catch my thoughts. They're running everywhere right now, and his house just looks at me, its quaint front porch almost seeming mocking in the face of my anxiety. I take a deep breath. Inhale for six seconds, exhale for eight.

After Declan texted me that he was still awake, I wiggled into my binder, not even bothering to put clothes other than my pajamas back on over it, slipped on my shoes and a black hoodie, and grabbed the car keys. On my way out, Lucas asked where I was going, and I just told him a friend's house.

"It's important," I said. "I'll be back in, like, thirty minutes. Maybe an hour."

"Be safe!" I think he called, but it was hard to tell while rushing out the door.

I don't know why I rushed. Maybe I figured that if I got here before I could think about what I even want to accomplish from this, I would come up with something instead of overthinking the entire ordeal and talking myself out of it.

And now I'm here.

Just sitting in my car.

Staring at the house.

"What the fuck am I even doing," I say to myself. Then I take out my phone and call Declan.

He picks up on the second ring. "Gael?"

"Hi." I smile nervously, even though he can't see me. "Um. Sorry to bother you so late."

"No, no, it's all good." There's a sound on the other line like he's getting up and moving around. "So . . . um . . . what's up?"

"This is gonna sound weird, but . . . I'm outside your house. Do you think you could come outside and we could—talk?" I get it all out in a rush, but the last word catches on its way.

There's a pause. I see the curtains in one of the upstairs windows get pulled back, and then a vague form that I realize is Declan a moment later. "Oh, wow. How long have you been sitting there?"

"Like, five minutes. I left right when you said you were up."

"I'm good to talk, but do you wanna come inside instead?"

"I, um." I hadn't thought of that. I think maybe cars are just my go-to space for heavy conversations, so I'd assumed that's what we'd do. "Yeah. If that isn't gonna bother your parents, or . . ."

"It should be fine. They're just downstairs watching a movie with my sister. I can ask them if it'll make you feel better."

"Please."

He laughs. It calms some of my anxiety; at least I know he's not so upset that he can't still laugh. When he returns to the phone a minute later to let me know I'm good to come in, I take another deep breath, get out of the car, and make my way to the front porch.

When I get to the door, Declan opens it, a soft smile on his face. "Hey."

"Hi."

We look at each other for a long second. Then Declan beckons me forward. "Come on, we're letting the cold in."

I slide my phone into my hoodie pocket and follow him inside.

Being in Declan's room causes another kind of anxiety, something new on top of the other stuff, that I can only identify as the nerves that must come from being in the guy-you-like-and-have-kissed-before's bedroom.

But other than that, being here is . . . I don't know. I'm noticing all the things I didn't the first time. There's a dent on the back of his door that I know must come with a story, and I want all of it. Every story.

Declan sits down in his desk chair, spinning around so he's facing me. I close the door behind me and stand with my back to it, unsure. "Um. So, here's the thing. I'm sorry for not responding to your texts all week," I start. "And for being all weird at school. I wasn't . . . The truth is, uh, something big kind of happened with my mom, after you dropped me off, and I wasn't sure how to face you after that because I felt like it was my fault since I was with you when it happened, so I just didn't respond and I wanted things at school to be normal so I just acted like nothing had happened at all and—that wasn't fair to you."

"Wait." He holds his hand up. "What happened with your mom? Is she okay?"

I run my finger over my eyebrow and tell him the story.

It's a shortened version of what really happened—because it always has to be, when I try to let it out—but I do give him more details than I did with Nicole. I try to let him know more, to not find the words so frightening as they come out, to tell him how it felt, if only in simple terms. And before I've even finished, he's gotten up from his seat and pulled me into a hug. I wrap my arms around him. He smells nice.

We don't pull away for a while, but once we do, he says, "I'm so sorry."

I laugh a little. "*I'm* supposed to be the one apologizing."

"Well, we can both apologize, then." He says it like he's joking, but I can tell he means it.

I grab his hand, and he lets me just hold it for a second before going to his bed, leading me by our still-joined hands. My heart rate kicks up, but all he does is sit down on the edge, and I sit next to him. Our knees touch. That helps ground me some.

"Would it be okay if I just . . . talked for a moment?" I ask. Declan nods and intertwines our fingers, squeezing once.

So I do.

"Obviously you know I have problems with—I don't know. Opening up. I was . . . really lonely for a lot of my life. I didn't have a lot of close friends. Up until I met Nicole, I didn't really have anyone to turn to. And it was like . . . I convinced myself that I didn't need anyone else, or that it wasn't worth it to make friends unless they made the effort first like Nicole did, or that it was better if I was just quiet and by myself and alone. But I think it's because I didn't want to get hurt again. I was hurt so much by my parents, their constant fighting, and then my mom's first suicide attempt, and then my dad hurt her with the affair, and then he left us and Mom and I were on our own, and it was sort of like . . . what's the point in letting anybody get close to you when they're either gonna hurt you or leave?" I punctuate the sentence with a laugh, the kind reserved for when something really isn't funny.

"And then—oh God, on *top* of all that, there's this thing I have with my body and my dysphoria and—" I wave my hand around vaguely, searching for something. "All of this stuff that makes it feel like I can't have anything romantic. Like I don't deserve any of it. And I know you know that, and I know you like me anyway, but it's like . . . because of all this, I've never wanted to tell someone everything. I've never wanted to risk it, because, you know, the more people in your life, the more people that can hurt you.

"But I . . . I want to risk it now. With you. I want to tell you—stuff I can't tell other people. And I want you to know those things about me that I don't let other people know, and I want you to see me, and I want to know everything about you too, and do you know what's really weird? I'm not even scared that you'll get to know me now and decide you hate it. I'm not. I know you wouldn't. I'm just scared that, eventually, down the line . . . something will happen. Something will change to make you see me differently. You'll stop liking what you see in me, or maybe I'll do something shitty like I did this week, so shitty that you could never forgive it, or maybe . . . I don't know.

I'm just scared of the leaving.

"My mom—she got *so* close to killing herself last week. Like, if I'd stayed out in the car with you for a minute longer, she . . . she could be gone. And knowing that, that I almost didn't stop it, that she almost . . ." I take a deep breath. "That was the most scared and alone I've ever felt, and I couldn't face you after that. Getting so close to losing someone I love so much, and then putting myself in another position to get hurt felt—naïve.

"And I guess it *is* a little naïve, setting myself up to get hurt. But I think I want to, anyway."

The entire time I spoke, I was staring at the floor. But now I look at him.

"Also . . . I *really* liked kissing you."

He laughs. It's watery, and he scrubs the tears from his cheeks with the hand that isn't still holding mine. "For what it's worth, I'm just as terrified of getting hurt as you are."

Then his smile fades a little. "But not hearing from you all week, Gael . . ." He's quiet for a moment, looking at our still-linked hands. "It's just . . . It was pretty freaky, you know? Things were so good that night, and then suddenly you were just gone, and at school, it was like—even when you were there, you weren't *there*. And I was just sort of left to wonder if I'd somehow messed everything up without realizing it."

Guilt prods at me, sharp and quick. "I'm so, so sorry. I know it wasn't the right thing to do, and you didn't deserve it. I guess . . . I guess a part of me thought that if I pushed you away, it would help, somehow. It would keep me from getting hurt or hurting you even more. But that wasn't fair to you. I wish I could take that back."

He squeezes my hand. "Just promise you won't ghost me again." He says it like it's a joke, a small smile in place, but I can tell he means it, too.

"I can absolutely promise that I'll never ghost you again," I say. "I'm sorry I did that to you."

He nods, and some of my guilt dissolves—not all of it, but some. "I know, and I forgive you. And, about all this stuff with your mom . . . you know I'm always here for you. I could have . . . I would've helped you. I want you to feel like you can trust me with your problems, you know? So we can get through this kind of stuff together. I want to be able to help you when you're struggling."

I squeeze his hand gently. "Yeah, I get that. I'm gonna try to get better about opening up about things like this. But, Dec, I don't want you to feel like you always need to fix my problems. You don't have to be helpful for me to like you. It's enough to just have you here with me. Okay?"

He looks down at our hands. "I guess we both have things we need to work on, huh?"

"I guess we do." I smile.

For a moment, we're quiet. We sit there on his bed, knees knocking together, fingers still intertwined, and I can't help loving how his hand fits in mine.

"So . . . about what I said about liking you . . ." I say. "Does this mean we can be scared together?"

He smiles. "Yeah. I think it does."

"So, does this . . . also mean we get to try kissing again?"

Declan laughs, clear and real and open. I decide, right before kissing him, that it's my favorite sound.

Twenty-Eight

WHEN MOM COMES HOME TWO days later, she seems fuller than when she left. Not just physically, but mentally; there's just a little more of her there. The moles and freckles painting her face don't wash her out, and the way she carries herself to the car worries me a little less.

The moment she'd seen me at the hospital, she'd pulled me into a hug, as warm and safe as ever, and I'd been reminded just how much—just how *badly*—I'd missed her.

From the corner of my eye, I could see Lucas standing behind us, hands in his pockets and a fond smile on his face, unsure of his place in all this but relieved all the same. Something rare seized at my chest. I managed to wiggle out of Mom's grip and wave for Lucas to join us.

It was the first time my family had hugged in years.

Now, in the car, Mom makes small talk with Lucas. It's the same type of thing they talked about when Lucas and I went to visit, but this has an easiness that only comes from the relief of being back.

They talk the whole drive home with only minimal silence between topics, and at the apartment, Lucas helps get Mom's things back in her room. It's not until we're seated around the dinner table that night that things get genuinely uncomfortable. We all know that it isn't normal for Lucas to be included here. But dinner isn't quiet. Mom tries her best at conversation, asking how Lucas is and what his job is like. I have little to say and little to add, so I stay mostly quiet.

My phone buzzes.

declan: Hows your mom?

gael: i think shes doing a little better. but its hard to tell this early on

gael: they set her up with a therapist while she was there so shes going to start seeing her every week now

declan: That's good!

gael: yeah. i was also thinking about maybe seeing someone

declan: With her or on your own?

gael: probably on my own

gael: maybe family therapy at some point too

gael: we could probably use it

declan: It's worth a shot at the very least!

Lucas clears his throat: a stiff, awkward sound. I look up from my phone.

"So," he starts. He switches his fork from his right hand to

302

his left, pausing. "I should probably head back tonight. I don't want to overdo my stay."

Mom nods. She's not looking at him, just at her food. I take a bite of my macaroni. Lucas cooked tonight.

We don't say anything for a moment too long, and Mom finally peels her eyes away from her plate to glance at me, giving me a small, reassuring smile when our eyes meet. Lucas shifts again, clearly anxious, but the fork stays in his left hand.

"I'm gonna pack after dinner," he says.

I look at him because Mom won't. "Okay."

Lucas looks like he wants to ask or tell Mom something. It's a familiar look. But he doesn't, and we just keep eating, his impending absence a weight on us.

After dinner, I head to my room and text Declan.

> **gael:** is it ok if i call u in a minute?
> **declan:** Sure!

"Hey," I say when he picks up.

"Hey yourself," Declan says. "Is something wrong?"

"No, nothing's wrong. I just wanted to talk to you, I guess."

"You '*guess*'? You don't *know* that you want to talk to me? Rude."

"If you're going to be annoying about it, I can hang up."

He laughs, loud and clear through the phone. I love it. I haven't yet gotten used to being able to actually think that and not feel guilty, so I try to think it as much as I can. *I like his laugh. I like talking to him. I like kissing him. I like* him.

"Okay, okay," he says. "So. How was your day?"

"Weird."

"Good weird or bad weird?"

"Kind of both. It was just . . . weird. Having my dad here with my mom too, instead of just one or the other. He's packing right now, then he's gonna head back to his place later tonight."

We don't say anything. Declan's waiting for me to continue.

"Sometimes I think he regrets leaving," I say quietly.

"Is that good or bad?"

"Both, maybe. I think . . . I don't know. Sometimes I think he's trying."

"Do you miss him?"

The question catches me off guard. But I have an answer.

"Sometimes, yeah. He's my dad. I mean, he's an asshole and he hurt me and my mom, but I still miss him sometimes. I still . . ." I think about it. "I still want him around. Just sometimes."

"That's what you want?"

"Yeah. That's what I want."

I only hang up with Declan when Lucas comes to my room to say goodbye.

"I'm heading out," he says, leaning against the doorframe, his suitcase next to him. He looks tired, but not quite as exhausted as he was the first few nights after Mom was admitted.

"Okay."

I'm not sure what else to say, and Lucas seems a little unsure, too. We look at each other for a moment, neither of us moving.

It's only when he turns away to leave that I get out of bed and hug him. He pauses, surprised, before hugging me back.

"I'll see you later," he tells me, patting my shoulder gently. He says it like he's just heading out to work, like he'll be back before I know it.

I pull away.

"Yeah," I say. "See you."

He gives me a small smile one last time before leaving, his suitcase rolling behind him.

Two weeks later, I get a call.

"Hello?" I hold my phone between my ear and my shoulder, my hands busy crocheting. I'm almost done with that blanket.

"Gael," my dad says. I stop, but only for a second—then my shoulders relax. I make a loop.

I pull.

"How are you?"

"I'm okay," I say. "I'm okay."

Epilogue

I DON'T REMEMBER A LOT from the first day after top surgery, but everything past that is vivid.

The healing process is painful. I'm wrapped up in bandages, my entire body aches, and even just standing feels like someone's trying to rip open my chest for the first week. And that's not even the half of it. I have to sleep sitting up, there are drains attached to my side that have to be emptied of the blood pooling there twice a day, I can only take sponge baths, I can't lift anything over two pounds, I can't move without someone else's help, I'm in pain every second of the day—

And it's the happiest I've ever been.

Lucas stays over with us for the first few days that I'm healing. He's there when I come out of surgery, his face swimming into focus above me, wearing an expression that I've never seen on him before. I don't know why it makes me so happy, in my still-high state, but according to Mom, I smiled at him and talked to him like I haven't since I was a kid. Funny what meds will make you say in front of your parents.

He still lives in Bellevue, and he doesn't come around much, but when he does, it's . . . not so bad. He and Mom have been getting along okay. It's mostly just a little uncomfortable. We're trying.

Mom and I are trying, too. Since she was hospitalized in November, she's been in therapy every week since, and I started going soon after. She has bad days—I do, too—but they've been less intense, less catastrophic. In therapy, I talk about some of the stuff I talk about with Plus: my issues with my body and the feeling-not-like-myself that's apparently called dissociating. I talk about my parents, too, and stuff with Declan as it comes up, and my panic attacks and bad dreams. I always figured I had some kind of anxiety disorder—I've had too many panic attacks to *not* have something going on—but it's nice to have the official diagnosis of generalized anxiety. And we made sure I'm seeing someone who's trans friendly. My therapist was really supportive as I approached my top surgery date, encouraging me to work through some of my more complicated feelings about my dysphoria and how much this surgery means to me.

A month after surgery, Nicole and Dakota get everyone together at a café downtown. Since it's summer, official Plus meetings aren't going on, but that doesn't stop them from hosting *un*official meetings. Thankfully, I'm just healed enough to go, and Nicole, Jeremiah, Annie, and Jacqueline are already there when Declan and I show up.

Nicole gets up to greet us. "You made it!" She's careful not to squeeze too hard when we hug, and I hug her back lightly. Everything still aches a lot.

"Not even a major invasive surgery can keep me away."

Almost everyone that usually shows up for Plus is already here; there are about fifteen of us in total, including Nicole's girlfriend McKayla. We're spread out across several tables, taking up most of the coffee shop.

It was a week after Mom got out of the hospital that Nicole told me she was talking to the owners of the Gazebo Inn. After the gala, they decided they wanted to support Plus in more consistent ways, and Dakota met with them to talk about becoming sponsors. It wasn't a fix-all solution, but it wasn't anything to brush off, either. Plus still struggles, and they're of course still looking for more sponsors where they can, but they're surviving.

Declan and I sit between Nicole and Jeremiah. Jeremiah nudges my elbow with his. "How are you feeling? Still hurts?"

"Not as bad," I say.

"Little less like you've been run over by a truck?"

I smile. "Only a little."

Annie stands up. She's across from us, next to Jacqueline. "I'm gonna go order a drink. You guys want anything?"

"I'll get in line with you," Declan says.

They head off, but not before Annie pecks Jacqueline on the cheek. Jacqueline and Maggie broke up soon after winter break, and Annie and Jacqueline started dating two months ago. As a couple, they're almost as obnoxiously sweet as Declan and me. Jeremiah gives me a look that says he's thinking the same thing,

308

but I know he's happy for them, even if he *does* tease them about it most of the time.

We stay there, talking and sipping our overpriced coffees, for close to two hours. None of us want to leave. We're not saying it, but I know all the seniors are thinking about how this is the last time we'll all be together like this. It's a bittersweet meeting, a soft goodbye we're trying not to admit is a goodbye.

I still remember what Nicole said when she first dragged me to Plus—that I could leave whenever I wanted. But now that the time has come to let it go, I want to stay.

After the last few people have trickled out of the shop, Declan and I drive with the windows rolled down and a playlist he made blasting through the speakers. When we pull into the park, there's nobody but us around. It's been several months since the last time we found ourselves here, but other than the grass growing out, it looks the same as it did our last visit.

Declan parks and waits until the song ends before he cuts the engine.

"So," he says.

I don't wait for the rest of the thought before I unbuckle and start to get out. He helps me climb out of the car; even though the pain has lessened with time, too much movement still hurts, and if I'm not careful, it sometimes feels like I've just been stabbed all over my chest. I'm glad he gets that. He was so sweet when I was first recovering, texting me nonstop when I needed him to distract me from the pain, dropping by the apartment every couple of days just to hang out with me, fetching me things like water and more painkiller and the remote. Obviously healing from any surgery is going to suck a lot, but it was easier with him there.

The air smells like summer. The weather has been in the eighties since my birthday in April, but it wasn't until a month and a half ago that school let out for summer break—our last summer break of high school.

Declan will be eighteen soon, the last one of our friend group. I'm already trying to come up with good birthday gifts for him.

"What were you gonna say?" I ask once we're at the swings, sitting side by side. Streetlights surround the park, but he turns on the flashlight he brought specifically for nights like this, when we disappear alone together just to talk for a few hours. It's an activity I hadn't expected to become so common, or so loved.

He writes something on the ground with the light, pushing himself back and forth with one foot lazily. He starts, "College."

I agree, "College."

"Sewanee and MTSU are only an hour from each other," he says. "It won't be hard to see each other on weekends or off days or when we don't have a lot of work. . . ."

He trails off. This isn't anywhere near the first time we've talked about the future, but he always seems more nervous about college than I am. He got into Sewanee, majoring (of course) in English, while I decided on Middle Tennessee State University. My major is still undeclared—I'm going to focus on gen eds this first semester and see where it takes me—but I've been thinking about what I would need so I can work with nonprofits once I graduate. I'm pretty excited for the fall. It'll be new and different and strange but—I'm hopeful.

There's no way to be physically close when we're on separate swings. I stand up and motion for him to follow. He does, helping me up onto one of the jungle gyms, and we settle down at the top of a bright-yellow slide, our thighs pressed together.

"Hey," I say. "What are you so worried about?"

"I'm not worried."

I give him a look. He manages to hold out for a total of five seconds.

"I've just never done long distance, even if it's not *super* long distance, and I guess I'm just kind of worried you'll get . . ."

"Get what?"

"Bored, I guess." He shrugs.

"Dec . . ."

"I know, I know, I'm being silly."

I nudge his shoulder. "I just don't want you to worry about something you don't need to worry about."

We're quiet. I glance at him. His hair is pulled into a loose ponytail at the base of his neck. I try to make out the line of his jaw in the dark and find that I don't have to. I have it memorized.

"We already text a million times a day," I say. "And it's not like an hour is that long. It won't be the same as it is now, obviously, but I mean, I'll drive it every day if you ask me to. It's more than doable."

"Sappy," he says, but the assurance seems to have worked

away at least some of his anxieties. On the mulch beneath the jungle gym, he draws what might be our initials with the flashlight's beam and leans his head on my shoulder. His hair tickles my neck, but I like having him here. The closeness is nice.

"I'm not going anywhere," I promise. "You know how I am. Once I'm in, I'm in."

He laughs, something small. I slide my hand into his.

"I like your laugh," I admit easily.

"Thanks," he says. "I like yours too."

He laces our fingers together, and it's comforting. Familiar. I wonder how many times we've done this since we got together. I doubt either of us could count, and I find that I'm okay with that.

"So, we're really doing this," he says.

"As long as you want to."

"*I* want to." He squeezes my hand and looks at me. "Do you?"

"Yeah." I smile. Squeeze back. "I want to."

Acknowledgments

I WROTE THE VERY FIRST draft of this book when I was sixteen, and in the seven years since, it's been through more revisions than I could count—all for the better. They say it takes a village, and this book wouldn't have been possible without the love, support, encouragement, guidance, and feedback of so many people.

To my agent, Pete Knapp—thank you so much for believing in me and this book. Since our very first phone call, I knew you understood the story I was trying to tell, and I can't thank you enough for championing *If I Can Give You That* the way that you have. I couldn't ask for a better agent.

To my editor, Karen Chaplin—thank you so much for taking a chance on Gael and me, and for always helping me make the necessary revisions. This story wouldn't be what it is without you.

Thank you to Alex Albadree for the beautiful cover art,

which I fell in love with from the very first sketch.

I want to thank my sister, Marcie, for brainstorming with me, for reading even this book's earliest drafts, and for being an amazing sister. None of the Plus plotline would have been possible without your help, including that two-thousand-word fundraising guide you wrote just for this. I still think you should be in a writers' room somewhere, but in the meantime, thank you for helping make my books more compelling.

To Max—thank you for being a wonderful little brother, for listening to my writerly struggles, and for pursuing your own artistic dreams. I can't wait for your books to be out in the world someday, too.

To Mom and Dad for being the most loving and supportive parents a person could ask for. Thank you for raising me with such grace and compassion, and for always believing in my art—whether that be Mom sewing my overly complicated cosplays back in middle school or Dad creating nerdy, creepy, podcast-inspired music with me during lockdown, you've both always supported my creative interests, and I can't thank you enough for that.

To Noah, for taking author photos that actually make me look good, and for generally being a pretty awesome guy.

To my professor, Dan Rosenberg, for all you've taught me. I wouldn't be the writer I am without your guidance and feedback, and I can't overstate enough how much impact you've had on me as a student.

Thank you to Hayden, Riley, Ally, and Bean for sticking by my side all these years. I can't imagine who I would be without you all as friends. Thank you for listening to me complain, for making me laugh, for getting on phone calls with me for up to twelve hours at a time, for driving with the car windows down and music blasting. Here's to many more *D&D* sessions and late-night Cook Out trips.

To my Wells friends and my Odd/Even crew: thank you for making my time in college so memorable and weird and fun and worth it. You all mean so much to me, and I can't wait for our next movie night. (Ian still doesn't get movie-picking privileges back, though.)

To my boyfriend, Ian—for being there for me, for believing in me, for loving me. It might only be a coincidence that our love story mirrors Gael and Declan's, but I'd like to think it's the universe saying something. It's kind of crazy how much I love you.

To my cat, Hermes, for being the cutest creature on the earth.

And, finally, to all the trans people who came before me, and to all the trans people who brought me into their community when I was first discovering myself. The fight for our rights continues, but I believe in us. I believe in our worth. I believe in our strength. I love you all.